Smolder

by
Rayna Noire

Chapter One

Ireland 1915

THE BONFIRES ON the beach picked out the colors on the gypsy wagons causing them to glitter in the setting sun. The craggy hills provided a backdrop in the lengthening twilight and created solid arms that embraced the crescent shaped beach. The deep roar of the waves swept through Meara moving into her blood and bones. As she stumbled from the water, Shona's strong arm wrapped around her shoulders, and Rosemary's arm encircling her waist prevented her from going head first into the surf. Ardan lifted a weary hand to the people on the beach and shouted, "We made it. At the end, I was sure the sea had decided to take us for her own."

"They're here." A shout went up and people spilled out of the wagons. Some ran toward her while others picked up instruments and played.

A woman with wild curling hair glowing red in the twilight walked to them with a smile while gesturing for the others to follow. She must be Red Monesha that Destiny, the fortune teller, had mentioned would take her the next step of her journey. A hand of uncertainty squeezed her chest as she worried that she had lost the emerald necklace that would serve as her payment for the ride in the sea. The weight of the emerald necklace swung underneath her shirt reassured.

Meara unlooped her payment from her neck and put them in the redhead's hand, held open discreetly at hip level, almost buried in her skirt.

Her smile brightened as her fingers closed over the necklace. "Welcome, welcome to the second part of your journey. We were told you would be coming in farther down the coast." Her hand flattened over her heart. "Monesha knows better than to listen to the words. I listened to my heart instead and waited here. It's time."

She held out her hand to Meara who took it.

A few dark-haired men, barefoot and pant legs rolled up, waded into the surf to help the others to the fire.

The ordeal of fleeing the convent, along with being kidnapped, escaping, and subsequently almost drowning caused Meara to collapse by the fire. The welcome heat warmed her while stiffening her ocean-soaked clothing as it dried. A large-eyed toddler peeked from behind her mother's skirt to stare.

It didn't take a mirror to know she must be a sight, something spat out of the sea. Her lips tipped up not wanting to scare the curious girl. The child grinned back, causing the adults to laugh in response.

The mother ruffled her daughter's hair, resulting in a small heart pang for Meara. If her mother had lived, would she have been the type to drop an affectionate hand to her child's head?

"*She would and most likely a kiss, too.*" The voice echoed in her head. Somehow, her father made it to the far shores of Ireland, too.

"You're here."

She must have said the words aloud, Everyone standing near in the firelight stared at her. She gestured to the avid faces that watched her. "I, ah, meant all of you."

No one responded, but voices from outside the circle of those surrounding her carried.

Ardan spoke to the red-haired woman. "No, I saw it with my own eyes. She called the birds with her mind. I saw them flock together, then swoop down and attack."

"If nature does her bidding, this is a sign of great power. She could be one of the chosen."

It felt like that the intensity of the gazes sharpened as she squirmed on the log, wondering if she could be the person wanted her to be. There had to be a mistake. Did no one realize she'd been convent raised and had no information about the world. How could she possibly be of service?

A few high voices carried over the chatter.

"I don't see what's so special about her."

"I was making good money in the city before Monesha decided we had to leave in a hurry."

Someone hushed the voices, but not before Meara realized not everyone was happy about their detour. Normally, this would worry her, but right now, sitting took all her concentration.

The gulls dipped in the falling light, making a final raucous cry before settling down to the beach. The wave-generated breeze caused her to chafe her arms. A flurry of hands dropped blankets and shawls still warm from their bodies around her shoulders.

Rosemary, who sat across from her, managed a short nod. Was her friend regretting her decision to chaperone her to Ireland?

In the disappearing light and flickering flames, her friend managed a strained smile. "So, this is Ireland." Rosemary glanced around at the various faces. "Everyone here is so friendly and nice to look at."

Her last comment caused the group to nudge each other and chuckle. One man whistled long while another hooted. Meara let out a long breath, grateful for a friend who could lighten the mood.

Rosemary continued to talk. "I don't know much about Ireland. What's best about it?"

Several voices shouted enthusiastic replies.

"The food."

"No, the music."

"The poetry and the magic of the tales."

"Ha, that's a good one, and you tell a mighty tale, too."

Perhaps a story, might put off whatever great and miraculous thing she was supposed to do. Never mind, she didn't know how to accomplish it or even what it was.

Meara pointed to the bearded man who boasted about the tales. "Could you tell us one? It would be welcome, especially after the trip we had."

"I could." The man inserted his thumbs under his suspenders and puffed out his chest, but glanced in the direction of the talking couple. "Might as well since Red Monesha is still deep in conversation with your friend. Well now, ready yourselves."

A few hooted and whistled, while someone shouted, "Make it a good one, Rom."

The self-proclaimed story teller's name was Rom. Meara glanced around to see if there were any other bearded men. Some, but not too many, and the others had grey beards, while Rom didn't.

He held up one hand gesturing to the group and then flattened his palm and moved it in a horizontal fashion. "Once very…"

"Long ago," the crowd chimed in.

Instead of being upset, Rom grinned, indicating this was a familiar routine. "…there was unrest in the land. Many called themselves king and their lands were their kingdoms, but there was talk that one king uniting all would help the isle prevent any greedy raiders from stealing from the sons of Ireland."

"Still unrest," a voice in the dark grumbled.

A grunt followed indicating the original speaker may have received a good nudge for the comment. "Be still."

A woman offered steaming bowls of stew to Meara, Rosemary, and Shona. Meara murmured her appreciation and dug into her fragrant stew thick with potatoes and onions.

Rom viewed his audience, dropping his hand and turning. Once assured all eyes were back on him, he started again. "The kings all voted who would be their one ruler. Once the vote had happened, they all took a knee and swore their loyalty, all except Lir. He turned his back on the group, packed up, and headed home."

"Ooh," a nearby woman exclaimed, "there's going to be trouble.

Men don't take that insult lying down."

"You're right, Briana. Those who swore their allegiance wanted to go after Lir, bring him back for killing, but the newly elected king forbade it. He knew he'd need Lir's help to govern the land. He'd rather have the man on his side. The best way to do that was…"

"With a woman." Several people shouted, obviously familiar with the story. A few laughed while one man shouted, "Run while you can, Lir."

Meara glanced away from the fire and could still see the silhouettes of Ardan and Red Monesha against the setting sun. The couple glanced back and moved farther away, making it impossible to hear them. The waving hands indicated whatever they were talking about elicited strong emotions. She hoped it wasn't her. All she wanted was to make it to her uncle's people.

Rom's expressive voice drew her back into the tale. "The king knew Lir had no wife or heirs, so he picked out three beautiful sisters of high estate and sent them to be Lir's bride. He picked Eva and married her. They had two children and then twins. Eva dies giving birth to the last. Grief overwhelmed the man, making him take no notice of everyday life." Rom held his hand, pausing his tale.

"Go on!" Shona shouted the command almost in Meara's ear.

"Aye, I will. Some say the king was worried about him and sent him another sister to wed, but I think it happened somewhat differently. The sister, Aoife, was jealous of Eva. After all, she married a noble man, who adored her and gave her children, while Aoife remained unmarried in her father's home. One day, Aoife appeared to look after her sister's children. She explains how much she loves the wee ones, although before this she had not been around to visit.

"Aoife always looked her best and made her manner as sweet as honey, but still that did not tempt Lir. Finally, she resorted to a Druidic wand she stole from her father's house and caused Lir to agree to wed."

A Druidic wand? This was the first Meara had heard of such a thing. If her father had one, why hadn't he held off those who stormed his land?

"Bewitched, he married the tricky sister, and all was well for a while."

Meara leaned forward as Rosemary asked with an avid expression, "What happened next?"

Rom spun around to face Rosemary. He held up a finger to his lips and whispered loud enough for most to hear. "It's a secret, but I might be persuaded to tell more if you graced me with a smile."

A wide grin pulled Rosemary's cheeks tight.

He splayed his hand against his chest and announced, "Ah, the lass wants to hear more. I must obey."

The crowd chuckled, while one man added, "You were going to go on all along. Be done with it. Put us out of our suspense."

"Very good, then." He bent, placing his hands on his knees to put himself at child level. "Lir loved his children. Perhaps more because they reminded him of his departed wife, Eva. Each day, he'd draw them on his lap and hug and kiss them. Aoife considered this the act of a good father, but eventually she grew jealous. All his love he lavished on the children. As for the spell, it got her married, but really nothing more. A nefarious evil bubbled up in her heart. Something so vile and black, she dared not tell it to anyone."

A flurry of whispering sounded as Rom paused for breath. Meara found herself caught up in the tale. Stories like this had never been told at the convent, and the tales she'd heard since had not been as skillfully rendered as this one. "What evil?"

All the eyes that had been on Rom were on her. It wasn't a situation she wanted. "Please continue," she urged. Her voice sounded thready and weak.

"The children were all wonderful swimmers. Some say they turned into fish when they hit the water. They had no issue going to the river with their stepmother. She led each of them to the shore and prodded them with the Druidic wand, turning them into swans one by one. The last child pleaded with her stepmother to at least leave them with their voices so they could talk to one another."

Meara looked around at the heads nodding. No one looked shocked or surprised as he told the ending, perhaps there was more. "Is that it? What did the father do?"

"He looked for his children everywhere, but couldn't find them. Finally, one swan went to her father and explained what happened. The spell couldn't be lifted, and the father visited his children faithfully. Six hundred years had passed before the swans were blessed by a monk releasing them from their spell."

The group gave a collective sigh and muttered something about the dangers of women scorned.

A chill swept over her. What if Druids were evil? Perhaps, her father had the ability to turn children into swans. If that were so, shouldn't he have been able to turn his attackers into livestock? Maybe the letter Simon received about her father being killed was just a tale, not real at all. Despite the several jackets and shawls piled on top of her, a shiver started at her feet and worked its way up to her ears, chasing away the warmth. Had she been tricked somehow? Had the bearded man talking to her in her dreams been an illusion?

The hatred Adelaide directed her way after Braeden took an interest in her felt very real. Maybe she would have been forced to leave town anyhow, especially with Adelaide's father being mayor.

Rosemary's voice sounded above the others. "I don't understand. Druids aren't bad. As far as I know, they aren't running around turning children into swans or bewitching men."

"Aye, you're right." A high clear voice called out from the back of the crowd. The crowd parted and allowed a tiny, white-haired woman through. She walked with the help of an ornate staff, and the firelight played across her wizened face. Her dark eyes reflected the light as she moved forward, stopping in front of Rosemary. "You do well to question such a shabby ending. Once the priests came, they changed our stories to suit their own purposes. Even took our beloved Brigit and made her into a sanctified saint in clean robes."

She shook her head emphatically and continued her explanation. "That's not our Brigit. She's happiest with her sleeves pushed up and laboring over the forge." She held up one finger. "That's the first Brigit. Sometimes people consider Brigit to be three sisters who are the same age and face. Others consider Brigit to have three distinct aspects. The smithy is only one."

Rosemary spoke. "What are the other Brigits known for?"

The wizened woman smiled at the query and held up two fingers. "The second one is well known to all Irish wives and daughters. She is queen of the hearth and helps with midwifery and healing."

Feeling a bit emboldened by her friend's actions, Meara called out, "What about the third?"

Before the revered crone could answer, Rom did. "Ah, she is beloved of bards, actors, poets, writers, and singers since she provides inspiration." He gave a little bow, earning some light clapping for his efforts, but the white-haired woman was not a fan. She gave him a narrow-eyed look that had him stumbling backward. "Many pardons, Grandmother Biddy. Please, go on."

The woman gave a sharp nod and continued. "As for the Druids, they ended up in the story because the Jesuit Brothers wanted to be rid of them and all the old ways. It served their purpose to change some tales, which worked well since only the brothers could write. The way I heard the story, the children were restored to their normal selves by a faery."

A faery, that sounded right. Meara's shoulders relaxed some, but her teeth still chattered, causing the old crone to stare in her direction. The side that had faced the fire grew tight and uncomfortable as it dried. Her back, especially her backside, was still wet and chilled despite the coverings.

"The gel is freezing. Have you fluff for brains letting her sit here in her wet clothes? Go get her changed." She nodded in Rosemary and Shona's direction, too.

A couple of older women along with a young woman close to her age, stood and hurried toward her. The three of them herded Rosemary, Shona, and Meara as if sheep toward the colorful wagons.

One gave an anxious glance back in the direction of the fire and muttered low enough for Meara to overhear. "Grandmother was right. When Monesha hears of this, she'll be displeased since she doesn't embrace the old ways."

The remark made Meara wonder who really ran the group. They were greeted by a woman named Red Monesha. The crone who many called Grandmother Biddy wielded her own power, which wasn't too surprising since respect was usually given to the elderly due to their years. Now, Monesha might be angry? This was so confusing.

They reached the wagon painted with purple and red flowers with curly vines, closed red shutters, and bright yellow stairs. One of the older women motioned to the young woman. "Jane, you go ahead and light the lantern. Find something," she tapped Meara's shoulder, "appropriate for her to wear."

While the idea of clean, dry clothes appealed, Meara didn't care for the thought of depriving someone else of their wardrobe. At the convent, she only had one shift. "Don't go to too much trouble. Anything would be fine. All I need to do is wash out what I have on and let it dry, then I'll return your clothes to you."

The younger woman slung back her long straight hair as she turned to face Meara. "I am honored to have you wear my clothes. Just think, when I'm old like Grandmother Biddy, I can tell tales around the fire about how I leant my clothes to…" She cocked her head and pursed her lips before asking, "What is your name?"

"Meara," she answered softly, unsure if she should attach a last name. Her father's name, which she could have claimed remained unknown to her. All she knew for sure was his first name had been Fulmen, which meant lightning. Her mother, Sorcha, had declared to her brother, Simon, that Fulmen stole her heart just as fast as lightning struck. Still, she could lay hold of her mother's maiden name. It could serve her well since she was trying to find the family. She cleared her throat and repeated her name, a little louder. "Meara Cleary."

"Meara, of the sea, which seems fitting considering the sea brought you to us." The young woman crinkled her nosed and opened the arched door to the wagon. She stopped in the middle of ducking through the low opening. "I forgot to mention my own name. Jane of the Fox clan."

Shona and Rosemary were guided to a different wagon, just as gaily decorated, but the colors were different. Her friends entered their wagon and disappeared. For a heartbeat, desolation swept over Meara, making her knees weak, forcing her to put one hand against the wood frame to hold herself up.

The remaining woman rushed up and wrapped a supporting arm around her, urging her inside the wagon. "Sweet Brigit. What fools we've been to overlook your condition. We'll get you dressed and tucked in bed."

"That sounds wonderful." Even though she should have tried to stay awake, at least a little longer until Ardan came back and explained their situation, sleep offered a sweet respite from the out of control turn her life had taken. Maybe in the morning, a solution would present itself.

"As it should. Most of us sleep outside when the night isn't too severe."

She nodded, not sure if an answer was expected. Clean clothes and a blanket would serve well enough. The starlit sky could keep her company as she analyzed all the bizarre things that had happened so far. Just maybe, her father would enter her dreams and explain everything. "I understand."

A colorful skirt and blouse appeared in Jane's hand, which she held out to Meara. "This should do. There will be no sleeping outside for you. Gypsies are known for their hospitality. You get to sleep inside the wagon."

The older woman, who Meara assumed was Jane's mother, stood outside the wagon on the steps, but it didn't stop her from joining the conversation.

"It's best you stay inside for everyone's safety."

The ominous phrase hung in her head as Jane patted her bed to indicate where Meara would sleep. Best for everyone, which had to mean whatever the threat had been had followed her. The young Romany woman patted the bedding and grinned at her.

"Off to dreamland for you. Perhaps, you'll meet a tall, handsome man in your sleep."

The image of Braeden before he told her goodbye and left to fight the Germans came unbidden. She thought of her sweetheart plenty and their almost non-existent romance. A few kisses and a promise to wait for him was all there was. Her intentions had been to stay, but after Eleanor's isolated cottage was attacked and burned because the woman had befriended the orphan Meara, it was clear she should leave.

With any luck, Braden's brother would explain to him, but she doubted it. He, too, was under the pampered and vicious Adelaide's thumb. The wagon darkened as Jane turned down the light and bid her goodnight. Meara echoed the sentiment as she closed her eyes and willed herself to think of happier things.

Chapter Two

THE WOOD SMOKE AROMA, the soft babble of voices, and the distant sound of hammers on wood pulled Meara from her slumber. The door and windows were outlined by the early morning sun doing its best to come inside uninvited. She blinked, trying her best to hold onto the rapidly fading dream.

Braeden had visited her in her sleep. He appeared so handsome in his uniform, which was peculiar since she'd never seen him in uniform, except in her dreams. The beginnings of a beard had shadowed his face, and his eyes appeared weary. He still took her hand and led her to a valley where he had spread out a blanket upon which a picnic basket sat. The two of them sat and conversed. Braeden refused to talk about the war because he wanted their time together to be pleasant. To keep it so, she decided not to mention her dash across England, even though she had the opportunity to do so.

Instead, they teased one another, laughed, and flirted as they consumed their lunch. Even the weather had cooperated for the dream picnic, making it perfect with a cloudless sky and a gentle breeze. As the sun moved across the sky, she knew their time together was ending. Braeden had jumped to his feet in alarm and pointed to a snake weaving its way through the grass.

The slender serpent didn't appear that threatening to her, but when she glanced back to where her sweetheart once stood, he was gone. It was then the sounds of the day carried her to wakefulness. Perhaps, she didn't want to stay in a dream where Braeden would be scared off by a simple grass snake. His behavior would be peculiar from any man, but especially Braeden, who knew the forest and its inhabitants.

A spritely knock sounded, followed by a familiar voice. "It's Jane. I brought you some tea."

"Come in."

The young woman ducked automatically to clear the low doorframe and knelt beside the bed, waiting for Meara to push herself up before handing her the steaming cup.

A fragrant steam wafted off the cup, hinting at exotic lands she'd never known existed until months before when an accidental bombing forced her out into the secular world. "This smells wonderful. What are the spices?"

"This is Grandmother Biddy's special tea, and she guards the ingredients, but I can taste cardamom, ginger, and cloves. Do you like it?"

Meara took a sip, allowing the flavors to rest on her tongue, then swallowed. "Yes. It's even better than it smells."

"Good." Jane adjusted her skirts and eased into a sitting position. "Did you dream last night?"

"I did. Even dreamed about a tall and handsome man."

Jane clapped her hands together. "Ah, I wish I could have had your dream. Instead, I dreamed of spices." She gave a long sigh, then wrinkled her nose.

"People like spices. Wouldn't that be a good dream?"

"I wish. It means I'm guilty of boasting and over-exaggerating. What I say can't always be relied on."

It didn't make sense. Meara put her cup on the floor to inquire more. "Why do spices imply lying?"

"I didn't say lying. It means making things bigger or grander than they truly are. On the other hand, another person who dreams of spices tends to exaggerate the consequence of simple mishaps. A stumble becomes a full-face fall into a thistle patch. I'm not like that."

Having known Jane less the day, it would be hard to say what she was. "How do you know what dreams mean?"

Her companion's shoulders went up in a shrug. "Doesn't everyone know the dream symbols? Even as a very young child, my grandmother would help me work out the symbolism in a dream. When we are asleep, those who couldn't reach us while we were awake often can as we sleep. Instead of words, images are placed in our dreams. Sometimes, they are warnings. Other times they are confirmations that you're on the right path. Sometimes, the dreams can nag you to finish something. Tell me your dream, and I will interpret it for you." She waggled her eyebrows playfully.

"Well, I, um…" She hesitated, not knowing if she wanted to share her time with Braeden. "When I left England, I had a sweetheart who is fighting the Germans. In my dream, he comes dressed as a soldier."

"Hmm, a soldier that can be a good omen. It means your friends will stand beside you. If you're betrothed, it means you'll be going abroad soon."

"I just got here."

"Maybe your dream was late in coming or you have somewhere else to travel. Tell me more."

"The sky was clear and the weather warm. We were enjoying a picnic in the meadow, and I remember a sparrow singing nearby."

"All good signs showing happiness." She tilted her head as a sly expression crossed her face. "And fertility. Who knows? You and your sweetheart could end up having several children."

The possibility caused Meara's brows to shoot up. "Oh, I don't think that is what it means." She'd never given too much thought to being a parent. Never having a mother meant she'd never had anyone to model maternal behavior. The only mother figure she had was the cold, humorless Mother Superior who ran the convent with an iron fist, prohibiting even the smallest show of humor. "There were other things in the dream. Odd things."

"Tell me."

Jane's first dream analysis hadn't been too horrible. Maybe Meara should tell her the rest of the dream, especially because it confused her.

"There was a snake in the dream."

"A snake?" An index finger tapped her cheek as Jane's eyes rolled upward. "Did it bite you or chase you?"

"No." She shook her head, remembering her calmness in the dream. "It was just a small grass snake. What surprised me is Braeden jumped up and pointed it out as if afraid. I turned away to look at the snake. When I looked back, he was gone."

"Is Braeden afraid of snakes?"

"I don't think so. He lived on a farm and tromped through the woods hunting mushrooms. He had to encounter snakes, but never mentioned a fear of them. What do you think it means?"

"This puzzles me." Jane splayed her fingers against her chest. "The sighting of a snake can mean disturbing news is on its way. The fact that your man reacted more than you could mean it alarmed him more than you."

Being shot at in the war, possibly on the front line, gave Braeden all sorts of fears every day. "Why wasn't I alarmed? Is the unwelcome news for me or Braeden?"

"Dreams can be like the Tarot cards, revealing shadows of what could happen. It would be great if they told you exactly what would happen so you could avoid it. Alas, we must deal with what we know."

"I'm not sure that I know anything." Her happy mood brought on by seeing Braeden in her dreams and waking safe in the wagon drained away. The more she knew the less she understood. Why did everything make the future blurry as opposed to clear?

Jane's lips tipped up slightly in a sad smile. "Ah, I know what you mean. Fate may have dealt roughly with you, but consider you made it here. That has to say something."

Although her natural desire was to argue it was all serendipitous, she knew better. Every time someone meant her harm, she and Rosemary had escaped, even when they foolishly accepted a ride from Taylor, believing he had been sent by her Uncle Simon. Sure, she and Rosemary were naïve country girls, but she should have been suspicious. How would her Uncle even have known she was coming or what train she would be on? Instead she accepted the ride. Only the birds saved her from whatever end Taylor and associates had planned for her.

Her mother was Celtic, while her father was a Druid, but why did people expect so much of her? "I'm not sure what incredible thing I'm supposed to do? I've lived my entire life in a convent. I know nothing of the world."

"The Fates don't always pick the most likely. Could be you were the easiest to work with since you haven't hardened your heart and became set in your ways. Then there is your innocence. Your purity. Often, that quality either made you a priestess or a sacrifice in various faiths."

"Priestess? Sacrifice?"

Jane pursed her lips and inhaled deeply. "I don't consider myself an expert on ancient religions, but I have heard of plenty that had virgin priestesses or even oracles. While those with no respect for feminine power were always sacrificing the pure to appease the various gods and monsters, I'd be thinking they weren't too appeased since they kept on having the need for annual sacrifices."

In the convent, she heard a great deal about Christ being a sacrifice. Being the son of God hadn't spared him pain or death.

"All I know is I don't want to be a sacrifice, and I have no experience being a priestess. Sometimes, my deceased father talks to me in dreams and every now and then in the waking world. When I'm in trouble, the creatures of nature, such as the bees, birds, and even fish come to help me."

Jane's eyes grew large as she whispered mainly to herself. "It is true." She gestured to herself. "Forgive me. I'm a little in awe of you. I've never known anyone who commanded nature. I suspect Grandmother Biddy can, but I have never seen her do it. Tell me, did you ask the animals to do your bidding?"

A good question since she hadn't even had time to consider all that happened. "When I was running from Adelaide, I may have prayed, even begged my father or the faeries for help. I can't remember all that happened. The bees came out of nowhere and attacked Adelaide and her friends. The birds I did call, but the fish I didn't. Still, they held me up in the water when the boat capsized."

"You are blessed." Jane reached for her hand and tugged on it. "You must come with me and talk to Grandmother Biddy. She can tell you what to do. There is much you need to discover about yourself and your destiny."

If Grandmother Biddy could give her advice about how to proceed with her quest, she'd gladly listen. Meara pulled on her borrowed clothes and followed Jane to a small campfire in front of the most ornate wagon in the caravan. Red and blue flowers bloomed on it, surrounded by gold curlicues and the occasional odd pair of eyes peering out from dark spots.

Gesturing to the wagon, she said, "What an incredible wagon."

The stooped woman exited the wagon and used her long walking stick beside the steps to balance as she moved slowly down the three steps. Jane stepped forward and put out her arm for Grandmother Biddy to take. The two made a slow processional to the fire circle. Sawed chunks of woods served as chairs while one ornate wood chair stood out. Meara automatically sensed that it was Grandmother Biddy's chair.

She moved closer to the chair as Jane escorted the woman to it. When Grandmother Biddy sat and composed herself by twitching her dark skirts to her satisfaction, she looked up to the two girls. "You have come for my advice."

"Yes." Meara stepped forward and gave a short head bob, not knowing the protocol for such a situation. "I would be happy to hear your wisdom."

Grandmother Biddy placed her wrinkled hands together and looked down at them as if praying, then she glanced up and caught Meara with her piercing black eyes.

"I'll not give you advice."

Her initial impulse would be to ask why. Better yet, why had Jane even hinted at Grandmother Biddy dispensing such?

The elderly crone continued talking. "The universe has given you plenty of advice and continues to do so. Our part is to look at what you've already been given."

Here she came for help and received cryptic riddles for her trouble. "Excuse me, Grandmother Biddy, but I beg to differ with you. I have not been given any assistance."

"Oh?" The woman made the simple word into a rebuttal. "Did you hear that, Jane? The girl hasn't been getting any help from the universe."

"I did hear that."

Being spoken about as if she weren't there was tiresome and made Meara a wee bit snappish. "Explain what you mean, since you both seem to know."

Grandmother Biddy angled her head in Jane's direction, expecting her to speak, which she did. "You're in Ireland now. A girl who only recently left the convent managed to travel across a country under war. Not only that, you escaped those who meant to do you harm, which is no small thing. Despite the shipwreck, you still managed to reach the Emerald Isle. That wasn't just good luck or even smarts. It was the universe on your side."

"Well, I never gave it much thought. Too busy trying to get out of town before something bad happened to me or Eleanor. Although, I wasn't nearly fast enough to spare my friend, Eleanor's home. I foolishly believed I could stay with her until Braeden returned."

Grandmother Biddy angled her head toward the sea, not Meara. "You probably had signs that it was time to leave, but you chose to ignore them."

Meara's lips twisted to one side as she considered the tumultuous turn her life had taken. "The convent was bombed. Before I could even consider what to do, Eleanor found me and took me in at the bidding of my father, who compelled her to rescue me."

"A strong man on this side and on the next, too." Grandmother Biddy twisted in her seat making eye contact with Meara. "When did you know it was time to leave?"

"There had been several incidents, starting with my uncle coming to the convent to find me. Being chased by Adelaide and her friends, who were determined to cut my face so Braeden wouldn't find me attractive, gave me my first push, but I stayed for Braeden."

Jane interrupted by gesturing with one hand. "You told me Braeden left for war. Why didn't you leave then?"

She should have. It would have saved Eleanor the trauma of having her house burned. She shook her head thinking of everything she should have done. "Eleanor even told me it was time to go and that it wasn't safe for me there. Still, I liked living with Eleanor, who was teaching me about the faeries and feeding me delicious foods. I was helping her harvest the herbs and selling them at the local market. It may have been the unknown evil in the forest that finally forced me out."

"Unknown evil?" Jane varied her gaze from Meara and Grandmother Biddy.

Grandmother Biddy closed her eyes and slumped in the chair as if weary. "It's not an unknown evil as much as unnamed. All our actions carry energy. The good energy makes people happy and draws others to us. It opens doors and makes progress possible. The bad actions," she exhaled a deep breath, "carry a heavy dark energy that sinks into the ground, contaminating everything. Right now, with the war there is a wave of dark energy caused by lives cut down before their time, greed, hatred, and the desire to harm others for no other reason than they are different. This is what you're fighting, Meara."

No, the woman was confused. She wasn't a fighter. If anything, she was trying to escape the evil. "No, I'm not a warrior. Even if I were, what chance do I have against all those Germans who are invading every country in their path?"

"Good question. At least it means you're thinking. First, you aren't fighting against every German. They are many who didn't want a war. There are others who have grown tired of the war, and still others who are unsure of the purpose behind the battle. You're fighting the evil that inspired it, but you're not alone. You're never alone."

Rosemary and Shona, along with a few of the gypsy women, silently slipped into the fire circle and took a seat. Rosemary waved vigorously as if reminding her of her presence. It made sense for Rosemary to know what was going on, but the others Meara wasn't so sure of.

"I know my father is with me." She laid her hand over her heart.

"He is," Grandmother Biddy agreed. "As are the faeries, your ancestors, those you have met who wish you well, and some within the camp."

It was more than she'd envisioned helping her, but her mind grabbed on one word. "Ancestors? I don't know my people. How could they help me?"

Grandmother Biddy twisted in her seat until she was almost at the edge of it and leaned in Meara's direction. Her shining black eyes compelled attention, not allowing Meara to look away as she held up one gnarled finger for emphasis. "Just because you cannot name your forebears doesn't mean they don't know you and are working on your behalf on the other side of the veil. Your father, as I mentioned before, is strong and can communicate with you in dreams and thoughts, but the others are helping you, too. Keep alert and watch for omens and signs."

A road sign might serve her better, but even those were useless since the British either changed them to confuse the spies or took them down altogether. A few citizens removed their town signs convinced those that needed to know how to get there already knew. "Can you give me an example of what to look for?"

One of the gypsy women murmured a loud agreement.

A quick swivel of Biddy's head pinned the speaker with the basilisk stare. "Hush, Jaelle, or get back to work. There is plenty to be done around camp."

The chastised woman slipped away toward the shoreline, where the sound of hammering emanated from boat repair to Ardan's craft.

Meara straightened and kept her hands tightly clasped in her lap, determined not to interrupt. Grandmother Biddy turned back to her and continued her discussion. "Often as people we take a fancy to something. It could be a trinket, a person, even a job, but if the universe doesn't mean for us to have it then it doesn't fall into place. Do you understand?"

Did she understand? Not entirely, but she scrambled for examples to demonstrate she did get some of it. "I wanted to stay in England, at least for a little bit, but things kept happening to push me on my way."

Rosemary nodded, aware of all that had gone on, but was smart enough not to say anything.

"It is as it should be. When you made the move to leave, did not everything fall into place?"

While her trip was never easy, things did happen when they needed to, from Rosemary arriving with the wagon, to Ardan and Shona ferrying them across the sea. Even the animals helped her on her way. "It did."

"That shows you're on the right path. It doesn't make it easy, but what is needed will come to you as it is necessary. Part of the universe conspires to make things happen, but another part is your ancestors watching over you." She reached out to touch Meara's hand. "You might not hear them whisper in your ear, but it doesn't make them any less."

"That helps." Not as much as she would like. Clear direction would be much more useful.

A raspy laugh escaped Grandmother Biddy's lips as she leaned back and lifted a necklace from the collection around her neck. She shook the necklace making tiny bells jingle. "My own mother gave me this when I was but a youngster. Mothers belled their children to keep them safe from demons and evil spirits. I want you to have it now. Come here, child."

Meara abandoned her perch on the log and knelt in front of the matriarch, who slipped the necklace over her head. A feeling of heaviness settled around her shoulders, making it somewhat difficult to regain her footing with grace. Her fingers stroked the delicate necklace, lifting to check the weight. Perhaps it was the combined weight of the new necklace with the one she retrieved from the convent's treasure box inscribed with her mother's name, Sorcha. If two such necklaces would create such a burden, then the tiny woman before her should not even be able to stand upright.

Observing her fingering the necklace, Grandmother Biddy cleared her throat, directing attention to herself. "It's heavy due to the magic. It's been my own since I was wee, and my mam's before that, and my nana's before that. If I'd had children, I would have bestowed it on my daughter. Instead, I have kept it for you. The necklace symbolizes protection. Combined with the necklace from your mother, which symbolizes love, you are very well guarded."

Well-guarded, protected, loved, she liked the sound of all that. In a time of uncertainty, a smile touched her lips. Grandmother Biddy made another guttural clearing of her throat.

"Don't make the mistake of getting cocky. Don't expect to walk through fire. These trinkets will shield you enough to come up with a workable plan. An intelligent woman always has a plan in place. Do not remove the necklaces even when bathing. Evil also surprises us when we are at our most vulnerable. Stop making it easy and start using your brain. No more excuses about being convent born. What happened to those nuns who didn't escape?"

"They died." She whispered the response not wanting to be reminded of the death of the sisters she'd spent most of her life with. How did the woman know so much about her because she hadn't told anyone in the camp? Rosemary knew a few things, but not everything. When she cut her eyes to her friend, she just shrugged.

Grandmother Biddy held up her boney index finger and wagged it as she spoke. "Some of the sisters may have awoken and thought either death was their divine punishment for some imagined spiritual stumble, or they expected someone to save them. Such thinking is not for you. Whether you want it or not, you've been chosen. Rather like that girl in France…" She paused and look to Jane who supplied her name.

"Joan of Arc."

"Yes, that one. Many followed her because she believed in herself and the message she received."

"I'm familiar with her, but she was burned as a heretic." Not an ending Meara wanted for herself even if the Pope had beatified Joan, assuring her entrance into Heaven and allowing her to intercede for those still on Earth. "Don't see how that made her any less dead."

Her comment caused a few laughs, which the matriarch's upraised hand immediately silenced. "Keep that attitude and you'll survive. I believe Joan's demise was caused by too much pride and not enough compromise. Heard she shouted down nobles and knights. It made her unpopular, and not too surprising, she ended up a prisoner of the English. She was put to death for a stupid reason. Jane, what was it?"

"Wearing men's clothing."

Surely that couldn't be true. She'd been taught that Joan of Arc had visions. The women of her region were sometimes rumored to have the sight. The difference was Joan acted on her visions even going so far as to tell the Dauphin how to run his war. "She was named a heretic."

Jane bobbed her head. "It's against Biblical law for a woman to wear men's clothing."

She knew it was, but burning someone at stake seemed a bit extreme. Before she could say anything, Rosemary did.

"I know plenty of women who wear their husband's pants under their skirts to plow the fields or ride astride. No one comes looking for them."

"True enough," Jane agreed, "but the charge of her wearing men's attire was real. It never seemed to bother anyone too much in battle, especially when they were winning. It's more of an example of people using laws, scriptures, and other rationale for their foul behavior."

"Well said." Grandmother Biddy clapped her hands together. She angled her head in Meara's direction. "Do you know what Joan's big mistake was besides too much pride and temper?"

The rough log irritated Meara's legs through the thin cotton skirt as much as not knowing the answer to the question. She shifted her weight, trying to think of an acceptable reply.

Even as a clairvoyant, Joan hadn't seen her capture coming. Meara didn't know the full tale, only what she was told at the convent. The nuns had a bit of a soft spot for Joan, having labored in a man's world and receiving no recognition for centuries. Perhaps, their high regard stemmed from embarrassment over the fact that their spiritual ancestors chose to roast a woman who had the gall to do a man's job, and apparently, did it better than most men. Sister Thomas had even whispered that the Cardinal had her burned twice since she died quickly from smoke inhalation.

Meara's slight brush with fire made her realize such a death must have been a fearsome thing. A shudder shook her body at the scenario. No need to look around to know everyone was watching her or at least those at the campfire ring. She needed an answer.

"Joan's mistake was she trusted the wrong people."

Rosemary nodded and gave her a wide smile, but Grandmother Biddy acted as if she didn't hear her, making Meara curious if she should repeat herself. "I said—"

Her gnarled hand went up stopping Meara from repeating her explanation. "Most would agree with your answer. As travelers, we know better than to trust those who promise to have our best interest at heart. We can only trust one another, and at times, even then we have been fooled. So, what do you say, Meara Cleary?"

She sucked in her lips for a moment, then spoke. "Trust no one."

Rosemary made an affronted sound from across the campfire while Jane directed a sad look her way.

The matriarch slumped back in her chair, closed her eyes, with the thin blouse moving slightly with each breath. She could be asleep, but that would be odd considering she was in the middle of conversation, although, the elderly Sister Matthew, who Meara had cared for, often fell asleep in mid-conversation. When Sister Matthew woke and discovered she wasn't alone, she usually claimed she was deep in prayer.

Grandmother Biddy had the right to pray as much as anyone else, but Meara suspected if the woman did so, it would involve a raised voice and dramatic hand gestures, not this soft slip into silence.

The object of her scrutiny's eyes popped open with a lively gaze that bore no trace of sleep. "Girl, if you aren't going to come up with a better answer than that, then I will for you. Trust your intuition. Call it your gut or your inner voice. That you can trust."

"Why didn't it stop me from getting in the car with the man called Taylor who had intentions of delivering us to someone?"

"Hmm." Grandmother Biddy rubbed her open hand over her face as she made a humming sound. It was a low, melodious sound like a bee buzzing in the garden. The noise stopped, she dropped her hand and spoke. "Did you not feel anything when the man approached you?"

"Confusion. He seemed so nice and well groomed. Even told us my Uncle Simon sent him, but I did feel something wasn't right. It grew as he drove. It just seemed too convenient since Rosemary and I had no clue what to do next to get to Ireland. The fortune teller, Destiny, told us to look for Red Monesha's clan once we got here." She shrugged her shoulders as she considered that the horrifying incident had happened little more than a day ago.

A slight nudge had Meara moving on her log seat to give Jane room to sit. Once the woman was seated, she nodded in Grandmother Biddy's direction. "This Destiny, I think I heard you speak of her."

"I have. She married a gadjo, an outsider, despite the prediction that her life would be difficult. When she was young, her name was Esmeralda, and all the young girls wanted to be like her. She could not only turn a card with skill, she turned all the young men's heads, too. Even though I didn't want her to leave, I knew it was meant. I'm not surprised she chose Destiny as her name. I realize now she had to leave to guide Meara and her friend here."

"It makes sense now." Jane leaned back a little on her log. "How long ago did she leave? I know I never met her."

Meara wanted to know. Rosemary's avid expression meant she too wanted to know the history of the mysterious fortune teller by the train tracks who not only knew their pasts, but their futures too.

Even though her rescuer, Eleanor, had alluded to meeting Destiny several years ago, Meara had dismissed the claim as shock after their midnight race across the countryside.

"Before you were born, long before. It's hard to remember exact dates. All I do know is if Destiny says something, take it to heart."

Goose bumps pebbled Meara's skin as her heartbeat stumbled before resuming its steady beat. Destiny had had a great deal to say about Meara, her family, even the trip, but most of it faded away the farther she traveled. What if it was information she needed to make it to Galway County?

As if sensing her distress, Jane clasped her hand and squeezed it.

All Meara had to do now was remember the cryptic information portioned out to her in drops.

Chapter Three

A RDAN STRODE CLOSER to the circle and shouted, "Shona, I need your help. We've managed the repairs on the mast, but now we need your sewing skills for the sail."

The woman pushed up from her seat to follow her father. She glanced back at Rosemary, "I'll want to hear everything later."

Meara watched Shona's upright posture as the woman strode away. Only days ago, she hadn't known a female who could sail and swim. In her small landlocked village of Hogstead, there'd be no use of either skill for man or woman. Still, the thought of a daughter helping her father in his chosen profession appealed to her. If her parents would have lived, she'd be out in the fields helping plant and harvest. Ironically, farm families expected as much from their children, but became horrified when a daughter wanted a real job in the city such as a clerk or even a nurse.

Sometimes, the parents would insist a woman's place was to be a wife and mother. Although there was never any backup plan for a woman who married an abusive man, or one who had never married, such as Rosemary. Even though her friend joked numerous times about only accompanying her to find a handsome Irishman to marry, she knew there was some truth to it.

The pull of Hogstead was not the village itself, especially since most had been afraid to befriend her due to Adelaide, the mayor's daughter, disliking her. Any show of friendship toward Meara could result in repercussions not only on the individual, but also their family. Rosemary had already felt the sting of Adelaide's wrath, which was another reason for her midnight departure.

The image of Braeden's smiling face shoved its way into her mind, not that it took much work. She thought of him every day, wondering how he was, where he was, and even if he was still alive. The thought of Braeden had kept her tied to Hogstead. The fear of him returning and not knowing where she was had caused her to stay where she was not welcomed. If she were honest with herself, Braeden had represented an acceptable, easy path for her, if not for Adelaide. Despite the fact she'd spent most of her life inside a convent, it didn't take long for her to accept that women married on the outside.

Even in the convent, the nuns served as brides of Christ and served an unseen husband. Mother Superior relayed the directives, which were assumed to be divine. It didn't take a fortune teller to predict that Meara wouldn't have made a good nun, especially with her curious nature and always asking why. Perhaps, she wouldn't make Braeden a good wife either, since she was neither biddable nor humble.

In an ideal situation, when the war ended, he'd return to her. They'd marry and live somewhere other than Hogstead to avoid the machinations of a spurned Adelaide, and all would be good. Maybe that wasn't her fate. It was the one she wanted, but trying to force it wouldn't make it happen. No matter how much you wanted something and tried to make it happen didn't guarantee anything. Adelaide served as proof enough when she decided on Braeden as her potential bridegroom. Braeden enlisted when he couldn't dissuade the determined woman otherwise.

Her lips twisted into a sour pucker as she realized how much she and Adelaide both had tried to force their surroundings into the outcome they had wanted.

Jane nudged her and asked, "What's the odd expression for?"

Not wanting to explain it, she shrugged. "Thought of something stupid I did. Makes me a bit regretful. I can be so boneheaded."

"Ha. I've done the same."

"Really?" Her brow furrowed as she considered the possibility. "You're surrounded by family. You have Grandmother Biddy to tell you what to do and not to do."

Jane laughed again and wrinkled her nose. "Oh, I've had plenty of people to tell me what to do. It doesn't mean I always listen." She shook her head. "Experience is often the best teacher. My da would always add saying 'fools would have no other.' He trotted that one out whenever I did something daft."

Her attention caught one word. "Does da mean father?"

"It does." Jane acknowledged with a grin. "There's a few other names, I could call him, too, but am smart enough not to."

"What's it like having a father?" In the convent, not only were they not allowed to talk about their past, but Mother Superior was especially against any talk about men, unless it was the disciples.

Jane rested two fingers against her mouth as her eyes rolled up briefly. "It's hard for me to answer that since my da has always been around. He taught me how to drive a team, how to throw a knife, fish, start a fire, and pretty much everything I need to know to survive. On occasion, when I got into trouble with my mother, he'd intervene. Not all the time. Sometimes I deserved whatever punishment I brought on my head."

"In some ways, your da is a teacher."

Jane's eyebrows lifted with the realization. "I never thought of him that way. He does other things, too. He earns money by sharpening knives, mending harnesses, and fixing pots and pans. Dear old Da might be the reason I'm not hand fasted yet."

"How so? Does he chase away all your young men?"

"Not exactly. Inside the camp, we all know each other, which means he knows the good and bad points of the various single males. They know him, too. My best chance would be to marry into another traveler group."

Would it be that easy to find another group? Perhaps there were dozens of such caravans crisscrossing the country. "Would your father be okay with you marrying someone who wasn't a traveler?"

A nearby woman whooped with laughter at the question. "She might as well marry an Englishman, then."

"What's wrong with an Englishman?"

Both Jane and the fellow traveler laughed so hard tears streamed down their faces. The show of hilarity had Grandmother Biddy tamping her walking stick for attention. In a powerful voice that didn't fit her small frame, she shouted, "Enough!"

The laughter stopped, and most of the women appeared chagrined, as they straightened on their log seats. It was easy to see who really ruled the group. The matriarch's gaze slowly went around the circle, focusing on each woman a moment before moving onto the next. A few bowed their heads, breaking eye contact. Meara vowed not to, since it would do her more good to be courageous as opposed to her reactive behavior.

When the dark eyes settled on her, she lifted her chin and returned the look. The lively intelligence and determination she saw in the old crone's eyes made her wiggle a little, but she refused to drop her gaze. She'd been schooled her entire life to keep her eyes downward. Such an action was a sign of humility as was appropriate for a bride of Christ. It didn't matter that she wasn't an actual sister. Meara had to follow the same rules. Sister Margaret explained humility was based on the root word, humble, meaning low or of little importance.

No. Meara refused to accept she was of no importance. Why had her mother struggled to get to a safe place before giving birth if she was of no importance? Why had her father worked so hard to reach her? Or compelled Eleanor to seek her out? Better yet, why were there those seeking her out to possibly hurt or kill her if she was of such little importance? It would make more sense for them to spend time on seeking someone else.

Her chin stayed up as her eyes met Grandmother Biddy's. Maybe, she didn't have a clue what her purpose was, but she would soon. Until then, she'd have to do her best to trust her instinct and watch for omens. Something brushed against her bare foot, forcing her to drop her gaze to see a small toad looking upward.

Jane pointed to the creature. "I've never seen any as bold to hop to a person."

Grandmother Biddy used her walking stick to point at the toad as she remained seated. "Look, Meara. Your first omen. What does it mean?"

Her hand covered her face, allowing her a few minutes to stall. Eleanor had spoken about animals being messengers of a sort. Usually the messages were good or encouraging, that much she knew. Often it had something to do with whatever was troubling the person at the time.

She peeked between her fingers and noticed the tiny toad held his place. What could he possibly mean?

Jane whispered in her ear. "Good luck. A change in fortune. A reminder not to doubt yourself and push forward."

Meara hesitated, wondering if she should repeat Jane's words exactly. She lowered her hand and observed the tiny toad, who acted more as if guided by an unseen hand. Once again, she felt the weight of the combined gazes. Her left hand reached up and wrapped around the necklaces, feeling assurance at the contact.

"The toad is here to remind me I'm never alone. Even though my fate has taken a turn I might not have wanted, it is a good one all the same. Good fortune awaits, but I'll have to do the hard things first before I earn this reward."

Some of the women in the campfire circle shot her a smile or a nod. A few murmured behind their hands, but they all turned toward the matriarch waiting for her response. Grandmother Biddy gave a regal nod and smiled at Meara. "Excellent. I should have known Jane would whisper to you the standard answer. I'm glad you didn't settle for it, but instead drew on your intuition for the meaning that applied to you."

Was that what she did? She had no clue. As if when she truly opened her eyes to the toad, she just knew.

"How can I learn to tune into this intuition?" It would be a handy skill to have on her side.

Rosemary thought the same. "I want to know, too. Can anyone do it?"

A hoarse chuckle emanated from Grandmother Biddy. She grinned, surprising Meara. The remaining women in the circle directed knowing looks at each other. A few worked their way to the edge of their log seats, leaning in the direction of the matriarch as if not to miss a thing.

Her fingertips swept up in a graceful arc and met in front of her face. Grandmother Biddy cleared her throat and gestured to Jane, who immediately stood, rushed away, and returned with a cup.

"Many thanks," Grandmother Biddy accepted the cup and drank deeply before she spoke.

"My children, many of you know what I am going to say. Some of you," she held up one index finger, "have forgotten or fail to practice. This is for you as much as it is for our visitors. Ask yourself if you rush into things without weighing the rightness of it? Does everything appear blurry when you turn a Tarot card as you can't read the meaning? If so, listen well."

Her dark eyes traveled around the group scrutinizing the women for a lack of interest. Finding none, she continued by stretching out her hand to one of the women. "Betha, what do you do when you wake up in the morning?"

The dark-haired woman looked thoughtful, answering slowly. "I give thanks that I am alive and have another day to call my own."

"Good. Gratitude sets the right tone."

Meara's lips pulled to one side as she considered her previous daily routine. Before the dawn rose, she'd been on her knees in the chapel chanting Latin prayers. She assumed they were prayers of thanksgiving but wasn't sure.

"What else?" Grandmother Biddy asked, with a certain imperious-ness.

Betha's eyebrows drew together as she pondered the question. Her finger rubbed her creased brow, but failing to come with any insights, she sighed loudly. "Grandmother Biddy, you know well that I have a man and three children to care for. There isn't any time for lying in bed."

A few others murmured their agreement until the stick stomping sounded again. "No excuses. How can you expect to get better when you refuse to do the work? Jane?"

"Upon waking, I simply breathe and listen. Sometimes I feel a shift in the universe. Other times I feel like something might happen, but I don't always know what."

Meara caught Rosemary's eyes across the circle. Her friend gave a slight bob. Had she too felt something the night they left? An urgency she'd put down to the growing strength of evil in the forest? Malevolence didn't confine itself to the forest, but streamed out everywhere polluting cities, countries, even soaking into the seas.

Her hand slipped before she'd even considered raising it.

"Meara? Do you have a question?"

"I do. What good is it to know something is going to happen if you don't know the details? I could get a feeling and decide to leave town, fearing the worst, when it was something good. I may have left the goodness behind."

"Good reasoning." She twisted in the chair and stretched her arms upward. "The ominous feeling of something evil heading your way is different from the happy expectation of something good. It benefits you to take the temperature of the day before your feet even hit the floor. If you're unaware there is a fortuitous event heading your way, then you can miss it."

Betha coughed and shook her head violently in denial.

The matriarch held out her stick toward the woman. "Betha, did you have something to add?"

"We are all governed by fate. We cannot change what is."

A swell of chatter rose as the various women reacted to her statement. Instead of stamping her stick, the elderly woman waited until the talking died down.

"Fate plays a part in our lives. We cannot choose our parents, the country we reside in, or even our children, but we can determine how we react to something. This is the importance of knowing or intuition. Without it, we miss out on opportunities, knowing when to push forward and to hold our tongue. Sometimes," she tapped her forehead with her finger, "we consider the decisions we make based on logic."

"True enough," a woman close to Meara agreed.

Did people act out of logic or intuition? She couldn't see the point in Adelaide announcing to one and all that she and Braeden were engaged when the man knew nothing about it. Did that make any sense?

"Did he know nothing about it?"

A voice she didn't recognize deposited a seed of doubt. After all, what could a man say to win her affections when supposedly engaged to another?

The sound of tongue clicking drew her eyes to Jane. "You don't agree."

"I do not. Just wait and watch Grandmother Biddy correct them."

A Tarot card appeared in the matriarch's hand. Meara leaned forward to distinguish what it was. A grinning skeleton holding a scythe and presiding over a dark landscape. "Do those who visit you for a reading react logically when you turn this card?"

A nervous laughter went through the group while one woman clapped her hands together.

"Oh, my, no. Many are afraid and accuse me of dealing the cards wrong and even threaten not to pay me unless I reshuffled the cards. When I explain it means change, they calm down somewhat, but not all believe me."

"That shows you should get your money first, Aine."

Another woman remarked, "Why do you bother telling the truth to the settled? They don't want that. If a woman comes to you, be she single or married, she wants to hear about some great love. You tell the men they will come into great wealth and will be the envy of all other men."

The crosstalk made it hard for Meara to determine who was talking.

"Lust, greed, envy, it all boils down to the same thing."

One woman shouted to be heard over the others, "Do those who seek a reading react from intuition or logic?"

All the talking, the noise, the disagreement, even though it may have been good-natured, bothered Meara. Her hands covered her ears attempting to shut out the voices. She squeezed her eyes shut, wishing that things could go back to the way they were when Grandmother Biddy was explaining.

"Everyone needs to stop talking."

Silence slipped over the group as if a low hanging cloud encompassed them all.

Meara opened her eyes slowly to avid stares. Each woman sat with mouth closed, which made her feel slightly ridiculous with her hands over her ears. Her hands slipped back to her lap, and she turned her head toward Grandmother Biddy, who regarded her with a frown.

"Meara Cleary, there was no reason to shout at us."

"I didn't." If anything, she did the opposite of shouting. She just wanted everyone to be quiet. She could remember thinking hard about it. Several faces said otherwise. Her elbow nudged Jane by her side.

"Did you see me say anything?"

"Nay, your lips never moved, but you shouted your intentions just the same. You said, 'Everyone needs to stop talking.'"

She had thought that. Well, that wasn't good if her thoughts broadcast to all and sundry. Destiny had warned her to put up barriers. "I'm sorry. The noise was all so confusing." Her skin reddened due the realization she'd told a group of women to be quiet.

"No worries," Jane assured her. "We travelers can be a noisy bunch and could benefit from being told to gentle our voices."

A few others agreed and started chattering again until Grandmother Biddy waved her stick. "Be gone, except for Meara. I suspect Monesha has jobs for all of you."

The women stood, some in pairs, a few alone, but they all hurried off, except for Betha. "You never told us if people act from logic or intuition."

"Neither. They act out of fear. A smart individual can use that fear to control the masses."

Betha nodded, then picked up the edge of her skirt and hurried away, leaving only Meara and Grandmother Biddy.

"Come closer, child."

A careful inspection of the empty circle yielded no other she could be addressing. Her knees trembled as she pushed herself into a standing position. Her feet felt like blocks she had to will in the direction of Grandmother Biddy. It wasn't that the woman frightened her. It was more what she might say that scared her.

Each day the world she knew changed. She changed in ways she couldn't even imagine. At times, Meara didn't even know who she was any more. Did she ever know who she was or had she just accepted what people told her?

The story she had accepted was a woman had collapsed at the convent, given birth to her, and then died. No more words were spoken about her mother, although the general feeling was that she'd birthed a nameless bastard who'd do well to serve the sisters in the convent.

On cat paw feet, Meara approached the ornate chair and finally, when she was near enough, she queried, "What can I do for you?"

"What can you do for me?" The woman sighed and rubbed her hand over her face before continuing. "It's not what you can do for me. It's what I can do for you. Without control, you can't achieve your goals."

"What are my goals? It would help if people would tell me exactly what I need to do."

"All in appropriate time. Think of yourself as the glue that unites the good things in the world. In times of great distress, people tend to forget the good and dwell on the bad."

She was the glue that held things together? Not a very appealing possibility, considering glue was made of horses' hooves, skin, and bones. Glue had the rank odor of death clinging to it. Her goal was to be as far away from killing and destruction as possible.

"Why glue?"

Grandmother Biddy held out her hand, palm up to Meara. "Look at your own hand. Without connective tissue, muscles, and skin, it would be of little use. It needs these things to work. In this world, there is much loss of life and snuffing out of hope. Part of this is people's willingness to obey without question, without searching their hearts for what is right. Those fighting on the behalf of evil aren't necessarily dark-hearted individuals. They could be average people with families, who enjoy a delicious meal and a walk through the woods like the rest of us."

"I don't understand what makes them evil." She'd always considered the faceless German soldiers as a demonic race with superior strength and red eyes driven by an insatiable desire to kill. Such images only fueled her fear for Braeden. How could he withstand such creatures?

"The same thing that makes anyone a tool of evil. The refusal to question what they know in their hearts to be wrong. The inability to stand up against that darkness. An Irishman said it best. No surprise since the Irish have always had the gift of eloquence. The only thing necessary for the triumph of evil is for good men to do nothing."

The words resonated inside of her. They had the weight and heft of truth. "There are people, good and true, that are currently doing nothing. For this war to cease, I must somehow unite these people?"

Grandmother Biddy gave the slightest incline of her chin as acknowledgement. Meara breathed in deeply. Although she had a rough idea of what was meant, it didn't mean she understood her part in the entire tapestry that was being woven around her.

"I'm supposed to unite all the good people?"

Even Joan of Arc had failed to do that, and she was a saint.

"You're the start and at times the end, too,"

Jane had warned her that Grandmother Biddy could make cryptic statements. At times, it felt like everyone made cryptic statements from Destiny to even Eleanor, her much loved rescuer. The only time things weren't too obscure was whatever order Mother Superior issued, which usually consisted of Meara, you need to do this, then she'd name some form of manual labor.

"How can I be the start and the end?"

Grandmother Biddy closed her hand and pulled it back onto her lap. "There are many who assume because they live in Ireland that they are safe. No need to worry about the Germans or possible harm. What they fail to see is the hate and disharmony bubbling up even in the heart of our own land. For some, encountering you will remind them the war is real. Evil exists. It will be more a poke in the side, forcing them from their comfortable belief that things might not be so good elsewhere, but all is right in their world."

"I'm not sure what I'm supposed to be doing. All I want is to locate my kin in Galway."

"You'll find them. Of that you can be certain. Remember when you wanted everyone to be quiet?"

Embarrassed that she'd somehow mentally shouted at the group, she replied in a soft, chagrined tone. "I do. I didn't really mean to do what I did."

"They're a noisy bunch. Sometimes, they do need to be told to hush. It isn't easy getting them to do so. Consider what you did close to a miracle. Still…" She brandished her index finger. "…you need training."

"Destiny told me I needed shielding. I thought I was doing that."

Grandmother Biddy released her walking stick, which tumbled to the ground and held out her hands. Meara took the outstretched hands feeling strength in the gnarled fingers.

"People always come to me, even those in my clan, wanting to know their future. Grandmother Biddy, will I marry well? Will I be rich? Well-liked? Powerful? I can't recall one single person, and I've turned the cards for thousands, asking how they could be a force for good. You have that magnificent opportunity."

It sounded good in theory, but many things did and turned out not to work in the real world. She shook her head. "I don't understand."

"That's why you're here. That's why Destiny and fate directed you here. I'm an old woman, much older than anyone in our tribe. Providence preserved me, so I could teach you. We travelers hold mainly to the Roman Catholic Church, but my forbearers also held to the land and the magic that accompanies the elements. This I'll teach you as we travel. It will give you the opportunity to practice in a safe environment. We'll start with an easy task. Dancing."

"Dancing?" Surely, she heard her wrong. How could dancing be a force of good? "Grandmother Biddy, I respect your knowledge and compassion, but how can dancing help?"

Her dark eyes sparkled, and she squeezed Meara's hands. "Dancing is a very powerful tool. Have you not heard the tale in your nunnery about Salome and how she danced before Herod?"

"I have. It was usually pointed out to me that Herod was depraved, while Salome was demonic."

Grandmother Biddy managed a raspy chuckle. "I'd expect no less from the good sisters. Salome was exercising the power of dance. At its simplest level, it can gladden the heart. To dance makes people happy. On the next level, it entertains or entrances people. It is also an excellent vehicle for magic."

"Pardon me?" While she would have claimed dancing close with Braeden was magical, she never considered it a work of magic.

"Dancing allows you the ability to work your way through a crowd without anyone being suspicious. It also allows you to move close to someone without them putting up mental boundaries. Dancing in some ways makes people open to suggestion." The matriarch's eyebrows arched.

"I think I understand. That's when Salome suggested she wanted John the Baptist's head, and it seemed reasonable to Herod."

"Not reasonable." Her lips pulled down in a frown as she continued. "I'd like to think beheading would not be considered an option. John the Baptist had been a thorn in his side, complaining about his relationships and how he governed. Pointing the finger at him and naming his sins. Herod wanted to be rid of John the Baptist and Salome provided the way."

Images of her dancing with Braeden morphed into an exotic dark-eyed young woman swirling her skirts, and when she made her final turn, she held up the bloody head of John the Baptist. "Why did John the Baptist have to die? Was he not the good in the world?"

"Everyone dies. Today, hundreds, perhaps thousands of souls slipped from this world into the next. Most go quietly and are soon forgotten. John the Baptist we still talk about and learn how to live and die from his example."

"Still." Grandmother Biddy wasn't understanding what she was saying. Why couldn't she make it clear. If someone was in the right and doing what he was instructed to do by a divine order, then dying such a horrific fashion should not be."

"I do understand. Sometimes, your manner of death gets a message through better than a long life can. Don't worry, Meara. Your job isn't to die just now. If you listen to your intuition, pay attention to what I teach you, you have many years ahead of you."

Many years cheered her and made her feel lighter. Grandmother Biddy still holding her hands, caught her eye and continued. "If you let your fears take hold of you and you find yourself constantly reacting to everything as opposed to anticipating it, then you won't last the year. Your companions, faeries, and even your father managed to keep you safe this far, but now it is up to you. What is it going to be?"

"Teach me."

Grandmother Biddy pointed to her stick on the ground. Even though Meara bent to reach for the stick, it quivered, rose from the ground, and hovered mere inches from her nose before dropping to the ground. How was such a thing possible?

"Will I be able to do that?" she asked, handing the stick to her.

The matriarch planted the stick into the ground to rise as she spoke. "You'll be able to do much, much more. Almost picking up a stick is no great feat. When I was younger, I could call the wind."

It certainly would be handy if a person needed a wind, especially a sailor. If she hadn't seen the stick move with her very own eyes, she'd suspect it was a made-up story, something invented for long winter nights to keep company amused. "Tell me more."

"First, let's go to my wagon. Even though I consider the tribe my people, they can at times be a suspicious lot."

Chapter Four

THE INTERIOR OF the wagon was just as fanciful as the outside. Sunlight filtered into the cabin from the open shutters. Drying flowers and herbs hung upside down between ropes of tiny bells and tassels. There was a drawing of the hand with several lines across it with cramped handwriting beside the lines. An ornate crucifix was hammered onto one wall. Beside it, someone had painted a tree with branches reaching upward and roots spreading out below. She recognized the tree from Destiny's house.

Couldn't remember what it was called. Just remember the fortune teller saying something about as above so below. She turned in the cramped space trying to separate the heady smells. Onion, she knew. Garlic dominated. Sweeter scents such as nutmeg, cinnamon, and ginger she recognized, but there were more fiery scents she didn't.

The acrid smell of sulfur had her turning in to witness her hostess lighting candles. Grandmother Biddy held a tiny stick to the lit candle, and it fizzled and flamed to life. The stick was used to light other candles. Noticing her attention, Grandmother Biddy smiled.

"Most of the travelers would not be caught using matches. My age allows me these small luxuries. Before you ask why I'm lighting candles during the day, close the shutters, angle the louvres up, which will allow the smoke out. What I'm about to teach you is only for you. No one else."

An outward reach to grab the shutters edges caught the attention of a woman walking by with a yoke across her shoulder that held two water buckets. Her lips went up in what Meara hoped was a smile. Once the shutters were hooked shut, she angled the louvres up, still puzzled why so much special instruction would be hers.

"Why teach me? I'm a stranger to you. Why not Jane?"

"I agree that Jane is a sharp one. Probably one of the sharpest in the caravan. She's had the benefit of much of my teaching. Still, she doesn't have the skills or the maturity to comprehend what you need to learn. Can I see your necklace? The one that belonged to your mother?"

Meara's hand went to her neck but paused. "You told me never to take it off."

"So I did. It was good of you to remember. Just pull it out from underneath your blouse. I can examine it without you removing it."

Meara's fingers rested on the necklace, absorbing the texture of the fine chain. Somehow, it managed to be strong and delicate. She held the pendant part closer to the light hoping it might make it easier to see.

A raspy laugh escaped the crone. "You're a kind one. I'd almost say you were too good for this world, but the pure at heart is what the world needs. I don't need to see it. All I need to do is touch it to see what I suspect is true."

Her gnarled fingers straightened and reached for the pendant. Only her index and middle fingers came to rest on it.

Grandmother Biddy's eyes fluttered close. Such a pose signaled immense focus as opposed to sleep.

For what seemed like forever, but had to be at the most minutes, Meara held still, and remained silent while the pendant was examined. Even using the special jewelry cleaner Eleanor concocted, the best she done was remove the grime of the years and lighten the silver enough to reveal her mother's name. What else could be hidden in the pendant beside the tiny pictures of her parents, which were now somewhat worse the wear after her ocean adventure?

Finally, Grandmother Biddy opened her eyes. "It is as I thought."

"What?"

"Your mother, Sorcha, is a descendant of the faeries."

Meara lips formed a mulish line, wondering why the woman was wasting her time talking nonsense. Here she thought she'd get some help, but instead, some rambling. Not unlike Sister Augustine, who declared she had daily conversation with her long dead namesake. She also claimed to have the ability to turn water into wine, but she never demonstrated it. Mother Superior's edict against strong drink kept her from using her skills or so she said, "I know faeries are tiny people, smaller than a flower blossom."

"Some are. There are many children of Danu. In the beginning of time, man and faeries were friends. They walked among the sons and daughters of Ireland, much taller than the Irish themselves, and all were fair of face. It wasn't surprising that many a lass fell for a faery lad and many a faery lass for a human lad. There was intermingling, but that caused a break between the two races. Still, the call of the faery exists in the descendants. No wonder the faeries were anxious to help you."

"I thought it was my father."

"That was a part of it. Your parents could have been drawn together by the faeries. They can see or predict what might happen, but even that isn't enough. People are a willful lot, never wanting to listen to good counsel but do as they please. Imagine your parents, if here, would tell you love brought them together."

"I want to believe that." There hadn't been a great deal of love in her life. There was plenty of mention of God's love within the walls of the convent. Right on the heels of the mention was a promise of punishment, usually involving a fiery pit and everlasting torture. It wasn't the thing to inspire endless devotion. She got glimpses of love when Eleanor talked about her family. On some level, she wanted to be in love with Braeden and believe he loved her. The fact he knew so little about her caused doubts, more than a few. As opposed to loving her, perhaps he only saw her as a better alternative to the petty, domineering Adelaide.

"You can. It does you no harm doing so." She tapped one finger against her temple. "I suspect the faeries caused some confusion, even mental manipulation to bring your parents together."

Well, if that hadn't happened, there'd be no her. "When my uncle and his friend showed up, they talked about my mother, Sorcha, being both beautiful and stubborn. No mention of her showing any interest in getting married, until she met my father, fell in love, and went to England."

"Sounds like magic to me, but only the best kind. Men and women often engage in an intricate dance when it comes to courtship. First, they circle around one another, deciding if they should make a move or not. How bonny a lass is or how fine a lad is part of the attraction. Then it goes onto finding out if the person is someone you'll want to spend your entire life sleeping next to."

The words reached her, even crawled into her head, and resonated with the other ideas percolating there. Was she part fey? If so, what skills did she possess? Could she call the faeries with her mind? If the faeries had brought her parents together, then for what purpose? Here she worried that Braeden confessed his love and intention to marry her without really knowing who she was, but did she have any clue herself who she was?

"If faeries helped my parents meet, what was their intention?"

The bony shoulders went up in a shrug. "Only the faeries know for sure. Faeries can be romantic and simply wanted your mother and father to be in love. I suspect since time passes differently in the faerie realm that they realized a dark time would be upon us and brought your parents together to help create you as an antidote to the evil."

Meara held her hands about a foot apart, palms facing each other, and gestured with them emphatically. "All this 'you're here for a purpose' I don't get. If I had such an important purpose why did my parents die? Shouldn't they have lived to raise me?"

"It would seem that way to most, but then your life may have turned out to be an ordinary one with you marrying a neighboring farmer and producing a child every two to three years until you were worn out."

"They died so I wouldn't have a normal life?" She dropped her out-stretched hands feeling a little poleaxed at the possibility.

"They died because there is evil in the world. It's the way of things that evil will attempt to extinguish the light and the good."

Back in Hogstead, she'd felt the darkness in the woods. Eleanor credited the feeling to someone have been murdered there. The normal serenity Meara felt surrounded by nature had been absent in that one spot. Most of the time the two of them had avoided walking that way, especially when the nameless force had reached out of the ground and grabbed them as they passed. A cold hand had wrapped around her ankle as the wind and rain slashed at them. Later, Eleanor explained the wind and rain were the water sprites fighting back on their behalf.

"This is so overwhelming. How can I fight back this darkness?"

Grandmother Biddy's dark eyes stared into hers as if trying to peer into her soul. The woman slumped back in her chair as if exhausted from her survey. "You can't."

"What was all this talk about having a mission and even coming here and meeting? You promised to teach me. Why bother if none of it matters?"

A heavy sigh filled the tiny space. "Ah, the same high emotion and drama as any other girl your age. I should have expected it. Listen first with your heart and spirit, before you despair."

"I will try. It's just that I have so many doubts about almost everything."

The sharp clap of Grandmother Biddy's hand along with the jangle of her bracelet punctured the pity balloon forming in her mind.

"Brush off your doubts." She made a brushing motion with her hands. "You have doubts or intentions. You can't have both."

"How so?" Maybe this was the teaching part she promised her, but she assumed it had something to do with dancing.

"Have you wished for something and then it happened?" Her crossed arms and smug expression relayed that she knew the answer.

Had she? While in the convent, wishes or dreams that did not fall into the narrow confines of their daily life were forbidden. Although at times, she had wished to be out of the convent walls, and she'd discovered a bolt hole. There were times she'd even wished to experience the outside world. Her hand flattened against her chest as she asked in a voice tight with horror, "I didn't cause the destruction of the convent."

"No. Evil caused it. Whenever men choose to war against one another, evil wields the whip."

That explained it. If Mother Superior were alive, she would have claimed, instead, that their purpose was to be martyrs because their God directed every action. "You know this using your magic skills?"

"No, child." Her hand went up to her head and patted it. "I used my brain. If you could consider intelligence magical, then it was magic. Maybe common sense is a divine power since so few appear to have it."

"How did you figure out what happened when you weren't there?"

"Simple. I took what I knew. Germans were waging war against England. Nuns in a nunnery do nothing more than pray and sing. They have no influence on anything around them. Why would the Germans bomb a nunnery?"

"It makes no sense. Hogstead is only a country village. The bomb came in the night, which meant whoever dropped it couldn't see what they were bombing."

"They could have been off course."

"I can accept that readily enough, but what about me escaping and all that?"

"That's when the magic happened."

Her midnight foray into the woods had started out as an unexplained urge, but soon turned dangerous after she bumped into German soldiers. "I think you lost me."

Grandmother Biddy reached for a shawl woven with vivid red roses and curling green leaves. She handed the soft shawl to Meara as she spoke.

"Look closely at it."

Well made, roses in all their different forms from a tiny bud to a full-blown rose on the edge of decay formed the design. On the underside was a reverse design, but she wasn't sure what she should be seeing. "Should I be looking for something?"

"Just one thread."

The garment must be composed of hundreds or thousands of threads. "Which thread is it? Any color?"

"Pick what one you want. Follow it through the weave of the cloth."

She brought the fabric in her hand closer to the candlelight. The edge of the shawl was fringed allowing her to pick out a navy thread. "I found one."

"Good. Can you see where it goes?"

If this was a magic test, she failed. "No, it mixes in with the other navy threads making a whole."

"Correct. This is life. There are many people, many thoughts, actions, intentions, even doubts that compose our daily life. Even when you thought you were alone, you were not. Others on this side of the veil and on the other are interacting with you."

"I understand that much. My father explained it to me, but what about the sisters? Was not anyone working on their behalf?"

Grandmother Biddy placed a finger to her lips and remained silent for a few heartbeats, just long enough to make Meara squirm. Finally, the woman dropped her hand to answer the question.

"I imagine some did escape. Probably those ill suited to take the habit and probably a few just waiting for such an opportunity. The others had long since learned to still the voices of their ancestor, considering it some devil's trick. So they died."

The way the old woman uttered pronouncement unnerved her, but Grandmother hadn't known any of the sisters and had no emotion about their passing. Talking or listening to dead people was so new to Meara. "Sometimes, I can hear my father, but not always. Why not my mother?"

"You will. I know this," she paused to tap her fingers on her chest, "in here. When people die and go to the other side, they leave with the only the knowledge they had at the time of their death. Your mother doesn't understand she has the power to communicate with you, but she will. Even now I feel a presence in this wagon."

No wispy form of a woman hovered in any of the corners. "I don't see anyone."

"Use your heart, your spirit, to sense these things. Too often people are fooled by what they see, but the heart never deceives. Remember in the circle, I asked the women what they did first thing in the morning."

She nodded, remembering the exchange.

"Everyone should open their senses upon waking to see if any changes occurred while they were asleep. Our ancestors did this which saved their lives on more than one occasion."

A crouching predator formed in her mind. It turned from a four-legged beast into a two-legged human armed with a heavy stone. Her ancestor rolled out of the way just in time. "I understand about hearing something? What else?"

"Our intuition or spirit picks up on disturbances in the air around you. It can register the weight of emotions. Have you ever felt someone staring at you before you turned around and confirmed it? When you met someone that you never met before, did you immediately sense they disliked you?"

She'd felt Braeden's eyes on her and was practically burned by Adelaide's dislike. "Yes, to both. Is that magic?"

"It's a start. Good trackers and hunters take the time to listen and truly feel. Our world is in transition before something happens. There are warnings. Old people like me are often looking to the cards or the sky for signs, but someone like you, who is on the move, must be on alert. Your job is to sense another's intentions. Do they mean you good or harm?"

"If they're a good person, then I can relax?"

"No. Remember your own words about trusting no one. Even good people can be tricked into doing wrong things. I'm sure there are many Germans who think the English are foul creatures who do not even deserve a country."

"Why would they think that?" It was so obvious that the average

English man or woman posed no threat.

"Because they were told repeatedly that it is so. It sounded right, familiar, after hearing it so many times."

How often had that happened to her? What did she believe that wasn't real? Meara pursed her lips and blew out a long breath. "It appears, the more I learn, the less I know."

"That's the start." Grandmother Biddy nodded slowly and withdrew a silk bag holding a rectangular shape.

Even though Meara suspected it was Tarot cards, the desire to know about her future didn't intrigue her as it would have a couple of days ago. She knew her past, so that didn't bear repeating. "What about the thread example? Was there something you were going to show me besides there's lots of thread in one shawl?"

"Yes." She reached out for the shawl, which Meara readily surrendered. "Show me which thread is yours?"

Her teeth clamped together. This she hadn't expected. If she had, she could have done something to make it more noticeable than its fellow threads. Her eyes stared at the patch of navy that made up the background and followed it to the fringe. *Universe, help me pick the right one.*

Guilt stabbed at her for asking for help on such an insignificant matter, but maybe that's what intuition was all about. The wrinkled hand rested on hers. Grandmother Biddy grasped the thread Meara was holding, wrapped it around two fingers and yanked.

"Oh!" The exclamation escaped her before she could even think to tamp it down. While she could sew a torn tunic or replace a button, she never had the skill that Sister Ignatius had at the loom, allowing her to spend long hours creating cloth to sell as opposed to doing the mundane tasks the other sisters performed. When she was younger, Sister Ignatius tried to teach her the art of weaving, certain her nimble fingers would be able to work faster than hers.

It hadn't been successful. The repetitive work often allowed her mind to wander, which resulted in an untidy weave. It did teach her that pulling a thread could damage a cloth, and if it was a poor weave she had made, the entire thing could fall apart.

The shawl lay on the table where Grandmother Biddy had spread it out. The stocky white candle lent its light to the section where a lengthy line interrupted the expanse of navy. The tightly woven material hadn't fallen apart, but there was still an obvious flaw.

"Why did you do that?"

"As a demonstration that every thread, every person is a part of the whole. If one person fails to do his or her part, then the whole is weaker for it."

That much she knew. "If I fail to do my part, then whatever everyone is weaving together may not work."

"That is so."

Too much responsibility for someone who before had only been entrusted with feeding the livestock and picking berries. "Where are these other people?"

"You've met some of them already. Eleanor, who took you in. Rosemary, your loyal friend. Ardan and Shona who heeded the universe and brought you here. There are many more you have yet to meet. While evil lurks in our time, so does the light. I'd like to read your cards now."

There was no gentle request as to if she wanted her cards read, which she would have refused, although she doubted anyone refused Grandmother Biddy. The woman untied the silk bag and withdrew ornate cards that showed wear at the edges. She shuffled slowly as Meara tried to prepare herself.

"You forgot about teaching me about the dancing magic." Which wasn't an entirely terrible thing.

"Ah, I see what you're doing, but I had forgotten. Dance is a magic all its own. It is joy, love, romance, and adventure wrapped into physical expression. We travelers love to dance. Well, most of us. There are a few who don't. Your job tonight is to get everyone dancing, except the guards."

"Guards?" She hadn't noticed any, but there had been men on the edge of the camp who didn't join the circle.

"We always post guards. Not everyone welcomes our caravan. Some even chase us away, afraid we might steal their chickens or children. I guess in the latter respect we're grouped with faeries, which is not an entirely a terrible thing."

"What should I do?"

"It's all about intention. It's not enough to have a thought in your head. It's important not to have any other thought in your head such as doubt about if it will work. Strong emotion fuels your intention. Think back to when you called the birds. What did you feel?"

"Absolute terror. I had a certainty if something didn't change, Rosemary and I would die."

Her hands tighten into fists, which she shook trying to shake off the dread she relived discussing the event.

"Very powerful emotion, but this time I want you to think happiness and joy when you think of everyone dancing. Keep the thought in your head that everyone should dance." Her fingers met in a contemplative pose.

"Is that all?" It didn't sound like that much, which made her speculate on why other people weren't employing intentions or maybe they were.

Grandmother Biddy lifted her chin and stared over Meara's shoulder. Her expression remained avid, and her head cocked as if she were listening to someone, then she nodded her head.

"Your mother thinks you should dance. It would only be natural that others would follow."

Why could Grandmother Biddy see her mother when she couldn't. "Did she say why I should dance?"

A gleam appeared in the old woman's eyes. "To feel joy, but also it would be strange if you didn't dance when everyone did."

Anticipation coursed through Meara's body as she considered the night ahead and her intention experiment. Doubt chased up her spine, too. She inhaled deeply, remembering there could be no true intentional work when doubt existed. It wasn't a question of she could do this. It was more that she had to. She had to be a thread in the whole. No way could she allow the fabric to unravel because of her inability to act.

Chapter Five

THE SOUND OF the cards being shuffled drew her attention. Her attempt to distract Grandmother Biddy from reading the cards only delayed the inevitable. The formidable woman fanned out the cards before stacking them into a pile and shuffling again.

"Meara, the cards can be a tool if used correctly, as can a pendulum. You need to know about both before I send you on. Emotions, usually fear, sometimes lust, stop us from doing what we should. They can cloud our judgement. It is good to consult another authority. That's why I use my pendulum or cards. Often, I do both just to be certain I'm not doing what I want to do as opposed to what is right. Everyone in the caravan depends on me for good advice. It will be the same with you."

"It's only Rosemary and me. So far, Rosemary has had the best advice."

"Your friend is a smart one because she relies a little more on her intuition than you do. That could come from living close to nature as a farmer. A person learns to read the many moods of the natural world. There is no reason you can't do the same."

Her inner world was telling her too much was happening at once. "Could we just concentrate on the dancing and save the cards for later?"

The thin lips pressed together as Grandmother Biddy placed the cards back into their silk bag. "I'll respect your wishes. Keep in mind you don't have forever to learn what you need to survive on your own. You'll not only be responsible for your own welfare, but for others, too."

The potential responsibility pressed down on her as if heavy hands landed on her shoulders. The sensation made her want to bolt. It also made her wonder if she'd made a mistake refusing the card reading. Part of her wanted to apologize for her words and ask for a reading. She neither bolted nor apologized. Instead, she lifted her chin and look directly into the questioning gaze.

"I understand. Tomorrow will be soon enough." Unsure of the protocol of the camp, she stood, not knowing if she should be dismissed. Waiting under Grandmother Biddy's intense stare caused her to shift her weight from foot to foot.

Finally, the woman spoke. "Stop that!" She clapped her hands together, emphasizing her point. "It will never serve you to broadcast your emotions. You'd do better to stay perfectly still and say nothing. Allow the other person to feel uneasy. Cultivate this skill, and you can hide in plain sight. Now, you should go find Jane. Ask her to teach you how to fish, clean the fish, and how to use a knife. These are all practical skills and should not tax you overly."

"I will. Thank you, Grandmother Biddy, for your instruction."

The woman gave a sharp bark of laughter as if Meara's words amused her. She gestured with her left hand as if shooing Meara away while searching for something. Not knowing what to do, she backed out of the wagon and descended the steps, hoping to find Jane nearby.

Never had she refused a directive, especially from such a formidable personage. What was happening to her? Her sudden expulsion into the secular world forced changes, which she'd expected to a degree. Never would she consider herself a leader or guardian, of sorts, meant to watch over others. How could she when she didn't even have the basic skills to survive on her own?

Eleanor had taught her to recognize edible herbs and berries in the woods. Being able to fish would be helpful, although knife throwing would possibly be even more important in her quest. Her mission, quest, or whatever it was, perplexed her. Her personal goal was to find the Cleary family and connect with them. In time, she hoped to discover her father's family as well.

Offhand, she suspected this wasn't her goal. Did she have no choice in the matter? Her steps slowed as she considered finding her family and hunkering down until the evil passed. She'd read enough scriptures to know that evil occurred in every century. Why would one evil be so much worse than previous evils? If she found a safe place, she could wait it out.

After her recent trials, the idea appealed. Not that anxious to find Jane and begin her survival training, her steps were slow and meandering. Braeden came to mind as he often did when she left open any space between her thoughts for him to squeeze through. His worried visage appeared with barbwire behind him along with the sounds of battle. His skin had a grayish tinge while the area underneath his eyes appeared bruised. His lips formed words she painstakingly tried to understand. Her inherent magical gifts weren't much help in lip reading, but she could decipher the last word was help.

He needed help! Someone needed to help him. Her hand flattened against her chest, which felt tight. Her pace picked up, but was stiff and jerky. Who was going to help Braeden? Why did England take its sons and put them in harm's way? Braeden was so young and had so much life to live. It was unfair putting a man used to working with nature and a plow and trying to mold him into a killing machine. Who was going to help him?

Meara's rapid strides carried her ten feet in one direction, then she turned and strode another ten feet. Repeating her actions moved her in a perfect square as she tried to deal with her thoughts. Part of the blame fell on Braeden. If he'd stood up to Adelaide instead of running, he wouldn't be stuck in battle pleading for assistance. As soon as the thought occurred, she felt guilty for thinking such a thing.

After all, Adelaide's family ran Hogstead and could make it uncomfortable for those out of favor. Hadn't Eleanor and she barely escaped when the house was torched? Even though she hadn't thought about it then, the townspeople's reaction would be no more than a slight curiosity about the event, and then it would be forgotten. If the locals stayed safe and unharmed, whatever happened to Eleanor and Meara was no concern of theirs. What if Braeden needing help was the result of something she did? If she chose to hide, which was her initial response, that help would never come. Sweet Mary, it wasn't just her life that was suddenly in her hands. Grandmother Biddy's words resonated in her head. She had to learn to teach and care for others.

Truthfully, she had no choice, unless she wanted people to die for her selfishness. Her impulsiveness at refusing a card reading turned her stomach. Why had she done that? She considered her actions bold, but not so much now. Fear had motivated her and carried her out of the wagon.

"There you are." Jane waved. "I've been looking for you. Grandmother Biddy told me you needed to know some practical skills about being a traveler."

Nothing had been said to her about being a traveler. Still any skills would be helpful. "Yes, I'd like that."

"I'll teach you how to dig up clams and capture crabs to begin. It's so much easier than hunting rabbits that have developed a healthy suspicion of traps and lures. Rom says we only catch the dumb hares now, and by eliminating them from the breeding stock, we're making the other rabbits smarter."

The thought of capturing one of the playful bunnies she'd observed made her uncomfortable. There had been little meat at the nunnery, except for the fatty pork they'd receive on the high holidays. "I thought you'd teach me to fish."

"I can, but it's not as easy in the surf. Sometimes, you can wade in knee high water, waiting for something to swim by and snag it with a net. Usually, it's easier to leave the net submerged to allow the fish to swim into it. This takes extreme patience and endurance since that water is chilly."

So far, nothing sounded easy or appealing. "Is there anything you can teach me that doesn't involve killing?"

"I could teach you to throw knives. It's a time-honored gypsy skill."

"Sounds good. Can we start now?"

"I need to go grab my knives."

Meara understood she might have to kill something for food to survive, but she felt even less ready to do that than to endure another Tarot reading.

"You'll have to toughen up, girl."

Her eyes searched around the area looking for someone who might have offered the advice. Jane strolled toward her wagon without a backward look. It hadn't sounded like Jane or her father. Were random spirits talking to her now?

"It's me, your mother."

Her heart gave a leap at the prospect. "Mother." She whispered the word, unsure if she should believe.

"Yes. I didn't know I could reach you until Grandmother Biddy mentioned doubt. I never believed I could reach you, but I decided to try."

"I'm so glad you did. There's so much I want to ask you."

"And me, you. It is hard to pierce the veil. So tiring."

"Rest then." She heard nothing else and assumed either her mother decided to rest or no longer could make her voice heard. If those who died could communicate with her, why couldn't she reach them with her thoughts?

Jane popped out of her wagon and walked back to her, carrying a long rectangular box. "Who are you talking to?"

"My deceased mother."

Her new friend didn't even blink, but regarded her calmly. "Are you finished?"

"I think I am, for now."

"Good. We need to go far away from the camp to practice. I'm not sure how good you are, and we don't need anyone to carelessly stumble into the path of a knife. First, I need to tell Michael where we'll be. He's one of the guards today."

Meara matched her strides to Jane's long ones. If she managed to walk as fast as her friend, she'd get places in a hurry. Her walk broke into a jog to keep up. "Why do you post guards?"

"Many reasons. Nature has her own moods. A guard can warn us of approaching storms, even a fire. Sometimes, we must relocate because angry townspeople blame us for missing chickens or a man discovers his wife has taken a lover. They assume any mishap is due to us being camped nearby. The cuckolded man would never look to his brother as being the guilty party. A fox could have easily stolen a chicken. Many would have accepted that explanation if there wasn't a traveler's camp nearby."

"If they feel this way, how do you interact with the settled?"

"They all don't. Many look forward to our visits as a time to get their knives sharpened, the cards read, or even the opportunity to sit in the circle and listen to a fantastical tale spun by Rom, or to dance with the gypsies. We're known for our spirited dancing."

"I've heard."

"Tonight, I'll teach you a dance that all the young girls are taught."

"I'd like that." It would feed into her need to get people dancing, but did seizing an opportunity make it any less magic, or was magic based on using opportunities?

A stocky man in a billowy white shirt covered by an ornate vest rested against a wagon ahead of them. Jane pointed. "That's Harman."

His relaxed posture didn't reflect any type of guard Meara might have expected. No ramrod back, no weapon, and no constant swiveling of the head to check for threats. "Is he even paying attention?"

"I am." The man answered, turned in their direction and offered them a slight bow. "My hearing is one of my best attributes."

Embarrassed at being overheard, Meara blustered her way through the situation. "Your other notable skills are?"

"My accuracy with a knife and the ability to see through others. You two have approached me for permission to go afar to knife practice."

Her eyes widened, and her mouth may have gaped a bit, causing Michael to laugh.

Jane shook her head. "Ignore him. He recognized my knife box since he crafted it for me. It's no secret we can't practice in camp. He went with the natural assumption. The man does not have any magical powers."

"Shows what you know." He straightened from his slouched position, pulled the bottom edge of this vest downward, and puffed out his chest. "I expect you'll be up in the Alder grove frightening trees with your knife skills."

"They are formidable. I'll be teaching Meara."

He nodded in her direction. "Jane's a good teacher when it comes to knives, but if you need to know any of the gentler arts, don't expect any help from her."

Jane grimaced and gave the man a shove that didn't move him the tiniest.

"At this point, I have no need of the gentle skills," Meara asserted, feeling the need to stand up for her new friend. Country women were expected to chop wood and drive a plow just the same as a man. Then, they were criticized for not sewing a delicate seam or making a fluffy biscuit while most men didn't even have the foggiest idea how to do tasks in what would have been a fair trade of labor.

Harman emitted another barking laugh. "Another one, just like you, Jane, my girl. Off with the both of you."

They left the flat stretch of beach and headed for a rockfall that made a walkway of sorts to the grassy cliffs. Wild grass showed up in tufts, breaking up the smooth beach. A few jagged rocks protruded out of the sand, appearing more like they had pushed out of Mother Earth as opposed to washing out of the sea. The tide-driven wind tugged at her skirt as they approached the rocky slide.

Jane broke their mutual silence. "I hope you don't mind climbing."

"Not at all. At the convent, I was crawling behind blackberry bushes and wiggling through a bolt hole to get close to nature almost daily."

Jane firmly planted her boot on the first stone and leaned forward as she scampered up the slide. Her question trailed behind her. "A bolt hole?"

Meara's flimsy slippers made the climb a little more challenging as she searched for flat stones with no sharp edges to pierce her shoes. "It is a small hidden exit. I suspect nature and time may have created it as opposed to it being made when the wall was constructed."

Jane moved higher, gained a level footing, and held her hand out to Meara. "Sounds curious. Don't tell me you were the only person to know about it?."

"Then you won't be disappointed. The last night there I heard another sister using it before me." She grasped the outstretched hand and scrambled over the remaining stones. Inhaling, she glanced back to see they'd not come nearly as far as she thought. They continued onward with Jane covering the rugged path with no obvious strain.

"You were surprised?"

"Yes. No one ever spoke of the hole. I assumed no one knew it existed since no attempt was made to repair the wall. I have no clue how many sisters may have used it over the years."

"Why?"

Grandmother Biddy had already mentioned that the travelers were Roman Catholics, so she assumed they knew all about nuns. A sister in the family was always an honor, while a priest was like having an ambassador of Heaven in your midst.

"Some of the nuns didn't care for being sisters, but there was no other avenues for them. They came for assorted reasons. Some were widows with no real purpose in their lives. Many had suffered a great disappointment and hoped turning to the church would heal the void in their lives. Still, others may have been encouraged, due to the honor shown families who have a child in God's service."

"Were you a nun?"

The prospect made Meara laugh, but it came out a bit breathy due to the vigorous nature of the climb. Her chuckles came out in gasps as she moved up behind Jane. Finally, they both reached the edge of the grassy cliff. Jane pushed her box over the edge and boosted herself up onto the ground, then held out a hand for Meara. Once they both were on the top of the cliff, they laid back in the grass to rest and watch the puffy clouds shaped like wooly sheep float overhead.

Jane's voice broke into Meara's contemplation. "Did you want to be a sister?"

"I would have made a poor sister. The spirit of obedience was not with me. I wanted to know the reason why we did what we did. Mother Superior didn't urge me to take the veil, either. I probably would have been an unpaid servant my entire life if the convent hadn't been bombed and if my Uncle Simon hadn't shown up. Whenever I crawled through the hole and sat underneath a tree listening to the birds, I considered leaving. After all, I was already out of the convent walls, but I knew nothing about the area. I even thought lions and bears existed in England."

"Even I know better, and I don't live in England. Why didn't you know?"

Why hadn't she known? A good question, one she hadn't spent too much time on since she'd been outside the convent busy experiencing new sensations. When she wasn't experiencing new wonders, she was in an all-out fight to survive. "I guess no one expected me to need to know. Since everyone else had lived in the outside world before they entered the convent, they must have assumed I already knew. Then there was a rule about the sisters could not speak about their life before entering the convent, and they'd made a vow to leave all that behind."

"Did people actually do that? Did no one talk about who they left behind and what their lives have been like?"

The disbelief sounded in Jane's voice. It made Meara smile a little. Those who had never lived in a convent had no clue how it was run. She couldn't even be sure if her convent had been the same as all the others. "Most did. A few new sisters spoke freely of what they had left behind and were reported for it. They were disciplined."

"Where they whipped?"

"No. It depended on the offense. Sometimes they were denied a meal or forced to stay in their cell and pray. Mainly, they were shamed in front of the other sisters. We had so few physical comforts that there wasn't much that could have been taken from us."

"It doesn't sound like something I would like to do. I guess I'm rather like you in that I don't follow rules well, unless I can be made to see the reason behind them, such as reporting to the guard where I'm going."

"Are the women in your camp carefully watched?"

"Not necessarily the women, but the children, the elderly, and anyone who might need assistance, which would include the sick, and Olio."

"Olio?"

"Sometimes, I think he lives in another world since he has very little interaction with the other travelers. When he was born, he had the caul, the birth sac, intact, which signals he is an oracle. All of us have waited for some great insights, but the only things he has offered have been weather predictions and where to hunt. He has been right on those matters. He could be more of a common-sense seer than someone who tells of dire happenings."

"No actual prophecies, yet?"

"He may only have one real prophecy, but it could save our entire group. We include him the best we can and not just because of what he might do. That's how travelers are. We take care of our own." Jane pushed up into a seated position on the last words.

"I didn't mean you wouldn't include Olio." She scampered to her feet, feeling somewhat defensive. "After all, you took us in."

"Which is highly unlikely, considering not only are you outsiders, but you're English, too. Nothing good has ever come from the two."

The words splashed over as if freezing water, rooting her to the spot. "What do you mean?"

Jane slowly got to her feet and touched Meara's arm. "Don't take on so. Now that I know you, I realize there is no black heartedness to you or the arrogance we normally associate with the English. Most Irish think of themselves as an independent sort. People who can make their own way, but the English don't see it that way. They had a desire to take over countries in the name of the king." She spat, emphasizing her point.

"Not our king, the English king. We were given laws, not of our own making and forced to pay taxes not to our own country, but to England. This has chaffed for a long time. There are those who would throw off the yoke of English oppression."

Not knowing what to say, Meara stood silent. Never had she heard anyone rant against her country, but then again, the sisters never had the luxury of ranting. Since they were all British, they had no reason to do so. Perhaps it would be better to know where she stood. "Do you feel this way?"

Jane's shoulders went up in a shrug. She smirked and then laughed. "That type of thing does not bother a traveler. We go where we will. Since we never settle, we aren't stuck paying taxes, either. Let's go find a fair size tree to aim at."

As her friend turned and headed in the direction of the alder grove, Meara hurried to catch up. "Why did you welcome us? Why were you exactly in the right place? We had no clue where we'd end up at, and yet you were here. Could it be coincidence?"

"No. Grandmother Biddy told us where to go. Even to the point of running the horses, so we'd be here in time."

The birds stopped calling as they entered the shady copse, unsure if they were predators. Jane circled around the trees, finally picking one on the outside of the grouping. "This one. It will allow you enough room to practice distance throwing."

Meara rammed both hands into her hair, pushing it away from her face. "I don't have any type of experience long or short distance."

From her kneeling position beside the open knife box, Jane grinned. "I know that. Why else would we be here?"

The knives were similar in size with wooden stocks. Some were or- nately carved, others had a plain base, but they all shared a wickedly sharp-looking blade. "They look dangerous."

"They can be, but often it's the only protection a traveler might have." She picked up one knife and tossed it in the air.

Meara took a step back and gasped as Jane reached for the knife, smoothly grasping the hilt as opposed to the point.

"Are you always fighting off those who would hurt you?"

"Usually not. Most travelers can talk their way around the settled. They use a combination of charm and flattery that often leaves those who wanted to threaten them bemused. Sometimes, a knife comes in handy. Most of the time, it is a threat just as a dog might growl at you to keep you away."

"Can you hunt with a knife?"

"Some can. It is more luck than anything else since you must get close enough to throw the knife. Take this one." She reversed the knife and surrendered it hilt first.

It felt heavier than the knives she'd use to cut up food, but the handle fit her hand well. She turned and eyed the tree.

"Not yet. You're not ready. A few things you should know. The knife is balanced so it will spin hilt over tip until it reaches its target." Jane reached into a box for another knife and flourished it.

"You look with your eyes, but you won't hit your target unless you line up your throwing hand with your eyes." She moved the knife at the same height as her head and flicked with the slightest wrist motion.

The knife thudded into the desired tree. It looked easy, but Meara soon found it was anything but. As the afternoon wore on, she learned to throw with her fingers and wrist, not her arm. Her initial throws went wild, causing her to search for the knife among the undergrowth. By the time the sun reached its apex, she managed to hit the tree, not where she planned, though.

"I'll never be as good as you."

"I've spent years perfecting my skill. It might take more than a few hours for you. We can practice as long as you're with us."

There it was again, the mention of her not being with the group. Soon she'd be pushed out like a fledging bird expected to fly on her own. Also, Rosemary could take a shine to one of the dark-eyed travelers and decide to stay, but that was unlikely since they didn't welcome outsiders.

"I'll do that."

"You'll need a sheath for your knife." Jane raised her skirt, exposing a red leather sheath strapped to her leg.

"My knife?" As far as she knew she didn't have one.

"The one in your hand, unless you'd prefer another."

She looked down at the blade she'd been using. "This works."

"As well it should. My father is an expert in creating well balanced knives. He trades for the steel. Many of the settled, especially the young men, want gypsy knives."

"Does he sell to them?"

"He sells them some knives, but not as good as the one you hold in your hand. It would be foolish to do so, since you never know when it would be used on you. He also marks the knives to show they had been sold to a settled."

"Why?"

"One of the lads who was so eager to get a gypsy knife might get liquored up and decide to show off with his prize. Even though many might witness the incident of the knife going awry and killing an innocent, it is still easier to blame a gypsy."

"Your father is a smart man. Does every woman wear a knife?"

"They all do as soon as they are trained. My father created my sheath and gifted me with it when I was twelve. It meant I had reached a point where I could be more independent. The men carry their knives in a special pocket made in their boot."

People probably protected themselves in England in a similar fashion, but she didn't know anything about it. Were there animals she should be wary of? "Did you ever kill anything?"

"Once. A badger. I surprised him, and he charged me. The knife flew before I even thought about it."

"Did you feel bad about it?"

"No. I brought back food for the people, and the hide was made into a foraging bag."

Would she look upon the animals she'd been content to watch in the woods as food? Her lips pursed, because she realized it might come to that. There wouldn't always be a handy pot of beans about for supper. Every day her world was changing.

Jane knelt beside her knife box, rearranging the knives. "It's best if you return the knife to the box since you don't have a sheath."

Meara complied, watching the implement go back inside the cloth-lined case. "Does every woman have several knives?"

Jane latched the box and tucked it under her arm. "No. Knives, while important, are costly. Each woman owns one knife. Sometimes, it has been passed down through the family. My knives represent my wealth. Many a man would think to marry me and get his hands on them. That's not going to happen."

Women were expected to have a dowry of some sort. It was regarded as a start for the new couple on their married life together. Sister Thomas, who was one of the few sisters who spoke freely about her outside life, regarded it as a bride price, something a father would pay not to be burdened with a daughter.

Jane led the way down the rock slide. Meara followed, slipping every now and then, but catching herself as she compared herself to Adelaide. Not only was Adelaide's father mayor of their small town, but he also owned extensive lands. Many a man would be fortunate to inherit that. Yet, none were tempted to marry the demanding woman. More accurately, none she preferred desired her in return.

From her high point on the rocks, Meara could see the sailboat bobbing in the water. The sail was furled and the mast repaired, although it looked somewhat shorter than before. Shona waded into the surf, carrying a package on her head.

"They'll be leaving tomorrow with the morning tide. We'll send them off with a big celebration tonight."

Meara hadn't expected them to stay. Ardan and Shona had briefly entered her life and would vanish as swiftly as they appeared. The celebration would give her a chance to work on her magic, but she wondered if Grandmother Biddy had given her an easy task. It may be much harder keeping the wandering folks seated as the music played than dancing.

"We'll probably be leaving soon, too."

"You will?"

"We only came here for you. We're in an exposed area, which makes us unsafe. Even though the shore belongs only to God, there are plenty who consider it theirs. Once they gather up their fellows and their gumption, they'll try to run us off. What they fail to realize is we were leaving on our own."

"Will I be going with you?" She hated to ask, but it would be better to know, than to wake up one morning alone.

"For now, you are. We won't travel into County Galway. It's too close to where the anarchists are. Normally, travelers don't shy away from a fight, but we know well enough not to get involved with their kind. It would only end up with being thrown in gaol. A traveler can't survive in a cage. That's the secret to remaining free. Avoid troublesome situations."

Easy for her to say. It seemed to Meara her life consisted of going from one difficulty to another. In between, she was supposed to learn to manage everything that was thrown at her. "Do you think it's me?"

"What?"

Jane had reached the edge of the rockfall and was looking in the direction of the sea. It was hard to tell if she had heard her at all.

"The sea is so big," Meara said, instead of repeating her question.

Her companion turned and put a free hand on her hip and stared out at the white capped waves.

Meara clambered down the last rocks and stood beside her friend. Might as well say what she had to say since she had the feeling Jane would worm it out of her.

"All that is happening. Is it because of me?"

"It's because of everyone and everything. We all contribute to the world we live in. We all have a part to play. Didn't Grandmother Biddy give you the thread talk?"

"She did." If the woman was content to sacrifice her shawl as a demonstration tool, then it was surprising it wasn't more threadbare.

"Then you know we all have a part to play, even if we don't fully understand our role."

That about summed it up. At least the dancing would provide some fun.

Chapter Six

THE SEA ROARED in the background, and the fire grew higher as two grinning men piled on the wood. People sat around the circle in a good mood after polishing off a stew thick with fish and clams. Beans, garlic, and a handful of fiery spices rounded out the dish. The sound of a fiddle being warmed up and a few pats on a drum meant there would be music and, naturally, dancing.

Tonight, everyone will dance. The young, the old, the happy, the sad, everyone will dance. She mentally chanted the words to herself, not feeling any magic or power. Closing her eyes to limit her distractions, she recited her intentions. *Dance. Dance.*

Music swelled around her in a lively tune that had people clapping their hands. She kept her eyes tightly closed as she worked on her intentions. Involved in making it happen, she hadn't heard anyone approach until her hand was snatched from her lap.

Jane's amused expression met hers as she firmly held onto her hand and tugged. "You'll not get out of dancing by pretending to be asleep. I promised to teach you."

Would that prevent her intentions from happening? It would be difficult to concentrate while following Jane's example. Then again, what if her dancing encouraged others to dance? It could be that some didn't dance, thinking they didn't have to skill to do so. Seeing someone as clumsy as she was might encourage them. It was hard to know, since she never tried to manipulate people before.

"It looks like you won't take no for an answer."

Jane gave her one good tug and pulled her off her log perch. Travelers whirled around her. Some of the men clapped their hands together as they moved in a tight circle. The women swished their skirts as they moved in a loose formation often making the same gesture at the same time. Children spun in giddy circles, often staggering to the log seats after too many twirls.

"What do I do?" Dancing was easy when Braeden wrapped his arms around her and guided her where she needed to go.

"Follow me. Just copy me. Sometimes it helps to feel the earth under your feet." She stomped her feet to demonstrate.

Meara stomped her feet, drawing eyes of those still seated and felt awkward doing so.

"That's good. Now, you need to stir up the fire inside of you." She clapped her hand together three times and shot a meaningful look at Meara who followed her example.

"It's time to call the wind into the dance. You can do this by spinning, or swishing your skirts, or both." Jane grabbed the edges of her full skirt and spun. As she slowed, she gave the material a swish with both hands. Others pushed off their log seats and joined them in the dance.

Knowing what was expected of her, Meara spun and swished. She found herself stomping, and clapping, and trading grins with other travelers as they circled one another. She meant to ask how they expressed water, but forgot in the frenzy of dancing. Every now and then she got a glimpse of Rosemary dancing, which didn't surprise her. She figured her friend was a more likely candidate to dance than she ever was.

Even the musicians abandoned their seats and whirled around the circle while playing their instruments. The music, the heat, the upraised voices circled around her. As she turned, she searched the logs for any of those who were not dancing. Only Grandmother Biddy sat in her chair and greeted her with a nod. The matriarch brandished her walking stick and stood. Planting it in the ground, she did a lively step around it, causing all to cheer.

The realization settled on Meara. Everyone was dancing. Euphoria raced through her, causing her to spin faster, stomp harder, and laugh as if she just discovered how.

Eventually the blaze settled down, allowing the night to creep back. One by one the dancers found their seats, leaving only some of the couples dancing together in the firelight. Meara found a seat as Jane dropped beside her.

"You did good. I think you got some of the old mothers up who hardly ever dance. They'd not let one of the settled outdance them."

Settled would hardly describe her, but she understood the meaning. Maybe it did take her dancing to get the others to dance. It's possible Grandmother Biddy knew this, but would not tell her. It was something she had to learn on her own. She'd asked her on the morn and use her best manners, also asking if she might have her cards read. Most likely, the crone would refuse as she should, since Meara had been so ungracious about it.

"They can rest easy since I didn't outdance them."

"You gave it a good try."

Her friend waggled her eyebrows, making her laugh.

"I did try. When we started you told me something about stomping for the earth, clapping for the fire, spinning for the wind, but nothing for the water."

"Did you feel any emotions when you danced?"

"I felt happy, excited and at times, a little fearful that I was doing things wrong."

"There is no wrong with dancing. It's joy. You were awash in emotions, which is the same as being sunk deep in the water."

"I get it now."

"This is why dancing and music are so important to us. It puts us in touch with all the elements. It really is a form of worship, but I better not say that too loud. There are those who would not approve."

As the couples stopped dancing and sought their seats, she could see in the flickering light a tall, blond man standing and staring at her.

Amid so many dark heads, he stood out like a beacon.

"Who is that?" She didn't want to point. "Over there. The flaxen-haired male."

"Oh, that's Olio. He tends to look at people like that, all intense. It makes you wonder what he's thinking. For the most part, he does not speak. We keep waiting for the prophecy."

He walked slowly across the circle, causing people to hush their chatter as he approached Jane and Meara. He stopped in front of Meara and pointed to her. "I will go with you."

Then he turned and left. When he left the firelit circle, darkness swallowed him up, the chatter resumed. Puzzled by his behavior, she turned to her companion for explanation.

"What did he mean when he said I'll go with you?"

"It looks to me like you'll have an escort." She uttered the words very matter-of-factly as if it was a done deal.

"I'm not sure about this. I need to talk to Rosemary."

"No need. It is always better for women to travel with a man than alone. This could be Olio's purpose, and he has spent his life waiting for you to appear."

She shook her head, not wanting to be teamed up with this Nordic lookinggiant, which made her wonder about his heritage. "Will he leave his family to go with us?"

"While we consider ourselves to be family, Olio truly has none. His mother was a transient who stayed with us for a time. Since he is older than me, I only got the story secondhand. She arrived pregnant, had her child, and when he was about two, she vanished, leaving Olio alone. He was never a talkative child, but he spoke even less after his mother's disappearance."

"How could a mother abandon her son?"

"His mother was intrigued by a settled man. She used to sneak off in the night to meet him, much to the disapproval of the group. The settled have no respect for the travelers. They consider us to be beneath them. Some think she ran off with the man, but others believe she was killed by her lover. If she'd carried a knife, she would not have been such an easy target."

Would the women have been able to stab the man for whom she'd developed a crush? Meara didn't feel she could ever wield a knife in anger, but maybe if it was a matter of her life or Rosemary's, it would be a different matter. After all, she'd called down the birds when she needed help, but had been unaware how that help would present itself.

"I can see the benefit of having a knife. Maybe Rosemary should learn to throw, too."

"Yes." Jane agreed. "Two women armed and trained is better than one alone."

"How about Olio? Can he throw a knife?" She assumed he could since all the travelers appeared to have the skill.

Jane smirked at her. "He never has a need of a knife. In the towns, men usually avoid him. I heard him called a Viking giant once. The fact he almost never speaks tends to make people anxious. He's a bit like the badger in never knowing if he might strike. The settled don't know how to act around him. Despite the fact he wears our clothes, he does not look like us. He doesn't act like us. Perhaps, the settlers think an enormous trick is being played on them. Still, considering Olio could easily pick up a settled with one hand, they do their best to get out of his way."

If Jane's intentions were to make a case for the man, she was accomplishing it. A giant that people hid from could be useful, while her natural compassion wanted to shelter the oracle from all who would ridicule and fear him. Maybe all he needed was a place to fit in. She didn't know where that place was, but maybe he needed to try and find it.

"I have a lot to consider. Are you ready for bed?"

"I am." They strolled off arm in arm in the direction of Jane's wagon.

"How come you have a wagon when the other unmarried girls sleep with their families?"

"Ha! I wondered when you'd point that out. I sleep by my family and everyone knows my skill with a knife. My pretty wagon and horse were a gift from my grandmother. When she died, it came to me. She could have given it to my father, but she thought to make me more appealing to any who would marry me since I came with a home and a horse to pull it."

"Did it make you more popular?" If there was anything for her family to leave her, would it make her a more attractive matrimonial candidate?

"Oh, yes, to all the wrong sort like the shiftless ones who never worked hard enough to earn their own wagon. My father discouraged them. I keep hoping I'll find a different group with someone I might fall in love with. It hasn't happened yet, and I'm getting old."

"You're not old."

They continued to argue about what qualified as old as they climbed the steps of the wagon and climbed into their pallets. Just before falling asleep, she wondered if she were too old to interest a marriage-minded man. Of course not, she reassured herself. Braeden had asked her to wait for him until he came back from the war. That had been her plan until circumstance sent her fleeing Hogstead in the middle of the night.

Chapter Seven

THE SHUTTERS WERE open on Grandmother Biddy's colorful wagon. Meara hesitated at the stairs, not sure if she should knock. It was so early in the morning. After the revelry of the night before, she could still be sleeping.

"Come in. Don't stand on the steps all morning debating what to do."

Meara grabbed the door handle and swung it open. Inside the narrow wagon, the elderly woman sat beside the table, dressed, and nursing a cup of tea. The Tarot cards were prominently centered on the table.

"Good morning," Meara started, but was halted by a slashing hand motion.

"None of that chitter-chatter. We have much to do. I saw everyone dancing." Her withered cheeks lifted in a pleased expression.

"I'm not sure that was me."

"Stop it. No doubts. Maybe things didn't happen in the way you expected, but they still happened. That's good enough. Don't complain about the method as long as you get the results."

The woman had a point. What she wanted to happen, did. That should be good enough. Meara slid into the chair on the other side of the table and glanced at the battered cards she'd worked so hard to avoid the other day.

"Are you ready to learn how to read Tarot?"

Did that mean she didn't get a reading today? "What do I need to know?"

Grandmother Biddy reached for the deck and picked it up. "Many of my customers believe the deck is enchanted, that some spirit inhabits it."

Meara kept her lips pressed together since she thought something similar.

"It would be handy to have a magical deck, but then there would be no need for women to pay me to see if they'd soon be married or to discover if their husband is unfaithful."

"Do you tell them such things?"

"I usually confirm what they already know. Hearing their thoughts come out of someone's mouth makes them real. Let's start by turning the cards over and looking at them."

Meara fingered the deck, then picked it up and dealt out the cards face side up. The card faces were elaborate with each inch of space covered. There were powerful figures, menacing and mysterious ones she didn't know how to take, along with the cups, wands, pentacles, and swords.

"Do you know the meaning of the suits, child?"

She shook her head. If she knew what everything meant, it wouldn't be so intimidating.

Grandmother Biddy tapped a wand of five. "This stands for fire. What can you tell me about fire?"

"It's powerful. It burns whatever is in its way."

"True. It can also stand for the passion you have to do something." Her finger smoothed over a blindfolded woman. She raised her eyebrows asking a question without opening her mouth.

"The woman is blindfolded. This must mean she is being fooled." Meara knew she had no clue what she was saying, but knew her teacher expected some answer.

"Not fooled, although I guess it could happen. A blindfold means lack of information. Something could happen, and you don't understand the cause. It doesn't mean you're stupid, just unaware. There are mountains in the background. What do you think that indicates?"

"Obstacles?"

"Some might read it that way, but I see it as knowledge. So, the blindfolded woman has knowledge at her fingertips." She picked up the card and waved it. "This could be you."

It was her, even if she refused to admit it. Instead, she held up a card with dark clouds. "Could this mean trouble?"

"It could, but not necessarily big trouble. It's conflict. Anyone born on this earth encounters conflict."

There were things to look for in the cards, hidden meanings she had to memorize. "If I learn these meanings, will I be able to read the cards?"

"That's only part of it. Each person comes with a question, a need. Someone will tell you, others won't. You have to apply the cards to their question."

"How can you do this if they won't talk about it?"

"Instinct, the same feeling that tells you to take a different path or that someone following you can also guide you to the right answer. I won't go over all the cards today. It would be too much. Instead, close your eyes, think of a question, and pick a card."

How do I proceed? She knew where she was going, County Galway, but was unaware of how to get there. Her finger landed on a card, and she opened her eyes to reveal a strong warrior on a spirited white horse.

"You've chosen strength. Always a good card. It means you have enough inner strength to reach your goals. It can also mean someone has come into your life who is very strong and will help you. He can be trusted."

Meara picked up the card and studied it. The warrior did look a bit like Olio. Having help would be useful, but she needed something more and reached for another card without prompting. A proud woman stood with a crown on her head and a sword in one hand.

Grandmother Biddy leaned forward, peering at the card. "Ah, the queen of swords. She is a strong, independent woman who gets things done. On the surface, she appears alone, but is also loving and welcome. She's not one to ask for help, even when she needs it."

Was she the queen of swords? Her lips pursed as she considered the possibility. All through her journey, she hadn't wanted other people to tag along, certain she was taking them from their own mission. What if helping was exactly what they were supposed to be doing? If she refused help, they couldn't do what they needed to do. Her desire to control others' interactions could be hurting others and herself. Why hadn't she seen that before?

The blue veined had covered hers. "You couldn't see. It takes time. Now, how about I show you a simple three-card spread?"

"I'd like that." The hand left hers, and Meara helped gather up the cards for shuffling. "What is a three-card spread?"

"It can be about almost anything. A problem you're having. A relationship. We'll start with the most common: past, present, and future."

Her fingers hovered over the spread cards trying to get a feel for which one would be the right one. She plucked one card out, keeping it faced down, and moved it away from the others. She did the same with two more cards.

"Turn over the first card you picked. That will be your past."

A woman stood listening to a troubadour sing while a huge full moon rose in the background. There was a crayfish near her feet. It wasn't an unpleasant card, but the woman looked uncertain, without a smile or any real animation in her face. She wasn't turned to the troubadour, but looking away from him.

"The moon card. What do you think it means?"

"There is a moon. The moon is associated with the waves, so could it mean emotions."

"It could. It could also mean intuition. You can tell by the woman's stance that the troubadour does not charm her. Her thoughts are consumed by her swirling emotions, doubts, and insecurities. Often, she has no clue what to do next. Does that sound like your past?"

Meara closed her eyes and inhaled. It sounded all too much like her past, even when her past was simply a day ago. "It does. I assume the next card is my present."

"It is. Turn it over."

Her fingers rested on the card while she wrestled with what she might face. Not knowing didn't make it better. Maybe it wouldn't be something too frightening. With knowledge, she could move ahead. She flipped the card over to an archer shooting arrows or wands.

"Eight of rods or it can be called eight of wands."

"Does it have a bad meaning?" Perhaps, someone would shoot her with an arrow or maybe she should learn to shoot along with her knife throwing lessons.

"No. None of the cards has a bad meaning. They are a way of relaying information. The archer has shot three wands into the air with another in his bow and another four waiting. The wands are messages. He is sending information out into the universe. Even now, you're receiving knowledge from a variety of sources. Along with the information comes opportunities. Knowledge, even if it's unwelcome, is always useful."

It wasn't as bad as she imagined, even rather mundane, considering she'd almost drowned during the crossing. Knowledge she could deal with. "I'm ready for the last card." She flipped it over without any prompting.

A man gathered swords on a snowy hillside as a unicorn watched. It perplexed her. Swords could be useful. Should she be gathering them?

"Ah, the thief in the night." Her companion steepled her fingers. "I expected something like this. Your reading was too calm for a girl who worked her away across a war-torn country and sea."

"What is it?" Her top teeth came to rest on the bottom lips. She regretted her temporary bravery that made her decide to know was better than not knowing.

"The thief represents trickery. Someone will attempt to fool you. They could be motivated by jealousy. You need to guard yourself and valuables. We already know there is a powerful evil abroad that is determined to stop all those who do want to fight it. You can pick another card for a clearer meaning."

The next card she turned over was a warrior holding up two swords while three were planted in the ground. Behind him two women were talking.

"The five of swords, which confirms the previous card. You have an enemy, who could be known or unknown to you. This person is determined to harm you in some way. Be on your guard. It's good that Olio is going with you. He is good at sensing unseen dangers. We will miss him and his unusual skills, but you need him more."

The scenario grew worse as she turned each card. Still, there had to be some good in the future, even a glint would help. She fingered another card, hesitating before turning it over. What if it was bad.

"Go ahead."

A mature man rested against a rock, staring off in the distance at two grazing unicorns. Two wands were behind him while one was in front. It didn't look like an ominous card, but she hadn't though the other cards were either.

"Three of wands. The man is reflecting on his past experiences. It means you're at a crossroads, the past will be behind you. Now is your opportunity for a fresh start, even a new love."

Much less gloomy than before, but so far, she hadn't even settled on an old love. The only enemy, she knew of, was Adelaide, and she'd left her back in England. Maybe none of this meant anything. It only had value if she gave it value.

She pushed uspfrom the table. "I need to say goodbye to Shona and Ardan."

"They already left on the morning tide. It gives them the best chance of reaching home before dark."

An emptiness filled her at the leaving of her new friends and rescuers. Was this how it would be? Would she meet people, work beside them, only to have them vanish in the night? It wasn't an appealing prospect.

"I need to go all the same." No reasonable excuse came to mind.

"Don't leave in haste because the cards weren't to your liking. Every day they change."

Meara threw up her hands, rattled at the life changes and the unreliability of the cards. "Why even read them?"

"To gain insight. Today, you might leave with a desire to be more aware of anything you could do that might arouse jealousy. Your carefully guarded actions might never inspire jealousy, and the cards I read today could change by the morrow."

That certainly sounded promising. "There's the glint of sunshine I was looking for in the entire situation."

As she swung the wagon door opened, Grandmother added in a faint voice, "They could remain the same, too."

The best thing to do was to pretend not to hear. She held up her hand as she left, made her way down the stairs, and bumped into Rosemary. "Good morning."

"Good morning to you, Meara."

"Where are you headed in such a hurry?"

Her friend flashed a grin, gesturing to a faraway wagon. "I'm helping Luca with the children as the women get the washing done."

"Oh, that's good of you."

"I don't mind. I love children, especially these brown-eyed darlings, who are so quick with a quip and light on their feet. In some ways, they're like tiny adults, only much cuter."

"Aye, I'll have to think on that." The past twenty-four hours had been spent mainly with Jane and Grandmother Biddy. For all basic purposes, she'd ignored her friend. "Where did you sleep?"

"Out under the stars with the older children. It was lovely having the ocean sing me to sleep."

While her friend did not seem upset by her impromptu camping outdoors, Meara didn't feel the same. Every night she had the luxury of sleeping inside and not once had she wondered about Rosemary or even Shona and Ardan. Never had she been responsible for others, but if she was expected to lead, then she would be expected to look out for the welfare of those who followed, too. It was no longer all about what she wanted.

"You make it sound poetic, but I feel bad about you being outside."

"Don't. I enjoyed telling the children stories until they fell asleep and listening to their soft slumbering breaths. It made me feel somewhat like a mother. I loved it."

"You don't have to do this. I can easily trade places with you."

Rosemary fisted her hands on her hips. "Now that I've revealed the charm of sleeping children, you want to take my place. We'll only be here so long. I want to enjoy it."

The sound of galloping horse's hooves had both women turning. A traveler flew through the camp shouting, "Pack up. Be gone. There's an armed group coming this way."

Women flew out of their wagons, taking down lines with clothes still attached. Others pulled the caldron off the fire, lidded it, then as a team of two used a wooden yoke to carry the heavy vessel.

Some men broke down temporary work sheds, sharpening wheels, and the forge they'd erected. Others moved the horses into their harness and walked them back to the wagons.

Even children had jobs, picking up stray objects that tumbled to the ground in the rush. A few older ones rounded the small flock of chickens into crates. As a toddler waddled by carrying a large cat, Rosemary took the cat and took his hand, leading him to the right wagon.

In a matter of minutes, the camp was dissembled, and the horses harnessed including Grandmother Biddy's. Olio climbed onto the driving bench of Grandmother's wagon while Jane shouted at Meara. "Come on. We need to go. You can ride with me."

Meara bent to pick up a forgotten doll and then climbed up beside Jane. The first wagon lurched into motion. Each one followed, creating a slow-moving chain of colorful wagons.

"We left in such a hurry. Are we in danger?"

"Not so much. The guard made a judgement call that those headed our way weren't in the mood to have their fortunes told or barter some goods. A few are carrying rifles."

"They could be hunters."

"Others are carrying pitchforks."

The wagon had reached the incline that reached up to the cliffs. The narrow path barely looked wide enough to accommodate the wagon.

"Look ahead. It will worry you less. Going down was the greater challenge."

Her eyes focused on the wagon in front of her that careened near the edge, causing dirt to crumble underneath its rear wheel.

Jane poked her with her elbow. "If we have three wheels on the road, we're good."

"What if we don't."

"Then, you get out and push."

Jane grinned at her, making it hard for Meara to decide if she was serious or not. The wagon in front of them stopped, allowing a few travelers to dismount. They circled around to the side of the wagon and walked.

"They're not pushing."

"Not yet. They're reducing the weight. It's a hard grade for a horse to pull. Maybe you might like to walk, too."

This time she knew Jane wasn't joking. Meara took advantage of the pause to step down and walk beside the wagon. At least the road wasn't as steep as the rock fall they'd used yesterday. One of the advantages of being able to drive a wagon was you didn't have to walk uphill. A few more yards and another pause had Jane asking Meara to hold the horse's head as she put the brake on the wagon and scampered down.

"It's not fair to ask Seymour to pull my weight when I can walk. I'll release the brake and you start him forward."

Meara moved to the horse's large head, and he regarded her with large liquid eyes that she would have sworn showed doubt. She gripped the halter. "How do I make him go forward?"

"Just walk, he'll follow."

She made it sound so simple. They had a cart mule at the convent who could be more than a little stubborn. Just leading him seldom worked, but she'd give it a try. Her feet stirred up some dirt and rocks as she shuffled forward, and to her surprise the horse followed.

"He's walking," She called back to Jane, who had released the brake and came up beside her.

"Of course, he is. It's his job." She patted the horse's flank and then reached for the halter, taking over the guiding.

It's his job. Well, not all animals thought they had a job to do and did it without complaint. From what little she'd observed about the world, not that many people did, either. Instead, most people wanted what they wanted and did not consider the consequences. The current war resulted from a thirst for land, money, and power and never mind the consequences. Her heart gave a little extra squeeze since thoughts of war always pushed Braeden into her mind, front and center.

The memory of his thick hair, trusting eyes, and up tipped lips right before he kissed her made her smile and sigh a little.

"I know walking uphill to escape a bunch of hooligans didn't cause that sigh. What's his name? Spit it out."

Should she? It would be nice to talk about Braeden. Get a feel from another woman. Once she found out that Rosemary once fancied Braeden, it killed the idea of discussing her confused feelings about the handsome farmer with her.

"Oh, it's silly, really."

"Love often is. Since I haven't been blessed in that department, I'm content to listen to others. Maybe their luck will rub off on me."

"Not sure if I can say I've been blessed in that department, either. If I am, I'm confused." She glanced back over her shoulder, but her view was blocked by another wagon. "Should we even be talking about this when we're running for our lives?"

"Running for our lives. That's a good one. Go on, I'll explain later." Jane snorted and shook her head.

No one acted too concerned about their flight. There were a few tight-lipped faces that showed more anger, possibly resignation as opposed to fear.

"Over a year ago, I was living in the convent totally cut off from the world by the stone walls. The only men I knew before my uncle showed up were the bearded statues of the various disciples scattered throughout our building."

"Oh my! I find that hard to believe. You were talking about your true love."

"What I am trying to say is I knew almost nothing about anything. During my stay with Eleanor, I started to question what little I did know. So much had been hidden from me. I knew nothing about my mother or father until my uncle came and very little after." Her nose wrinkled at how easily she had accepted whatever she'd been told. Didn't necessarily like it, but she didn't feel there was an alternative either.

"Don't be too hard on yourself. What else did you know? You still haven't gotten to the good part where you're swept you off your feet and fall hopelessly in love." She wiggled her eyebrows as she clucked to the horse.

"I don't think it was like that. I was a new girl, someone Braeden hadn't met before. It could have been the novelty of someone new that attracted him."

"Don't you love him?"

She sighed and dropped her chin. "That's part of the problem. He's handsome, and he treated me well the few times we've seen each other. I worry about him, but I have no clue about what love even is."

"I think that is true of everyone."

The comment had her turning her head in Jane's direction. "You're wrong. I've seen more love in this camp than I have experienced in my lifetime. It's obvious parents love their children. Every one of you respects and honors Grandmother Biddy. There's affection between couples and friendship between most of the women. Almost all of this is new to me."

"I never thought of it that way. The convent must have been a dreary place. Does this mean you're not waiting for Braeden?"

"I tried to wait until circumstances forced me to leave. Eleanor told me if it was meant to be, a mere ocean couldn't keep us apart. I truly want the best for him. What if the best isn't me?" It was the first time she verbalized what she had been feeling ever since her handsome suitor left. A farmer would do well with a woman familiar with the land and the planting seasons. She could learn, but it would take a while.

Jane led in silence for a while. "If you want what is best for Braeden, then you are more loving than most. There isn't much you can do with the war on. Time and distance might change your feelings for one another. After all, he's the only boy you've kissed."

"True. Eleanor said something similar about not marrying the first boy who showed an interest in me. Do you think I should kiss some more?"

"I recommend it. I'm sure he has kissed more girls than you."

"Sometimes I think he showed a marked interest in every girl in town until Adelaide labeled him hers."

Janes's eyes sparkled with interest. "Who's Adelaide?"

It wasn't something she wanted to talk about. Meara crinkled her nose. It wasn't that she'd thought the girl would appear just by the mention of her name, but why take chances. "Oh, someone back in England."

"There's more than that to the story, especially when you mentioned that the man you may or may not love belongs to another." Jane arched her eyebrows. "I never thought of you as that type of girl."

"I'm not!" She shot Jane an indignant glare depite she sensed it was meant as a joke. "Adelaide told everyone he was his without bothering to ask Braeden his opinion. I'd rather talk about kissing."

"Who wouldn't?" Jane chuckled. "How can you judge your sweetheart's kisses to be the best when you have nothing to compare them to? You may find he is the better one. If he is, you'll count yourself lucky."

The thought made her smile, but before she could drift off into the world where Braeden and she had dream picnics and sunset strolls. Jane shifted subjects, explaining their flight.

"Those who thought to scare us only wanted us gone. When it came right down to it, most realize they'd lose if it came down to fighting. A good many of them are clumsy and slow and would find a knife at their neck before they could pinpoint the last spot where they saw a traveler."

"If that's the case, why not stay and fight? You haven't done anything wrong."

"True." Her shoulders hunched forward, but she pushed them back. "You are quite the innocent. When you escaped from your home in England, had you done anything wrong?"

"No. I did catch the eye of a desirable young man that a certain female claimed as her own but nothing other than that. One of the dying nuns accused me of causing the destruction of the nunnery by being an evil bastard child, which I am not."

"Then you know what it is like to be accused of something you haven't done."

"I do."

"You didn't stay, even though you hadn't done anything because you knew there would be consequences."

"You know the story." It made her wonder why Jane felt the need to bring up what had already been discussed.

"It's the same with us. People call us riff-raff, the devil's children, beggars, and land lice. Some are afraid of us stealing their children as if we'd want their overfed, spoiled darlings. Strange thing is, I've never seen anything to merit these accusations. Because we've chosen a way unique to the settled, some fear us. A few resent us when a traveler manages to drive a harder bargain than a settled. Way too often, the settled men get liquored up and come to our camps, hoping to find easy women to ease their lust. What they find instead is mothers and grandmothers wielding cast iron skillets to keep the randy men at bay."

"No knives?"

"Knives serve a purpose, but in close combat a skillet works better. Our goal is to discourage, but never kill."

"Why wouldn't you kill if you were defending yourself?"

A long whistle pierced the air, causing Seymour, the horse, to tilt his ears forward. "You sure are bloodthirsty for a nun."

"I wasn't a nun. I asked too many questions to be a good one."

"The questions are only a minor issue with your desire to stab anyone who threatens you."

"That's not what I said. I just meant it could happen."

Jane shook her head slowly as she continued urging her horse forward. The visible flat land ahead caused the horse to give an extra push to get off the incline. They both broke into a jog to keep up. The part of the caravan that had already conquered the hill stopped to allow drivers and riders to climb aboard.

After they both were seated on the hard bench seat, Jane returned to the conversation. "Most of the time I've been alive or had the wits to observe much, I noticed our group always opts for running as opposed to fighting. One day I asked my mother why. She shushed me, but my father overheard. He decided it was fitting that I learned about my uncle."

The way she said the words made it sound rather ominous. "What about your uncle?"

"He was hanged for defending his betrothed."

"Why would they hang him? That makes no sense." She hoped if it came down to it that Braeden would defend her. She had no doubt he'd save her from a stampeding bull, but would he defend her to his mother who'd already accepted the gossip about the troublesome babe left at the convent?

"I agree with you on that." She gave the reins a flick that had the horse picking up his pace. In the distance, a ribbon of road beckoned, but the caravan continued to run parallel to it as opposed to moving to intersect.

"So, what happened?"

"This happened way before I was born. Uncle Nico was my father's older brother. It feels weird to say his name, a man I never met." She caught Meara's gaze and continued.

"Uncle Nico was tall for a traveler. The older women in the camp would talk about what a fine specimen he was. The men would talk about his skill with the horses. With just the right words, he could make a horse fly."

Meara's eyebrows lifted and her mouth half-opened, ready to question the flying ability. Jane corrected herself before she could. "He made the horses run fast."

"This was a dreadful thing?"

"Not in itself. He liked to challenge people to race against him. Money would exchange hands with people betting on the races. Nico always won. After a while, no traveler would race him. This caused Nico to challenge the settled who were proud of their horses and racing skills. The settled were confident and bet heavily, which meant they lost heavily as well."

"I'm not sure what that has to do with him being hanged and his betrothed."

"I'm getting there, and there's a reason behind all of this." She cleared her throat. "It's obvious you would have been a horrible sister, especially a silent one."

"I agree." That thought had preoccupied her a great deal right before she escaped. "Your uncle?"

"I remember."

The sound of a rider caused them both to look around. The man's over long dark hair was windblown, and his face was full of color. His teeth flashed white underneath his mustache as he slowed his horse and turned to address them.

"All is well." He flicked the reins and darted up to the next wagon to convey the same message.

"What did he mean all is well?"

Jane blew out a long-relieved breath. "It means we're not being followed, which is a blessing."

"Why would they follow you?"

Jane gave her a nudge. "I'm shocked that the Mother Superior didn't push you out of the convent long before now for your chattiness and tendency to interrupt."

"I'm sure she considered it, but as the youngest member there, I was able to do things the older nuns couldn't, such as climb on the roof to replace blown off ceiling tiles."

"I'll keep that in mind if I ever need a ceiling tile replaced."

"What about Uncle Nico?"

"There are a few who accused my uncle of living too fast and too easy. They'd never say that to my father, but everything came easily to Nico. His friendly manner, dark good looks, along with the wealth he'd gained racing horses made him a favorite among the unmarried girls and their families. Each one wanted him to pick their daughter for marriage. He naturally chose the most beautiful unmarried woman, Layla." She said the name with distaste as if trying to spit the word out.

"I take it you're not a friend of Layla."

"No one is. Layla was proud of herself and often teased the young men with long looks and swishing her skirts. In camp, nothing would come of it because her father and brothers would stare down any man who looked at her too long. Not so in the settled communities, where Layla gave more than one man a reason to hope she might return his affections."

"She didn't. Wasn't she betrothed to Nico?"

"She was, but she was also one of those women who could never have enough positive attention. One day after going to the village market to sell their colorful shawls, a man followed the women back. He kept calling to Layla, but she ignored. When they were almost at camp, the man grabbed Layla and forced her to kiss him. Like any smart female, she kneed him where it hurt most and pushed him away. They left the man moaning in agony, although one or two of the travelers took the opportunity to spit on him before they hurried back to camp. News of this incident spread through the camp."

"I can't imagine that went over well."

"Nico raged around the camp and said he'd find the man. Layla refused to give the name of, although she may not have known it. A few of the other women were more accommodating by describing the man. One even remembered which house was his. Nico stormed into the village, demanding to know who took advantage of his betrothed. The man who came outside to deal with Nico was not the man who kissed her, but his brother. My father followed as soon as he heard, knowing how Uncle Nico could be when he was mad. Most of the time people loved him, but when he was angry it was useless dealing with him. All probably would have been well, except the stupid, settled man said something about traveler women being whores, and what was a kiss, considering most did a lot more for a few coins. A fight ensued. Nico never meant to kill him, but when the man with the runaway tongue fell, his head struck a stone trough, which did the job."

"That's why he was hanged."

"It was an unjust hanging. No court, no judge, not that either would have favored Nico. Someone found a rope and strung him up on a nearby tree only feet from the dead man. My father arrived to find his brother swinging from the tree. They at least allowed him to cut him down and take the body."

The possibility that they wouldn't have allowed that shocked her a little. "What happened to Layla?"

"When my father returned with Nico's dead body strapped to the horse, the camp was taken up, and they all left. It was only a matter of time until the town folks decided to come after the rest of us. It was during the chaos of breaking camp that no one saw Layla slip away."

"What happened to her?"

Jane's shoulders went up in a shrug. "Hard to say. Everyone has a theory. Some say she went to the man who kissed her. Others say she killed herself because of the shame of causing her beloved's death. One thing was for sure, she had cut her ties with the travelers."

"This is why no one stands and fights."

"Yes, it is. We tend not to go into the village, but allow villagers to come to us. The women or even children will go into the village and tell the mothers and wives that the travelers are here to mend pots, fix harnesses, and sharpen knives. There's also the unmentioned benefit of having your palm read or picking up an herbal remedy."

"Why don't you mention it?"

"Come on. I know there wasn't any fortune telling in the convent. The Bible forbids it. Can't remember what verse. Something about King Saul consulting the Witch of Endor."

Meara's hand rubbed her neck as she contemplated all that she'd heard. "The Witch of Endor was always right."

"Yeah, being right doesn't always help. It often makes the situation worse. That's why Grandmother Biddy won't give any negative reports to the settled women who want a fortune told. People don't necessarily want the truth. They just want their ears tickled with good possibilities."

She wouldn't mind a happy report or two. When things got tricky she knew enough to change the subject. "Grandmother Biddy told me that the travelers are Roman Catholics."

"That's true. As is most of Ireland, except for the troublesome Protestants in the North."

"Why are they troublesome? Is it because they're Protestant? The people in Hogstead were but most were kind enough to the nuns with only a few malcontents."

A short laugh greeted her statement. "You caught me out. I was repeating what my da said without even giving it a thought."

"Why do you think most resent the Protestants?"

"I have no earthly clue. It's probably because they're different. Da says they're not true Irishmen. It's odd, really, that I was willing to dislike people I never met. Makes me no different than the settled who resent us because we're not like them."

A yell sounded up ahead, causing the caravan to shudder to a stop. There was some milling about toward the front, shouted instructions, but nothing she could understand. A cold chill swept through her body, and a feeling of wrongness invaded it. She chafed her arms, trying to push the cold away; the chill came despite the late summer sun beaming down.

"What's wrong with you? You're shaking? What's happening?"

The image of women crying and cradling dead babies filled her mind. She blinked several times, hoping it would go away. The grief-stricken faces belonged to the travelers. "Something bad just happened. I don't know what it was. A decision was made that will bring death to your children."

Chapter Eight

"STOP IT, MEARA. You're scaring me. If you're trying to sound like Grandmother Biddy, then you almost have it down. You have to talk a little slower and put space between words to allow people to inch forward to hear the next one." Jane tried for a smile, but didn't quite achieve it.

"I'm not playing around. I'm serious. I had a vision of the women of the camp holding their children and crying because they were dead." Even talking about it caused her to shiver. She hugged her arms tight around her body, but it did nothing to dispel the chill that went all the way down into her soul.

"What are you talking about? One minute you were talking about your protestant village. Now this? Why the change?"

"I'm not sure. When we stopped, the coldness crept in, and I had a feeling something bad had happened. Then I got an image as clear as the wagon in front of us as the women of the camp criying over their dead children."

"Stop talking about it altogether. Don't mention it to anyone. It would be more than enough to have you chased out of the camp with sticks. Travelers value their children and would let no harm come to them if they could prevent it."

"I never said they didn't love their children. It was only an image that came to me unbidden. It may not mean anything." The words were to reassure her friend, but Meara didn't believe them. If only she knew what monumental decision had been made that moment to change the fate of the camp.

Grandmother Biddy might know. If nothing else, she could help her reason out why she saw what she did. "When do you think we'll stop?"

"Not for at least a couple of hours. When we are made to feel unwanted, we do our best to put a sizable distance between ourselves and whoever wanted us gone."

"That's it." She clapped her hands together. "I know."

"Know what?"

Once she was asked, Meara realized she didn't know as much as she thought she did. "When you were talking about putting distance between us and whoever didn't like the travelers, I realized the death of the children was caused by someone who fears the travelers."

"Meara, you need to stop this now. No one wants to hear you talk about their children dying."

Normally, she might have been content to stop talking, but not today, not when she knew with absolute certainty her vision would come to pass. "Talk would be better than their child dying."

"Tell me how you are going to stop this great disaster?"

"I don't know yet." Meara chewed on her bottom lip, praying the knowledge would reach her in time.

The wagon shuddered as it went over hardened ruts as they crossed the main path and veered off into the fields. Blinding sunlight meant the orb had reached its peak and was descending toward the west where they were headed. Jane allowed the reins in her hand to go slack as Seymour, the horse, ambled at a leisurely pace.

"We should be stopping soon to water the horses."

"Will we make camp?"

"Probably not. Red Monesha knows where we can camp in peace. Her father mapped out the friendly areas, but that has been some years ago. It seems more and more wherever we stop, we're being chased away. People are even more fearful of strangers. Sometimes I wonder if it is due to the war. There's even talk about the English wanting to draft good Irishmen to fight their war."

"People generally fear what they don't know." She could see how the free roaming travelers would cause some resentment, especially with the specter of an enforced draft possibly happening. Those who didn't understand the hardships a traveler faced could imagine they had an easy life roaming the countryside and sleeping under the stars.

The vegetation grew thicker ahead, and it was a lush green. Sheep baaed in the distance, along with a solitary moo. Jane lifted her hand to gesture where the animal sounds came from.

"Livestock, so there must be water nearby."

"Usually sheep come with a shepherd."

"This is true, but often the shepherd is sleeping or otherwise engaged. Even if he wasn't, a caravan against one shepherd would scare most of them off. Running back to town to report being overrun by gypsies. With any luck, one of the girls can keep the shepherd talking while we water the animals. Normally, we carry water with us, but our time by the shore pretty much emptied our water bags. Even if the settled hadn't pushed us into leaving, we would have left soon. Red Monesha was just waiting for Ardan and Shona to sail away."

"I guess it doesn't matter that much, then. The speed everyone packed up with was impressive."

"It comes from practice, too much of it."

"Why do the people hate the travelers so much?" She understood they were different, but weren't most people, since no two people were the same.

Jane circled her neck, working out the kinks that came from sitting upright on a backless bench seat. Then, she twisted her shoulders and settled into a slightly slumped posture.

"I wish I knew. Once, I asked Grandmother Biddy the reason why. She told me people always needed scapegoats. Then, she told me some story about eight women being accused of witchcraft because some woman was having demonic fits where she cursed at the clergyman and threw Bibles at him."

"I suspect she was doing what some of the people in the village wanted to do, but dared not."

Jane laughed. "That's a good one. Anyhow, they convicted eight women on this cursing woman's word. Grandmother Biddy told me the woman probably either resented or envied the women she accused. What I can't get is why when someone acted in such a way that they'd even believe her?"

"People believe what they want to believe. When the convent was bombed and the resulting fire scared the villagers, they wanted a reason for the occurrence that would somehow keep them safe."

"What do you mean?"

"If it was a bomb, which I truly think it was, then they could all be at risk for another to fall. Instead, they decided the fire had to be some sort of divine punishment. Some even believed I caused it somehow by simply existing or some devious means."

"People actually said you started it?"

"Some did. Never to my face, although Eleanor never told anyone I was from the convent. Instead, she said I was a cousin who came to visit. You see how easy it is to accuse those you don't know for anything bad that happens in your life."

"I see that. Sometimes I think we travelers are like Celtic Jews, because we're landless, always moving, and never truly welcomed anywhere. There might be a few who are excited when we show up, bringing some change into their otherwise dull life, but others curse us."

The discussion about scapegoats and witches had momentarily distracted her from her vision, but it came rolling back again. Her shoulders were tight, her jaw equally so as she worked it back and forth. Why have visions if they came without instructions. Grandmother Biddy told her she should only trust her intuition. Were visions her intuition? She wished she knew where Grandmother Biddy's wagon was in the caravan.

Her eyes fell on the green field filled with the occasional boulder and tufts of weeds and thistles they bounded over. It would be simple enough to get down and search for Grandmother Biddy, but she could be in the front of the caravan. It would make sense to protect the matriarch.

There was a shout and the pounding of horse's hooves as a rider shot past them.

"Water stop!"

Jane pulled back on the reins, bringing Seymour to a stop. "Do you want to hold the reins or scamper back into the wagon for the water skins? It's best to fill up since we don't know when we might find water next."

Holding the reins to such a powerful beast wasn't what Meara wanted to do, but it happened to be the most practical. She didn't know where the skins were. "I'll hold the reins."

Jane pulled the brake on the wheel and handed the reins to Meara. "There isn't a great deal to do. With the brake on, it isn't like he's going to bolt. Probably grateful for the rest."

Her lips flattened as Meara hoped the animal wouldn't take advantage of an inexperienced hand on the reins. If Rosemary and she were to make it to the Cleary home, they had three options, horse, foot, or train. She didn't know much about the train system. The fact that their boat capsized meant she lost almost everything she had. Thank goodness, she had sense enough to wear her mother's necklace and the emeralds for payment to Red Monesha, too.

There were no funds for a train and none for a horse, either. It looked like they'd be hiking across the Emerald Isle. On the plus side, Olio's massive bulk might cause troublemakers to think twice before taking on the reticent travelers.

Jane came up beside the wagon, flourishing the empty water skins. "I'll go on down to fill them up. You can walk Seymour down when it comes our turn."

Her companion strolled off with a bag slung over each shoulder and another in her hands. A fly buzzed over the wide rump of the horse, landed, only to be swished away by an ample tail. Jane expected her to move this creature. In the convent, she had yearned for more contact with animals. Instead of a huge horse, she'd hoped to interact with the hedgehogs and the bunnies.

Still, Jane expected her to do it, which meant she must be capable. The wagon in front of her jerked, then smoothly moved away toward the watering spot. Think. What did Jane do? Meara kept the reins loosely in her right hand as she scooted across the bench to release the brake. Seymour didn't break into an all-out gallop as she expected. His head was buried deep into the grass, possibly checking for clover.

Meara stood to get a better view of the horse. It looked as if he were grazing, which she didn't think was possible with a bit in his mouth. It could be that travelers didn't use bits or maybe Jane didn't. It never occurred to her that she would have trouble starting the horse. Maybe it was more like a mule than she realized.

The rider that had dashed by before walked his horse slowly up the caravan.

"You have troubles?"

She was, but didn't like to admit it. Stubbornness, pride, or whatever she might want to call it, could have her standing here all day watching the horse eat his fill. "I can't interest Seymour into walking."

The man stood up in his stirrups and moved his horse closer to Seymour. He leaned over just enough to slap the grazing horse. The startled horse bolted, throwing Meara back into the seat. The action had her grappling for balance and the reins. When she found both, she managed to guide Seymour toward the wide creek that served as a water stop.

At the creek edge, Jane picked up the filled water skins, and turned. Seymour gave a welcoming whinny that had her stumbling backwards. "What are you doing here?"

Her eyes moved up to Meara who did her best to appear confident. "You told me to drive him here."

"I did, but I did not expect you to do it. Have you ever driven a horse before?"

"No, but I figured I should start sometime." There was an entire world of things she hadn't done. Maybe she should try some of them, especially if there was some truth to the business of saving the world and stomping out evil she was supposed to do.

"Aye. You should. Seymour is a good one to start with, seeing how slow and old he is."

Slow and old? His initial start denied the description, but the horse never broke out of a fast walk after the initial startle. Driving the horse to the water, which was probably where it wanted to go, wasn't as big of a deal as she initially figured.

After depositing the water skins in the wagon, Jane walked to Seymour's head and grabbed the halter leading the horse to the water. The horse placed his lips in the water and slurped loudly enough for Meara to hear.

"He's thirsty, as am I." She scampered to the ground after placing the brake on. Jane placed a hand on her arm.

"You don't want to drink with the animals. Go upstream a little way."

It made sense if she didn't want any horse slobber in her mouth. Farther up the water was bound to be clearer where it hadn't been stirred up by horses' hooves wading into the water or even people sinking their various vessels into it to collect some of the life-giving liquid for their journey.

The sound of chatter along with childish whoops of delight reached her along with the sound of splashing. A gaggle of women had gathered around one wagon discussing a fortunate find. Curiosity had Meara wanting to ask what had been found, but she didn't have time to stop and ask.

The best she could do was get her drink and make use of some handy bushes. Taking too long and the caravan might leave without her. She'd like to think Jane would wait for her, but then that might not be the traveler way. Most everyone was self-sufficient, even the children to a degree. They were expected to do daily chores. Every one of them, except for the babies, had helped to break down the camp and scrambled into a wagon. There were no mothers yelling for their missing children. With that in mind, she could do no less, considering not everyone was pleased with her presence.

She slipped off her shoes and waded into the cool water to a spattering of stones that encircled a still pool of clear liquid. The muddy water near the edge would have served, but she doubted it would have tasted good. The rocks teetered as she balanced herself to slowly stoop to reach the surface. Her first sip of water was sweet and assuaged the tickle that had been created at the back of her throat from sucking up dust created by the wagons in front of her. It also created a desire to drink more.

Her face was almost to the water when the rocks shifted. Her face plunged into the water with her body following. Meara stuck her hands against the rocky bed and pushed up. There were a few muffled chuckles coming from the shore, probably attracted from the large splash she made. By the time she turned, whoever had witnessed her humiliation had faded into the tree shadows. She waded through the creek to reach the shore, not at all careful of her trailing skirts since she was wet already.

On shore, a good twist eliminated a great deal of the water that weighted her clothes. All she had time for was a quick trip to the bushes, even that was interrupted by the rider moving up the creek bank.

"Moving out!"

She barely had her skirts decently down as she sprinted by the wagons. A few travelers noticed her wet state and yelled out comments.

"Did you take a swim?"

"This wasn't a bathing stop."

She ignored them. It would take too long to reply, and she had nothing to say. A stitch in her side forced her to push her fingers against it to keep running. As she passed one wagon, she would have sworn they had a wooly sheep lashed to it. It had to be something else since she hadn't seen any sheep in the camp.

Seymour, along with the wagon, was already in the caravan line. Jane stood on the seat shading her eyes showing more trust in the elderly horse than Meara had. She waved her arms in her friend's direction.

"There you are!" She made a sidestep that centered her behind the reins tied to a metal bar on the front of the wagon.

"Here I am." She grabbed onto the wagon and pulled herself onto the seat.

"I was worried about you. I never had a clue you'd decide on a swim."

"I didn't."

Her friend arched an eyebrow.

"I fell in."

"How could that happen from the bank?"

When she decided to wade into the center of the creek, it seemed like such an inspired move. Her initial walk upstream had her passing several people on the ground with their back ends raised to the sky as they struggled to drink. Others were simply filling their canteens and drinking from them. That should have been a hint. Her shoulders went up in a shrug, hoping that would be enough to discourage questions.

"You're wet all over. If you fell from the bank, I'd expect just your front to be wet." She held the reins with one hand and tweaked Meara's skirt as if testing its wetness.

Not wanting to talk about it, she remained quiet until Jane slapped her leg, causing water to squirt out.

"What was that for?"

"Just trying to get a reaction out of you. Go get changed. I have dry clothes you can change into. Hurry and you can get changed before the caravan starts moving."

Meara swung down from her perch and entered the wagon and shut the door. She'd located a clean skirt the same time the wagon lurched into motion. It looked like returning to her place beside Jane became more problematic.

Chapter Nine

LEAVING HER WET SLIPPERS behind to dry, dressed in a faded blue skirt and homespun top, Meara was ready to return to her spot. The only problem was the wagon was moving, not fast, but still moving.

Following them was another wagon. Not too close, but close enough for the driver to wave, thinking perhaps she was signaling him. She wasn't. Her eyes dropped to the grassy ground passing under the wagon. Thick and plush grass would cushion her fall. Spots of earth peeked through the grass and a few stones, too.

Her hands gripped the frame of the door as she balanced in the open doorway. After seeing a couple of the traveler men perform tricks on the horses, she imagined there was an agile move that could land her on her feet. Unfortunately, she didn't know any. Jane probably wouldn't appreciate everyone being able to see inside her wagon, either. She reached back with her right hand and closed the door.

Her only choice would be to work her way down the two steps and jump. It would only be a couple of feet. Add in the moving part and what should be simple became harder. Still maintaining her grip on the doorknob, she lifted one foot in the air while praying it would land where it was intended. An indecipherable shout went up from the following wagon. Feeling a little more confident when her foot touched the wooden step, she moved the other, but kept her grip solidly on the door handle.

It felt as if the wagon was slowing. That would give her the opportunity she needed. Since she'd made it down the first step she felt committed to try the second. To do so, she'd have to give up her death grip on the door handle. She sucked in her lips, trying to mentally prepare for what was sure to be a disaster. Unfortunately she had an audience.

Nothing for it, either she took a tumble or she spent the rest of the journey plastered against the back of the wagon. The travelers were never shy about commenting, either. Her insistence on remaining on the first step would be the talk of the camp, unless she returned to the wagon interior, which suddenly appealed.

Her mind made up, she let go of the frame, and tried to turn but the wagon jerked sending her flying into the air with a hard landing on the dirt.

Stunned, she stayed there for a few seconds, blinking up at clouds until she remembered there was a wagon behind her. Meara rolled to her feet just as Jane rounded the wagon.

"I heard the Foxes yell to halt, but I had no clue it was you we were stopping for. What were you doing?"

Not wanting to discuss it in front of listening ears, she grabbed Jane's elbow and pulled her to the front of the wagon. Her companion scampered up, taking her place behind the horse. Meara pulled herself up and sat, remaining silent, hoping that would somehow take away the burn of humiliation from her cheeks.

Once the wagon started moving again, Jane shot her a sideways glance. "Do you want to explain why you were throwing yourself off my wagon?"

"I didn't know how else to get off."

"Look behind you."

All that was behind her was a wagon unless Jane meant behind that wagon, which would be even harder to see. "What am I supposed to see?"

"There's a window behind us. You could have climbed through the window or simply asked me to stop."

When she said it, it sounded obvious. "How was I supposed to know there was a window there, and I had no clue how to get you to stop." There was no mention of acrobatic moves off the rear of a moving wagon. It would be hard to imagine Grandmother Biddy attempting such a move.

"All you had to do was hammer on the wall to get me to stop."

"I didn't know that. Besides, I'm not used to asking for things. I figured the whole caravan would stop."

"Wouldn't be the first time and besides, we're not traveling at high speeds. You have to learn to ask for what you need." She gave a little nod as if agreeing with herself. "Have you ever asked for anything?"

"I'm not sure." She tried to remember a time when it felt normal to ask for something. A vague memory presented itself. While the convent never approached what some people considered merry or festive, they did sometimes have a bit more on the high feast days. "Once a nun's family who were candy makers brought us all a candy cane for Christmas. It was so sweet that I gobbled it down while the other nuns savored theirs. A few broke them into pieces so they could make it last longer. Some even refused the canes, saying it was a temptation they didn't need. I asked for their canes. From the reaction I got you'd think I had asked for their immortal souls. Mother Superior claimed I was guilty of the sin of gluttony and made me stand in the courtyard with a sign around my neck that read gluttony, and I had to ring heavy hand bells. Whenever she couldn't hear the bells ringing, she'd stick her head out the window to have me start again. By the end of the day, I thought my arms would fall off, and I never made the mistake of asking for something again."

Just the memory of the heavy bells had her hunching her shoulders. It almost put her off candy, but since they never received another treat such as that, it wasn't a worry.

"I never thought much on nuns. We travelers don't run across them on a regular basis. The few I saw had sour faces. The lack of sweetness and brutal punishments must have accounted for their expression."

"I don't know if every convent is the same. Some might be better."

"Or they could be worse." Jane gave a pretend shiver, holding up her index finger. "If you're going to function in the real world—and you are—you must ask for things. When you do, you must be confident and determined. People will try to ignore you because you're a woman and young. Most men they interpret those characteristics as being brainless. Well, you don't have a man to do for you, which means you'll have to stand your ground."

"How do I do that?" Most of the time, she'd been lucky enough to have things given her, and a few times she took what she needed, but she had never asked for anything.

"It's attitude. Hold your head up and look the person in the eye. Don't make the mistake of smiling."

"Why not?" Once she discovered she could smile she liked it a great deal, even better when people smiled back at her. It was so much better than donning an expression of humbleness and piety, which she assumed was a type of blank expression or looked like the edge of falling asleep judging by the sisters' faces.

"Smiles are tricky things. Smile at a man and he might think you fancy him. Sometimes, that works in your favor, but usually it results in his thoughts straying and not paying attention to what you're saying. Smiles are for close friends and families. Don't go giving them away to anyone. Often when you smile at a woman, she thinks you're working a scam or are laughing at her for some reason."

"Why wouldn't she think I'm friendly? I am."

"I know you are. Friendships don't happen overnight. Sometimes, a person who smiles too much is trying too hard. In that case, a smile serves as a banner announcing your weakness. If you smile when you ask for something, it could result in unfavorable consequences. You could be charged too much."

"Hayden, the handsome, charming traveler, smiles all the time."

"True enough, and he is a con artist. Sometimes, I think he blinds people with his white teeth as he talks or dares them into betting against him. A bet they will lose. Surely, you don't want to be like Hayden."

"I don't."

"That's good. Our clan could not support more than one. Even one keeps us moving more than we like. As a woman, you'll come up against tales about women being weak. You have to show people you aren't."

She wasn't so sure about that, but up to now she'd survived, which is more than many had. "How do I do that?"

"Put your hands on your hips. Wait in silence. When asked any question, just repeat your request. Many times, they'll give it to you, simply to have you leave."

"So basically, I enter a village, say I want to buy a lamb, and they say they have none. I cross my arms and stand there until I get one."

"They might not have any. In that case, go to the next village or farm."

Meara tapped her chest with her hand. "Here I thought you were teaching me something. First you tell me, look them in the eyes, state your request, and you'll get what you want. Then you tell me, it might not work. What good is it then?"

"I didn't say it was perfect, but it could be to a degree. It depends on how much you believe in yourself. Did you learn any incantations before you left England?"

If she had learned magic she wouldn't be dependent on chance-met travelers to take her where she needed to go. "No." Meara held up one finger. "Eleanor did tell me about King Arthur and his knights. There was a woman in the story named Morgan Le Faye. Supposedly she was a great sorceress who first learned about magic in a nunnery. It definitely wasn't ours."

"I thought some might be helpful."

Her fingers smoothed over the chains hanging around her neck. "I have my mother's necklace and the one Grandmother Biddy gave me. I believe they're both magical."

"They're probably protection magic, which is good to have. It won't make people like you. A charisma charm would be useful, I'll have to look that up. It has to be something like the love potions the women come seeking."

"You have magic?"

"Of a sort, the magic of belief and sometimes confidence."

It didn't make sense. Eleanor made jellies that relieved women's pains often infusing them with the good health intentions. The woman didn't attend church or even claim any religious affiliation. Grandmother Biddy had warned her the travelers were very religious, which made it hard to reconcile any belief in magic, while despite their fear of any type of witchery, most believed in the Tarot.

"What about the verse in the Bible that talks about not letting a witch live?" More than one sister chanted it using the verse almost as an incantation.

Jane shrugged. "Oh, that. Well, any spiritual insights, any good, comes from God. That verse about witches was made up by King James a long time ago. Something about he had his fortune told and supposedly he would be killed by a witch or something. The man thought he could prevent it by turning everyone against the witches."

"Did a witch kill him?"

"I don't think so. That would have been remembered."

"Tell me more about how you make unlikable folks popular?"

Jane wrinkled her nose and waggled her eyebrows. "You are interested?"

"Some. I don't want to do anything weird such as swallow a live toad. I don't think I could."

A sigh sounded, while Jane shot her a look of disbelief. "I have no clue what they taught you at the convent, but magic never involves harm to another creature. All you need to do is write your full name on a piece of paper. Your full name is?"

"Meara Cleary as far as I know. Not sure if I have a middle name." If she did, then whatever Jane had in mind might require the use of it. "Does it matter if I don't know my middle name or even if I have one?"

"No. It's how you think of yourself. You write on the paper, 'Meara Cleary is well liked.' Write it three times, then burn the paper in a candle flame. The burning sends the message out to all."

How something so simple could be effective puzzled her. "Is that it?"

"The most important part is to believe. Without belief, then it won't work."

Her companion spouted the words as if they were nothing. All you had to do was believe. Sometimes belief was hard to come by, especially when people told you that you had some great mission to perform or listen to your intuition for guidance. Part of her wanted to just find a quiet place, maybe with a widow woman who needed someone who'd accept her help for room and board like the arrangement she had with Eleanor. The war would end, since wars always did, eventually.

Even as she considered the possibility, part of her rebelled. Something deep inside of her prickled up like a porcupine, even making her a little bit ill in its refusal to accept her plan to lie low. Perhaps it was the intuition Grandmother Biddy told her to trust. Obviously, it would not let her rest easy.

"I could do the name and the candle."

Jane's gaze remained on the wagon ahead as she answered. "You should. Everyone has enemies, those who envy or resent them for some reason." She pursed her lips as if considering something. "You probably have more than most."

"That I didn't need to hear. Despite doing my best never to harm or anger anyone, I think you're correct. I should do this tonight. I have a feeling I might have need of being liked sooner than later."

Instead of disagreeing, as Meara hoped, Jane nodded, saying, "Need to do it tonight. Would have been better to have done it yesterday."

The furrowed brow meant her companion knew something, possibly something Meara wouldn't want to hear. The smart thing would be to inquire, but she didn't. She would before the night was over. Just a few more moments of tranquility, if she could call bumping over Ireland in a wagon tranquil, then she'd ask.

Chapter Ten

THE ROLLING SLOPE of the land grew taller, becoming hills as the caravan journeyed on. Every now and then, they came across a stone wall they had to circle around. Jane nodded at one. "Not the friendly sort."

"He may want to keep his sheep in."

"More likely he wants to keep people out. Folks like us, wanderers and strangers."

It seemed to be a normal enough desire for a person to have until she realized she was one of the people the landowner wanted to prevent from getting too close to home and property. She'd never thought of herself as a threat in any manner. It was an uncomfortable feeling that led her to change the topic, hoping the feeling would follow, too.

"I heard some of the women talking about a lucky find."

"That means someone found something worthwhile. It could be anything from a few coins to a shawl that had been dropped."

"If they found it, shouldn't they try to find the owner?"

Jane's head swiveled her way as the woman blinked and shook her head. "How would they go about finding the owners?"

When put that way, it made her feel silly. Of course, the travelers weren't going to show up at the local gathering to report finding a shawl. "That was silly of me."

"Not silly. Just ignorant."

"That doesn't sound much better."

Jane nudged her with her elbow. "It is. All it means is you're not that familiar with traveler ways."

"I'll admit to that since I've never met a traveler before I encountered your group. Explain the traveler ways to me."

"That might take a while." She clucked and used both hands to snap the reins. "Seymour takes any opportunity to slow down."

The sounds of the wheels turning intermingled with bird song and the low hum of insects probably warning their brethren about the huge vehicles heading their way. Just when she decided Jane wasn't going to speak, she did.

"Luck and fate plays a strong part in the traveler's life. Although, some consider chance-found objects as blessings from God. If you're cold and walking through a field and happen upon a jacket or a blanket, then it is a blessing or a fortunate find."

"Do you not worry about the person who lost it?"

"If it were more important, the owner would have done a better job of caring for it. I know what I have is all I have. I'm not leaving things in various places. It could be that he or she has so much they don't know where their stuff is. Then again, there could be a leprechaun they offended, playing a trick on them. It could be the leprechaun is rewarding us, too."

It sounded a bit like stealing according to the commandments the convent had her memorize. Still, some would say the tithes the convent demanded for the upkeep of the sisters from struggling families could have been a bit like stealing. The box she'd found in the convent after it burned, yielded some funds. Taking them put her more in danger of hellfire than any of the travelers.

"What if you came across something you didn't want. Something nasty."

"I wouldn't be foolish enough to pick it up and would assume it was meant for someone else." Jane laughed at her comment.

"All right then, I think I get it. I remember one of the sisters telling me that God would provide for all our needs. I always wondered why he didn't think we'd benefit from a little more meat, but never made the mistake of mentioning it."

"It was probably just as well. I find when it comes to religion if you ask questions and folks don't know the answer to, they just get mad."

"True."

The afternoon waned as they passed farms, wooded areas, and rolling hills dotted with sheep. In Ireland, it was hard to believe a war was happening only an ocean away.

In England, the shortages, the blackouts, and even city folks appearing in the country all indicated something wasn't right. Here, all appeared normal. Her lips twisted as she realized she had no clue what normal looked like. The aspect of the ordinary brought her friend Rosemary—who had turned self-appointed guardian—to mind, although she had been slipping on the guardian part since they entered the camp. It could be she transferred her guardian duties to the children.

"Do you think Rosemary is okay? We left the beach camp in such a hurry, I never even saw her." Guilt sank its claws into her. Friends should know where friends were, especially when escaping riled townsmen.

"A smart mother snagged your friend to help corral her children. I know you've witnessed the man speeding back and forth yelling orders. He always checks to make sure no one is left behind. He would have noticed Rosemary."

"You're right. We can catch up at camp."

"That you can." The wagon moved along without the two of them saying anything until Jane spoke. "Have you considered the two of you might not be together always?"

"I have. Rosemary has made no secret of the fact she wants to marry. Back in Hogstead, it was hard to marry because a jealous Adelaide spread so many ugly rumors about her. They were all untrue, but people can be funny about that. They don't want to associate with anyone who has rumors spread about them as if it could be catching."

"I like to think the travelers are different, but I've seen people leave over misunderstandings."

"Where do they go?"

"Who knows? I guess it was rather like Destiny ending up all the way in England. I wasn't around when she left, and Grandmother Biddy suggested her departure because the other women resented her. If people believe God blesses you with a fair face or figure, wealth, talent, or a charming manner, then those without judge themselves lacking. We all know you can't be angry at God, but you can resent the person who so clearly shows what you lack by just existing."

"Did you think women resent you because you have your own wagon and horse?"

"I know they do. They also resent my closeness to Grandmother Biddy, why I've come to the realization that I'll never find a husband here within our group. My father refused all who wanted to woo me. Those he didn't refuse, I did. This makes things awkward. Women envy my wagon and independence while the men who wanted to take the wagon and independence away from me resent my refusal to accept their desire to do so."

Here Meara thought she was troubled and viewed Jane as having a stable life with no pressing issues. In many ways, they were the same, buffeted by circumstances, not knowing which way to turn. "Has your father spoken to you about passing over every man's marriage offer?"

"When you say it that way it makes me sound difficult and contrary. It wasn't my plan to refuse all marriage offers. I kept waiting to feel something for any one of them, but because I've grown up with them, I know too much to feel even mildly attracted."

"Such as?"

"Cam never washes his hands. I imagine he bathes even less. I wouldn't want him to touch me with those hands. Another has the habit of whining about everything. Every word that comes out of his mouth is a complaint. Sol cheats at cards while Hayden flirts with all the settled women. A few say he takes it beyond flirting, which could explain some of our rapid departures."

"Are there no suitable men?"

"Some are suitable, but they are like brothers. I'd hoped for a big meeting of travelers so I could meet people I hadn't grown up beside, but the possibility of that happening is getting less and less."

"Why?"

"The settled are afraid. We're finding less and less welcoming towns. There are rumors about travelers stealing people blind and seducing their women, although the last part with Hayden might be somewhat true. He likes to brag that if a settled man took care of his woman, she wouldn't fall for a smooth-talking traveler." Jane grimaced at her own words.

"I can see why you passed on him."

"Yeah. What amazes me is I considered him once. My mother warned me off him since she'd witnessed his flirtatious ways when we were in town. I was willing to fall under his spell like any other simple lass. He's good at making a girl feel special. I'm warning you and hope you'll warn Rosemary. All the other girls in the group have been. That puts him in the same place as me with having to consider another group for a spouse."

The sun had dipped behind the hills throwing up the last rays of light as the rider reappeared.

"Camp stop."

As he worked his way down the caravan, Jane sighed. "Thank goodness. I grow weary of these drives that last all day simply because someone is afraid of travelers too near them. You'd think we were midges."

"What?"

"It's a hungry insect that shows up in the wet, summer months. They usually show up in a group, biting and stinging folks. Sometimes I feel as unwelcome as that. It grows old."

The horse pulled them into a clearing with a copse of trees and a stream meandering through it. Hills curved around one side. It looked like a safe enough place to her, but Jane pointed to the hills.

"I suspect there is a city or a town on the other side of the hills. At best, a few farmers, who wouldn't mind us camping out here. Most might let us stay a few days. It's when we stay longer they get antsy. In the morning, or even possibly tonight, a scout might go out. They might even send Olio."

"Olio, really?" She wasn't sure how the oversized man didn't stick out like an illuminated beacon.

"He's very good at being quiet. If someone sees him, they never think he's with the travelers. Instead, they assume he's a confused tourist who has lost his way. There are a few of those around here, and he's clever enough to play the part."

"That's smart."

Even though she didn't know much about the man who had volunteered to go with them when they left, an admiration grew, especially when she discovered how he could be useful. That sounded petty, not how she wanted to think of herself. When he first declared his intentions to travel with her, she assumed from the way Jane talked it would be her job to look out for him. The more she heard about his abilities, the less she thought it.

Jane guided the wagon into the loose circle. She pulled Seymour to a stop, tied the reins, and applied the brake before jumping down. Meara joined her friend on the ground and helped her unharness the horse.

"We'll take Seymour to the grassy area where he can eat with the other horses."

There were a few horses already there grazing on the bright green grass. Jane indicated that Meara should hold the horse as she sunk back on her haunches and withdrew a rope of sorts and attached it to his front legs before pushing back to her feet.

"What was that for?"

"We have to hobble the horses or they could startle and run off. We might never find them again. Although, with Seymour, we'd find him. It's also a precaution against those who would harass us by running them off. If we're stuck without our horses, then we might be accused of loitering, which is a jailable offense."

"Seems unfair if the horses were spooked."

"I'd agree, but it is what it is. That's why we must take precautions."

The women were scurrying to surround an area with stones for a fire. Two others struggled to remove a cauldron from a wagon. Meara and Jane rushed to help.

"Here, share the load." Jane placed one end of the yoke against her shoulder while Meara tried to hold onto the fire darkened kettle so whatever was in it wouldn't spill out. The women worked together as they maneuvered the receptacle to the fire circle.

"The men might not like that we're warming up the porridge, but we can't waste it," one of the women commented.

The other snorted, then added, "They'll get over it soon enough as soon as they see what else we're having."

The women gave each other knowing looks, making Meara wonder what else could be in the supper works.

Rosemary descended from one of the wagons, carrying a baby. She cooed at the wrapped bundle and headed their way. Her friend grinned as she approached. "That was a delightful ride."

Meara exchanged a quizzical glance with Jane while one of the women behind them commented, "I noticed Megan was smart enough to have you help with the children."

Rosemary nodded. "Glad to do it."

"Saw you sitting beside Hayden holding that baby looking like a family."

The name rang a mental bell. If it hadn't, the shove Jane gave her along with the hissed words, "Talk to her," would have done it.

The two women who they helped with the cauldron continued to chatter to each other listing what food stuffs they had.

"Potatoes."

"A few leeks."

"A handful of radishes."

"Couple of parsnips, which should make a fine stew once we get Cam to butcher the sheep for us."

"We'll need to smoke the rest of the meat overnight to be able to carry it with us."

Meara listened to the conversation as she tried to think how she'd phrase warning off Rosemary. The little experience she had, came from Eleanor warning her about making big decisions on waiting for Braeden based on a few words and a kiss.

If Rosemary's over cheery mood was any indication, then Hayden had charmed her thoroughly. Meara fell in step with Rosemary as she walked with the baby, trying to keep it from fussing. Something about the women preparing dinner nagged at her. It was more likely she'd rather fix dinner than do what she needed to do.

"Did you have a good ride?"

"Wonderful." Rosemary somehow made the word sound even more pleasant than it normally did.

"I'm glad. My ride wasn't awful, except for the fall into the creek, followed by the fall off the wagon." She related the details exaggerating the specifics to make her friend laugh.

"Well, I have to say my trip wasn't that eventful, but it was pleasant all the same."

Here came the hard part, which she felt she had no right to say. Someone who knew Hayden should deliver the news. At least it would be believable coming from another traveler.

"Jane and I had a chance to talk a great deal today."

"Oh, no, here it comes." Rosemary's smile vanished, and her face pruned up.

"Here comes that?"

"Hayden told me Jane would warn me off him. I never suspected she'd use you to do it."

It sounded like the sly traveler had already taken some preventative measures. "She isn't using me. She did inform me that our sudden departure was most likely caused by Hayden flirting with settled women and sometimes more."

Rosemary's gentle stroll morphed into a hurried stride, jostling the baby in the process who fussed at the change. She slowed, trying to soothe the baby. "It's all rumors. I'm surprised you'd believe such a thing considering rumors had you fleeing your own home."

She had a point and a valid one at that. "You're my friend, and I worry about you. You're a smart woman."

"I am. That's why I refuse to listen to gossip."

"That makes sense. I'm sure you'll agree that Hayden is handsome."

"He is." She placed the baby against her shoulder as she directed a confused gaze at Meara.

"Bet you'd agree he is charming, too."

"That he is. This is strange since you appear to be agreeing with me."

Well, she managed to turn the conversation the tiniest bit, but not enough to be effective. What else could she say? "I imagine any girl would be proud to call him hers."

"That they would."

"The man is past the age of marrying. He should be married by now."

The angry expression had faded from Rosemary's brow, but showed a flash of returning. "Men can marry whenever they please. It's not the same as women."

"He could pick any unmarried woman he wanted from the caravan."

A smile tugged the ends of Rosemary's mouth upward. "He has. Me. He's just been waiting for the right woman to show up."

"The stupid one." Her hand covered her mouth too late. Rosemary turned with the babe on her shoulder and stomped away.

Jane slid from her place against the wagon to join her. "That went well."

"I wish. Hayden asked her to marry him or he did something that made her believe as much. Keep in mind that Rosemary came to Ireland to marry, and now she has her wish." It looked hopeless to her. It might just be her and Olio traveling to the Cleary farm.

Jane sucked in her lips, glancing in the direction Rosemary had taken. "Maybe I should have talked to her, but I felt she would listen to you."

"Wouldn't. He warned her against things you would say to sully him."

"Scoundrel. I guess we should have done that candle spell first. It couldn't have hurt. If she decides to join up with Hayden, she'll be crying in her pillow before a month is up."

"I have that feeling, too." Not knowing what else to do, she searched for Grandmother Biddy, to discuss her vision. She knew better than to mention her intention to Jane. "I'll wander around a bit."

She suited her actions to her words as she searched for the colorful wagon. It didn't take her long to find it. Grandmother Biddy was sitting in her ornate chair outside of her wagon. Her eyes lit up when she spotted Meara.

"I had a feeling you would come."

Of course, she did. "I need to talk to you about something."

"Do we need to go inside?"

Remembering what Jane had said about jealousy and rumors in the camp, she decided against the action. It might hint at favoritism or even whispered stories about other camp members. It would be better to talk about stuff in clear sight. It would make it appear less malicious.

Meara squatted by the chair to whisper her vision. Emotions shifted across Grandmother Biddy's face finally settling on concern.

"You did right to come to me. This vision came to you for a reason. It must be true. The question we have to ask ourselves is what would kill the children and not the adults?"

"An illness. Usually an illness takes the frail. The young ones are too small to fight against it."

"That's a possibility, but you saw none of the old dying in your vision?"

"I did not." She grimaced and swallowed. Why couldn't she make any sense of this? The smell of cooking meat caused her stomach to growl. "It's more than that."

"How so?"

"I had the feeling that whatever harm came from someone who disliked the travelers."

"We'd see anyone coming into our camp. We'd not be foolish enough to take an unwarranted gift from a settled."

"What type of gift could they give you that would cause illness?"

Grandmother Biddy stroked her chin with her veined hand. "When we barter, it is usually for coin or food. Although, this last stop didn't yield any bartering."

The unease in her stomach grew. It resembled the same sensation she had when she had the vision only more intense. She wrapped her arms around her stomach, trying to quell the feeling.

"What is it?" Grandmother Biddy placed a hand on Meara's feverish forehead. "You're burning up."

"It's my stomach that hurts, but it is spreading through me."

"Poison." She uttered the word with deadly calm.

As soon as Grandmother Biddy diagnosed her condition the feeling fled as fast as it came. Meara slumped against the wagon confused by the ordeal. "I don't know what happened."

"Someone in the spirit world is trying to get a message across. Poison has been brought into our camp and will be fed to our children. We need to figure out how."

It had to be deliberate, yet at the same time undetected. Guards were always posted on the camp so no one could have slipped in and poisoned their food supply. Grandmother Biddy pushed up from her chair.

"I need to warn the others not to eat anything."

"I'll help. Give me a moment to fetch my shawl."

Her stomach gave another growl, possibly reacting to the smell of bubbling stew. Across the camp, a begging dog stood around the cooks. One woman slipped him a bone that he ran with into the woods surrounding the wagons. Her eyes followed the dog knowing somehow it was important. The image of the wooly sheep flashed in her memory. It stayed even as she tried to pass it off as unimportant.

"Do we have any sheep in the camp?"

"None. Stupid creatures. Good to eat, but too much work to herd. Why do you ask?"

"I saw one strapped to a wagon."

"Peculiar. We had goats. Smart enough animals. You can milk them and use the leftover milk for butter and cheese.

Unaccustomed to goats, she threw Gradmother Biddy an apologetic smile. "Not real familiar with them. I'm sure I've seen them."

"Plenty of farmers have them. They can get by on poor grass and weeds, which makes them an excellent animal for a traveler."

"I may have seen some at the Hogstead market. What happened to yours?"

"They weren't mine, but when food got low the goat was the first to go.'

It seemed odd that the animal would take off on its own. Outside of the mule, cat and half dozen laying hens and rooster the convent owned, she hadn't had too much experience with animals. "They decided to leave?"

"If the goats had the gift of foresight, they would have taken off. Instead, they were eaten." Grandmother Biddy chuckled at own joke, then cocked her head, and asked. "Whose wagon did you see the sheep strapped to?"

Her shoulders went up in a shrug. Most of the wagons appeared the same to her despite the owners' hard work to make theirs the most beautiful with curving flourishes and colorful flowers. "Just one I passed on my way back from the creek. It could have been on my way there to."

As soon as Grandmother reached the her wagon, Meara offered her arm to the elderly woman to assist her with the steps.

A small boy ran from the direction of the woods moving as fast as his short legs would carry him. He screamed something that was indecipherable, but it red face signaled whatever it was mattered. Instead of veering off to the women cooking, he kept heading toward them. When he was close enough, she could understand his words.

"Blackie is sick. Come quick."

"Blackie," Meara repeated the name.

Grandmother Biddy pointed in the direction the boy came from. "It's the dog, Blackie."

An image of a woman handing the dog a bone came to mind. They must be cooking the sheep. It could have been poisoned." One of those fortunate finds wasn't so fortunate this time.

Chapter Eleven

MEARA STOOD FROZEN in place. Her eyes rested on the agitated boy as he begged for help.

"Hurry. Blackie is sick."

Grandmother Biddy reached out to place a hand on his shoulder. "Blackie's an old dog. When dogs get old they often go to the woods to die."

"It's not that. It's poison from the bone," Meara cried. "He didn't get that much just a little from the meat still on the bone. The dog can be saved."

Both the boy and Grandmother Biddy regarded her with dropped mouths. Something dropped behind her. She heard the metal ting. Sure, she'd surprised them, but she'd surprised herself more. It was hard to explain, but she knew without any doubt that the words were true. The three of them stood them for approximately three heartbeats until they swung into action as if hearing an inaudible bell.

Grandmother clapped her hands together. "Liam, go get me a bowl, two raw eggs, and a spoon." The boy scampered away to do her bidding.

Meara started toward the cooks, hoping she was wrong.

"My husband will be pleased with dinner tonight. It has been a long time since we had mutton."

The other woman patted her chest with her hand and gave a little laugh. "Same here. I think we should feed the children first. That way we can get them asleep in case our husbands want to thank us."

Meara exploded, racing across the last distance to the cooking fire as the women conversed and dipped out a ladle of stew. The first cook brought the ladle close to her mouth to taste the dish.

"No!" Meara shoved the second woman out of the way and knocked the ladle out of the other woman's hand, spraying the contents to splatter all over the both.

"Are you daft? That's a waste of decent food." She fisted both hands on her hips, narrowed her eyes and lowered her head.

For a split second, she thought the woman would charge her similar to a bull. She waved her hands, to distract her long enough to listen to reason. "The sheep was poisoned."

"Says you." The other woman, the one Meara shoved, came to her friend's defense. "There's no reason for carrying on the way you do."

"There is. There was." She pointed to the cook, with one fist planted on her hip. "You were going to taste the stew and likely die a painful death." A disbelieving snort sounded beside her. She pivoted to face the other woman. "You were going to feed the children first. They would all have died!"

Her vision made sense. If the children had eaten first, they would have died, alerting the adults not to eat the stew. Since the first casualty was Blackie, it allowed her the needed time to put the facts together. Neither woman appeared convinced. The first one nodded to the second one, who was hesitant to make her opinion known.

"You be spinning tales."

"Why would I do that?" Her voice broke on the last word as she realized she'd failed to convince the women of the necessity of abandoning the stew. In the distance, she could hear children's laughter and a horse's neigh. For all practical purposes, it was another afternoon. Unless she could convince the women of the harm that awaited them, it might be some of the travelers' last afternoon.

Sweat dampened her blouse as her gaze switched between the two women. If she could empty the cook pot, she believed that no one would eat off the ground. What of the wildlife that might try to scrounge a meal? A sliding step brought her closer to the pot, but the opinionated traveler must have guessed her intentions and stepped in front of the kettle.

The woman gave her a long glare and hoisted an eyebrow. "Ever since the sea spat you out, you've demanded all the attention. Everyone is hopping around to do your bidding."

That was so untrue. "I haven't asked anyone to do anything."

Even though her goal was to sound conciliatory, she failed. Instead, her tone was a shade less than belligerent, and her hands found purchase on her own hips.

"Aye, I'm not sure how it is done, but you do it just the same. Probably bewitch everyone you meet. How else can you explain Red Monesha deciding to leave a successful camp to go to the beach where we would make no money?"

"Not sure how I could have guided Monesha's movements since I was at sea or probably still in England. I'm more concerned about the stew and the health of your children." She pushed her hair away from her face as she regarded the two suspicious women.

One pursed her lips and wrinkled her nose. She stooped to pick up the dirty ladle, then she straightened and pointed the utensil at Meara. "You say you want to help. If you know so much, why didn't you stop me before I put the poisoned meat in the soup. Everything is ruined now. At the very least we could have had vegetable stew. Now, we have nothing."

Why couldn't she get these women to believe her. It sounded more as if they'd rather not trust her and take a chance on eating tainted stew. How could she lead if people refused to follow? The travelers weren't her people and didn't have any faith in her. Until a couple days ago she hadn't known any of them. Maybe that was it, she hadn't proven herself.

"Do you have nothing else you could make for the evening meal?"

Both women folded their arms as if on cue and shook their heads. Olio's tall form appeared from the side and walked toward them. He held up a hand in greeting. Having caught the end of the conversation, he responded. "You have food. I bartered for it."

"You can't make a meal out of that," one of the women protested.

Meara remained silent, aware that the sum of her cooking knowledge would fit into a thimble.

Olio looked unconvinced, but directed his eyes toward Meara, a silent plea for her to take over the arduous job of convincing the cooks while he told her, "Grandmother Biddy thought you'd want to know they managed to get the dog to vomit up the poisoned bone."

"Which dog?"

Before Meara could answer, Olio did. "Blackie."

"Oh, my. The bone I gave him made him ill?" Her defiant attitude melted away as concern colored her inquiry. "I hate to think I made him sick."

"You had no way of knowing." Words she thought would comfort the woman, instead had the female pivoting in her direction and shaking her spoon. "You who knows so much could have told me much sooner, or did you want my Blackie to die?"

"I don't want anyone to die or anything." She was about ready to give up on the whole situation when Rosemary rounded a wagon cradling a baby.

"What has you so riled up? I can hear you across the camp."

The second woman who had been content to listen, approached Rosemary and held out her arms. Rosemary surrendered the baby without a complaint. As soon as the child left her arms it let out a distressed cry.

The woman rocked the child, but its crying increased. "What have you done to the child?" She landed a baleful look on Rosemary, who turned to Meara as if she had a clue what was going on.

Rosemary shrugged. "Nothing. If you gentled your speech and didn't yell into the babe's ear, it wouldn't fuss."

She paced with the baby against her shoulder, muttering just loud enough for them to hear. "No slip of a girl tells me how to take care of a baby."

Olio reached for Meara's arm, managed to grab hold of her hand,

and pull her away from the upset women. "Grandmother Biddy sent me to retrieve you."

"I understand." She gave a backward look at the kettle still cooking over the fire. "Where is she?"

"I carried Blackie back to her wagon. You'll find her there."

A request from Grandmother Biddy was more like a summons from the queen. She had no desire to refuse it. "I'll go, but I have a favor to ask."

"What is it?" The man had a reputation for talking as little as possible, which he lived up to.

"I'm worried." She wasn't sure how to convey her concerns because it would sound as if she were criticizing the travelers. Her gaze swung over to Rosemary, who was still talking to the other women. Some of the natural boldness she'd admired in her fellow Brit didn't appear to be going over that well.

"I'm afraid if I leave Rosemary with those two they might put the baby down and resort to hair pulling."

"I'll see that they don't."

"Thank you. There's one more thing." She held her index finger, anxious to remind him about the stew. Meara angled her head in the direction of the stew pot.

"Done." He gave her a short nod as he moseyed closer to the fire. Even though she was anxious to see what he might do, Rosemary would relay any vital information to her later. A sense of foreboding settled on her shoulders, reminding her of how she felt before Adelaide and friend attacked her. She stood for a minute trying to open her senses to whatever it might be. A threat, a definite one, growing even stronger as she stood there.

Hadn't they just spent the day leaving behind those who disliked the travelers? Maybe the threat was the mutton still cooking in the pot. Part of her wanted to go back and check to see if Olio was successful in his endeavor, but the other part knew she had to see why Grandmother Biddy summoned her. What she needed to be able to do was split herself into two. Until she could, she'd run. Her feet flew across the ground until the distinctive wagon came into view.

The youngster she'd seen before came around the wagon leading a black dog that moved slowly, but still had enough energy to wag its tail. Grandmother Biddy leaned out the open wagon door.

"Come inside."

She ducked back into the wagon leaving Meara with no choice, but to follow. As she placed her foot on the first wooden step, she swiveled her head to see if anyone was watching. Her invitation to visit would serve as more evidence of favoritism. There was some movement near a tree, but whoever it was vanished before she could get a clear look.

It was probably no more than someone walking through the camp. To think she was being followed was sheer lunacy, but a mention that some resented the time she spent with Grandmother Biddy and Jane heightened her paranoia. Another possibility was if someone had been there, he could be watching the camp, speculating on when they would all die from tainted meat. She ducked to enter the narrow, arched doorway.

The white-haired matriarch glanced up from shuffling her cards. "Close the door behind you. I've already closed the shutters. Have a seat. Things are moving faster than the cards foretold."

Meara sat on the low stool next to the table. Even though all Grandmother Biddy did was shuffle, a sense of urgency filled the small space.

"How could the cards be wrong?"

"They're not necessarily wrong, but things change, which changes the time table." She placed the cards on the table for cutting, which Meara did. "Think of the immediate future. The now. I'm only going to do one card because there is so much I need to relate before you go and I go."

Meara's lips twisted as she tried to figure out the cryptic statement. While she knew she'd be leaving eventually, the ugly mood of the women made the possibility that much closer. True, she hadn't contributed anything to the group, except for the necklace she gave Red Monesha, though the gift probably wasn't common knowledge. Even in a tiny community such as theirs, there were still bound to be those who'd steal or use the knowledge of the necklace for their own benefit.

The shuttered windows made the interior close and heavy with the scented candle smoke. Jane had mentioned that the magical candles were made with rue that magnified whatever was done within its realm. Grandmother Biddy would use no other candles. Her hand hovered over a card in the spread. Turning it over would relate knowledge, possibly motivating her to an impulsive action.

She inhaled deeply, closed her eyes, and allowed her hand to drop to a card. When it dropped, it almost felt cemented there. For a second, she considered moving her fingers a little to the right, but her hand would not move, as if an invisible force was pinning it down. Maybe fate, or possibly her father, but why would he want to hold her hand down.

"Open your eyes and turn the card. Delaying will not change the image on the card."

It would do her no good to argue about how readings could change with the slightest alteration to the timeline. That could happen, but a certainty overwhelmed her that this was not the case today. She opened her eyes, and the candle flame grew a little higher, then guttered, then resumed its steady flames as before. The card she turned was an eight of wands.

"I expected as much." Grandmother Biddy tapped a yellowed nail against the picture of eight wands hurtling through the air.

"What does it mean?" The cards with people on it were much easier to understand. She couldn't remember if the wands were good or bad.

"There is no good or bad. There only is what is. Remember, soon I won't be here to tell you these things."

"You're leaving the travelers?"

"Not the travelers, but this plane. I waited for you to arrive, but once you leave, my time will be over. Before I leave there are things I need to bequeath to you, but first let's talk about your card. The eight of wands signifies travel, urgency, speed, and change."

"I expected to leave, but not you."

"It's my time, but I'll do you the courtesy of allowing you to be gone for a few weeks before transitioning to the next level. I do not want you to be blamed for my death."

"Why? Why would that happen? Why would I be blamed for your death?" Anyone who saw Grandmother Biddy would know the woman had lived past her time. She had to use a cane or a helpful arm to get around, and most of the day she stayed in her wagon, possibly reading cards or sleeping.

The woman managed a weary smile. "Some people," she shook her head before continuing, "need to blame someone even though a situation is a natural consequence."

Meara closed her eyes for a second, remembering some of the things she'd gone through. "I've met some people like that."

"Then nothing that is going to happen should surprise you."

A heavy pounding vibrated the wagon, chilling Meara. This was it. What she knew was coming, but hoped to avoid, had arrived.

Chapter Twelve

G RANDMOTHER BIDDY WAS the first to respond. "Olio, enough! I need my wagon to last a little longer. Open the door."

The door swung out. Olio inserted his head and upper torso, filling up the entire doorway. "Things are getting ugly."

An uneasiness slipped over Meara as she speculated on what could have happened in her absence. "I told them the food was tainted. How could they be mad about that?"

"It's not what they are saying. Word has gone around the camp that Rosemary poisoned the stew to kill as many traveler children as possible."

She slapped her hands on both sides of her face in horror. "Why would they say such a thing?"

Grandmother Biddy cleared her throat. "There are a few who resent our rushed trip to the seashore." She held up one finger. "Rosemary's accuser has a fondness for Hayden. Her father refused to allow the union and instead married her off to a more practical, but less well-favored man."

Jealousy could cause people to react in crazy ways. "Where's Rosemary?"

The last thing she wanted was her friend to come to harm. Guilt needled her. If only she had been paying more attention these last few days to what Rosemary was doing, maybe she could have been more aware. Still, the dangers of Hayden she'd only discovered today. If she had instincts, they hadn't done her that much good.

Olio answered in an even voice. "After I pushed over the stew spot, ruining the supper and setting everyone in an uproar, I managed to convey her to Jane's wagon. I came for you. We need to leave immediately."

On that she agreed. "I'm ready." She half-stood, but stopped when Grandmother Biddy's bony hand clutched hers.

"You're not ready, yet." She fixed her with a fierce gaze that had her dropping back to her stool. "Olio, come in, I need you to carry something to Jane's wagon.

The floor dipped and rocked back as the big man maneuvered his way around the cramped area and picked up a battered, padlocked case Grandmother pointed to. He pulled the case behind him and when he got to the door, he gave a backward look.

Grandmother Biddy gestured in a shooing fashion. "Be gone. I'll make sure she gets where she needs to be. Don't speak to anyone, not that you would, but even if they ask you a question, keep walking."

Once the door closed, the tiny woman reached for Meara's other hand as she spoke. "There's much I need to tell you. Normally, people undertake spiritual quests, and they find the needed information as it comes, but you don't have that kind of time. The fact someone would stoop to poisoning sheep, knowing good and well the entire camp could die, proves to me how much evil has spread. Years before you and I were born, the Goddess Danu, saddened by how the humans treated the faeries, vowed to leave them to their own devices."

"Did she?" Meara pressed her lips together, certain that faeries had helped her.

"She did for a while, but the faeries are able to forgive a lot. Even though they hid in all sorts of places, usually in liminal spaces where the land meets the water or the earth meets air. The faeries often sought out those who respected the land and all its inhabitants."

"I know my father interacted with the faeries. Perhaps my mother did, too, but how does this involve me?"

"Yes, they were the favored ones. Last night, when I slumbered, the entire story unfolded. Your parents did fall in love. They were intended for one another, but they were gifted with a horn by the faeries."

"A horn? The kind you blow?"

"Yes, but it was made in three pieces to be assembled and blown when faery help was needed. It was given to the three important clans in Ireland, Scotland, and England."

"Were the Clearys one of them?" Her uncle hadn't hinted at their family being important, but obviously they were.

"Neither your mother's family nor father's family was one of them, but as time moved on, people forgot about the faery horn, which made it easy for the faeries to steal them back. Not only did your parents share a deep love for one another, but they also honored the Fair Folk. They must have seen no hint of malice in your parents, because they delivered the horn to them in its three separate parts."

"If the three parts were put together, the horn blown, and the faeries were called, would the war end?"

If all it took was finding three bits and screwing them together, surely she could do that.

"I wonder. The impression I get is you must do it. It must be done. This is your mission. Faeries want to help, but humans must do their part, since faeries can't exist in the same place as evil."

A thrill of excitement unfurled, awakening her other senses. Her ears picked up the sounds of movement and voices outside. Her nostrils wrinkled as she absorbed the smell of heated candle wax and the various spicy herbs hanging inside the wagon. This is what she wanted, although she preferred a map to a mission. If she knew where to go and what to do, she could do it. "I've been waiting for this. Where is the first piece?"

"That I do not know, but only you can do this."

It sounded as if she was back to stumbling around the countryside, slipping away whenever danger presented itself on the horizon. "Why me?"

"Your parents had the horn, but made the crucial decision to disassemble it and bury the pieces in three different countries. While I did receive a dream I'm not sure if it came from your parents or the Goddess Danu."

"Where do you think the pieces are?"

Grandmother managed a lengthy sigh. "Logically, I would say your mother's old home, your father's home, or where they lived last. As for Scotland, that's a puzzler. They had to have visited to bury it, and they'd want to put it someplace safe. Your parents know, and I expect will guide you. That's why it can only be you."

"I was afraid you would say that."

"What is it they say in England? You need to maintain a stiff upper lip?"

She blinked. "I'll try, along with a dry eye."

Grandmother Biddy tightened her grip, causing the ornate rings to bite into Meara's skin. "You'll need a look away spell. By this time, those who want to be riled up will be. Do nothing to attract attention to yourself. Move outside of the circle to Jane's wagon, which should be pulled out of the circle by now. Are you ready?"

"I guess I am." Did she mean was she ready for the spell or to leave? It didn't feel like she had a choice in either, and it certainly didn't depend on if she wanted to.

"Look away now, there's nothing here. Attend to your business and let me pass."

Grandmother Biddy stayed in position with her head bowed and her eyes closed. It made Meara wonder if she were meditating. Finally, the woman opened her eyes and looked exhausted. She dropped her grip and slumped back into the chair.

"Go now. Remember the words because there'll be many times you'll need to move about unseen."

"I will." She reached out for the matriarch's veined hand. "I'll never forget you."

"I expect as much since I'm unforgettable."

The comment sounded much like the woman she first met, not this shell of a person. She pulled back her hand as she stood. "Thank you for everything."

Meara pivoted in the direction of the door, knowing it would be the last time she saw the opinionated woman.

"Wait."

Grandmother Biddy pushed to her feet. She wrapped her cards in a silk scarf and shoved them at her. "Take them. When I'm dead, plenty of the vultures will come and pick my wagon clean. Olio took most of the good stuff, but I refuse to allow my cards to go to some opportunist who mistakenly believes she could tell better fortunes with my cards."

The silk wrapped cards disappeared into Meara's skirt pocket. She gave a final tender look to the woman who taught her so much about magic and herself. She placed her hand on the door latch when Grandmother Biddy spoke again.

"You must watch your step because you're not the only one who is looking for the horn. Those without a pure heart hope to twist the faeries to their bidding, which we can never allow to happen."

"Can that be done?"

"I'm not sure, but it could be the reason the Goddess Danu chose to hide away her children. Many blessings. You will succeed. I saw it in the cards."

The parting sentiment was meant to reassure, but it didn't. Instead, Meara couldn't help but dwell on the past as she slipped out of the wagon. The time tables had changed. Couldn't her success in such a venture change, too?

Chapter Thirteen

OLIO STOOD IN the woods as silent and stalwart as the trees around him. If Meara hadn't been looking for him, her eyes might have gone right over him. As she approached, he took no notice of her, making her doubt his guarding ability. Had he perfected the skill to sleep with his eyes open?

Jane's wagon stood off in the shadows with an anxious Rosemary lingering beside it. Meara held up a hand in greeting being careful not to call out. No response. Everyone was acting as if they couldn't see her. Ah, the spell did work.

Since Olio was the closest, she reached out and attempted to pinch his muscular arm. causing him to jerk his arm back and swat the air. It was harder than she thought since he had no loose skin to grab ahold. Finally she succeeded in scratching him. The man acted as if she were a bee and swated again.

"Olio, it's me, Meara."

"Where are you?" He swiveled his head in both directions and even turned around to look behind him. "I can hear you."

"I'm in front of you. Grandmother Biddy did a look away spell on me."

He waved his hands in front of him until one touched her shoulder. "There you are. Better to go now while the spell is in force."

He headed toward the wagon, gesturing for her to follow.

Rosemary questioned him as he approached. "Have you seen any sign of Meara?"

"She's behind me."

"I don't see anyone. Have your wits left you? Those crazy women who accused me of poisoning their food may have grabbed her."

Rosemary's lips trembled, and a tear puddled in her right eye. "I was supposed to take care of her."

Meara gave Rosemary a slight shove. "Stop it. You'll have me dead and buried. I have a few years ahead of me if we can get out of camp safely. No one should begrudge us slipping away, considering they don't want us here, but who knows how they'll act, they're all so crazy."

"You're alive." Her friend lunged in various directions until she contacted Meara.

Meara returned the hug as Jane came around the wagon.

"I have Seymour in his traces. All we have to do now is wait for Meara." She did a double take at Rosemary, then commented, maybe more to herself than anyone else, "I see the famous look away spell is in place. We better go since it usually never lasts more than an hour. Rosemary and Meara, get inside the wagon. My goal is to slip away without anyone noticing. Not too many would remark on me moving my wagon. I can always claim that I need to be closer to my parents. In the end, it is time for me to move on. My parents expect as much."

Meara broke out of Rosemary's embrace when she realized the protective lengths Jane was willing to go through just for them to leave the camp. "You don't have to do this. Point us in the right direction, and we'll walk away. It should be easy enough to vanish with the night coming on."

"Get in the wagon. We'll talk after we get away." Jane gestured to the door that Rosemary had just opened.

Olio gestured to the front of the wagon and suggested, "I'll walk with Seymour and hold his halter. My night vision might be a bit better than his."

Meara entered the wagon and missed Jane's reply. It would probably be something about the senior horse not wanting to go anywhere, be it day or night. The sudden jerking motion had her reaching for something to stop her fall. One hand hit the rough texture of the wall while she braced her feet to deal with the rocking motion. The darkness made it hard to see anything, but she knew her friend had to be in here with her.

"Rosemary, where are you?"

"I'm sitting as you should be. Just lower yourself, and you're bound to find something to sit on. If you make the mistake of sitting on me, I'll let you know. Should have gotten in while there was some light from the outside."

With legs still braced against the motion, she squatted and patted the nearby area for a possible seat. Her finger encountered hair, causing her to draw it back.

"Hey. That's me."

"I figured as much." Before she could try again, a jolt off balanced her and sent her to the wood floor. "Oof."

"Are you hurt?"

"No." She pushed up into a sitting position. "At least, I found someplace to sit."

"Good. I'm not even sure what happened out there. I spent a lovely day playing nursemaid to an adorable baby. She was just about perfect, almost never cried." A sigh sounded.

"You have the touch when it comes to babies and children. It probably didn't hurt that Hayden kept you company the entire ride."

A throaty laugh filled the interior. "Didn't hurt one bit. He's such a charming man. If all Irish men are like him, this trip will be like a preview of Heaven."

"Don't get too excited about your potential celestial home. I suspect it is not filled with handsome men wanting to flirt with you."

"Well then, I'll have to enjoy my stay in Ireland. I can't understand why you tried to warn me off him."

"It could have something to do with every father refusing to accept Hayden as a potential son-in-law."

"Oh, that!"

Even though she couldn't see her face, Meara could well imagine her friend casually gesturing with her hand at the ridiculousness of a father not approving Hayden. If it were one father, or even two, but when the whole camp disapproves of the man's husband potential, that says something. Apparently, Rosemary would not be dissuaded.

"Never mind, it's neither here nor there. With any luck, we won't be seeing any of the travelers anytime soon."

"You're right." Another sigh sounded. "I just don't know what happened. One minute everyone wanted me to help them with their children, and the next I'm being hit with a wet ladle."

Worry grabbed Meara by the throat and squeezed. As far as poison went she knew very little. The extent of her knowledge was that you want to avoid it. It might be able to enter through the skin. "Did you get any of the stew on you?"

"I'm not sure. Maybe some splashed on my dress. Olio knocking over the tripod that supported the kettle, being attacked by a ladle-wielding crazy person, and the baby crying confused things for me. It's not that I've never been in a girl fight. I have, but it has been quite a long time ago."

"I'd never imagine you as a fighter."

"That makes two of us. Back when I was younger, I tended to fly off the handle. Took everything as a personal insult. I may have pulled a pigtail or two. I watched my boy cousins fight and discovered the benefit of knocking your opponent off his feet. My cousin, Harold, even taught it to me. I know the woman was already mad, but once I knocked her on her backside she was cursing me good. Olio ferried me away, which is just as well since I only had one good move. Still…" Her voice trailed off.

Meara waited in the dark, not sure if her friend had finished speaking. It never occurred to her how difficult conversations were without light to view the speaker. "Maybe we can find a lantern and some matches. At least, I could see you."

They could hear some yelling outside. It was far enough away they couldn't make out the words. A big jostle had her tilting, but she corrected by holding herself up with one hand. "What now?"

A tapping came from the front of the wagon, from the area where Jane would be sitting holding the reins.

Rosemary whispered, "That's our sign to be quiet."

The jingle of the horse harness and the thump of the wheel penetrated the wooden walls. Even though Meara strained her ears to catch a hint of the yelling she'd heard before, other than the travel noises, she heard only the evening chorus of bugs punctuated by a solo of a night bird.

Were they being followed? They might have been initially, but it was hard to tell. The darkness grew even blacker, which she normally would have assumed was impossible. It pressed down on her and had a physical presence. Her fingers went up to clutch the necklaces. Grandmother Biddy had taught her an incantation to keep evil at bay, but she couldn't remember it.

The bounciness of the wagon along with the rapid hoofbeats meant increased speed. Most people didn't travel at night. Did Rosemary know any more than she did? Even though she'd been warned not to talk, Meara suspected whatever she might say wouldn't be heard over the rattle of the vehicle or Seymour, the horse.

"Olio guided you back. Did he say anything?"

"Something cryptic about he had been expecting this."

Meara made sure to keep her voice low so she couldn't be heard outside. "I know the travelers regard him as something of a seer. Makes me wonder what he does see. Grandmother Biddy warned us to be long gone before she passed."

"She predicted her own death?"

Rosemary must have leaned forward since she sounded louder, then again in her surprise she might have forgotten to lower her voice.

"Hush. Don't speak of it. Not sure if I was supposed to tell anyone. She told me it was important to leave now. Some of the jealousy toward you came from the woman or women who were denied Hayden as a husband. Even though he had a reputation as a flirt, most still yearned after the man."

"I can believe that. Still, it wasn't all me or even Hayden for that matter. Some resented you, too. That much I heard."

"True. There are those who resented their sudden departure from a money-making area. Apparently, there are less and less places friendly to the travelers. Suddenly, they had to leave to meet us. I'm sure we weren't an impressive sight, staggering out of the sea."

A snort greeted her statement.

Meara continued as she tried to unravel the dynamics of the group, if only to herself. "Red Monesha or Monesha, I'm not sure which name she prefers, is the leader. For the most part, I saw her doing very little leading. The fact that people publicly announced their disagreement against the decision to go to the seashore shows no one fears her, while the group honors and respects Grandmother Biddy. With her gone, I imagine it will be harder to hold them together."

"I can't get over Grandmother Biddy telling you when she was going to die."

"It's peculiar, I agree. It's not that she is going to die in a couple of days. It's more that she has been dying and forced herself to hold on until we arrived." An oppressive weight settled around her shoulders almost as if someone was pressing down on her.

"I understand. She's a strong woman who could do anything she set her mind to. Did she tell you why some of the people had decided to give you the cold shoulder? How did you fall out of favor? On that first night, people were looking at you as if you were an angel that descended to earth to walk around the mortals."

Remembering the looks of expectation and her fear of not meeting them caused a remembered thrill of apprehension that almost rid her of the feeling of hands on her shoulders. "Rosemary, you don't have your hands on me?"

"No, why would you ask me such a silly thing?"

She exhaled slowly not wanting to frighten her friend. A presence had somehow entered the wagon. Still, Jane would know how to protect her private property and would have set up some barrier or charm. Grandmother Biddy would have shown her what to do. Perhaps she was imagining the presence. Not too surprising with everything they'd been through. When panic threatened to overtake her, she regained some control by breathing through her nose and counting her breaths.

Despite it already being dark, she squeezed her eyes shut and concentrated on her breathing. A high-pitched keening penetrated the walls, stealing any peace she'd managed to obtain through her measured breathing.

"What is that?" Rosemary cried.

Meara wanted to reassure her friend that it was only a train, but so far, they hadn't seen even a railroad track. The keening grew closer and louder.

Jane's voice urged on the horse, but there was no difference in speed. "Come on, Seymour. You can do this."

Meara sat ramrod straight, gritted her teeth as she strained her ears, trying to separate Jane's directives from the continuous howling. If it was the wind, it was like no wind she'd heard before.

"Get on down there, Olio. Be a man. If you take the halter and run, Seymour will be forced to run along with you."

"The beansidhe is howling, and the area is teeming with sluagh waiting to steal my soul."

Meara crawled closer to the front of the wagon where Jane and Olio were seated to hear better. Rosemary mistook her movement as an attempt to get close and grabbed at her. After frantically patting Meara's arm, her friend wove her fingers with hers as she spoke. "This is rather frightening. More so than the sea or the bird attack."

Even though her ears were waiting for the next bit of conversation from outside the wagon to determine what they might do next, she felt obliged to reply to the statement if only to confirm she was listening.

"Why is this more frightening?"

"Those others were unexpected. I remember even being happy, and it was daylight, too. Even when we were fleeing Hogstead at night, I thought of it as a grand adventure."

Before she could answer, Jane's upraised voice was heard. "For the love of God, get down there and run that horse, or we will never get out of this accursed area. Hold onto the horse's trace if you're afraid of being stolen away. Don't look at any of the lights, either. Go straight."

The wagon dipped and sprung back up on one side proving Olio had finally chosen to lead the horse. The vehicle sped up, but it could never be referred to as running. At best, Seymour had broken into a trot.

The tight squeeze of Rosemary's fingers on hers gave away her state of mind. Of course, she was scared. Who wouldn't be after practically being chased out of camp? If she were guided to Ireland for a purpose, and she believed she was, then shouldn't she survive the adventure? It made sense to her.

Seymour's bone jarring trot forced her to place her feet against one wall. If Rosemary did the same, and they sat back to back they'd have some stability as opposed to being thrown about as if leaves in the wind. It only took a few seconds to explain what she needed. Sitting back to back made it easier to converse as well.

"Back in Hogstead, my mum talked about The Green Man, brownies and lobs, but never a beansidhe?"

The Green Man she'd heard about was a presence in the forest, sometimes considered lord of the woods. Brownies she'd heard were helpful beings that often helped with housework. She said, "I've never heard of a lob?"

"I only have because I have relatives in Wales. It shows up like a dark storm cloud with arms. It's mischievous, always wanting to stir up trouble. That may be why people sometimes refer to troubled times as having a dark cloud over your head."

"He sounds dreadful. How can we avoid him?"

"He's attracted to arguing, so if we avoid that, we're good. He only comes out at night, too.

"It is night."

"I noticed that. Do you know what a beansidhe is?"

Meara leaned against her friend as she considered the word. "The fact that they wail doesn't sound like a pleasant entity to have around."

"My thoughts, too. When we stop, we can ask."

It felt as if they'd been traveling forever, but at best it was only a couple of hours. Instead of fighting against the movement, Rosemary and she were swaying with it. It certainly was a lot easier than struggling.

She blinked against the dark, thinking eventually she should be able to see something. Often when you walked into the room without a light, everything might appear black, but after a bit shape took on shades of gray. Nothing was taking shape, which might be just as well because she wasn't a real major fan of seeing what was pushing on her. A simple shoulder wiggle helped her evaluate if anything still was. Nothing.

"What are you doing?"

"Just checking. No broken bones from the rough ride." She wondered how long she'd mislead her friend. Maybe people always did this, never said what they really meant or were thinking. Instead, they came up with a nice safe lie. Something they believed people would accept and be comfortable with.

Even the possibility that the sisters had lied to her most of her life should horrify her. Was it a lie if they had been lied to? Most of the time they were only repeating what they were told. Oddly, she didn't harbor a lot of anger toward them. They were dead after all. It wasn't like it would do her any good to resent them. They were like her in many ways, just victims of circumstances that led them to the convent.

She moved her shoulders a little more, twisting one way, then another. Still nothing. Had she imagined it? Maybe she was making mountains out of mole hills. Had it been her intuition? If it was, why couldn't it answer in full sentences as opposed to leaning on her?

Rosemary interrupted her analyzation.

"Did you hear that?"

She couldn't hear anything. No wailing. No voices outside. Not even the evening chorus was making a peep. Her hands went up to her ears and rubbed them. Had she lost her ability to hear? Had she grown used to the keening noise? If she couldn't hear, then she shouldn't be able to hear her friend, either.

"I don't hear anything."

"I know. The screaming stopped, which I hope is a good thing." She relaxed a little against Meara's back. "It's been a day and a half."

"True enough." The day that had started with a Tarot lesson, soon turned into an escape from townspeople who may or may not have wanted them gone from the beach. Then it was on to a fall into the creek, to the fall from the wagon lip. She'd managed to finish off the day with a prophetic vision Jane had warned her no one wanted to hear. People didn't want to think their children were in danger, even if they were.

A stomach rumbled. It was hard to say whose it was since she felt close to starving, but Rosemary claimed it.

"I missed supper. I imagine you did, too."

"We all did. Not even sure those back at camp have cobbled together an evening meal. Even when I tried to explain the food could be poisoned, it was like they didn't want to accept it. They'd already put all the good vegetables into the pot. I'm not even sure they wouldn't have served the stew if Olio hadn't knocked it over. If the children had died, they would have blamed me. Called me some monster into child sacrifices."

"Ah, don't worry about that too much. They probably already do."

Despite the darkness, Meara twisted abruptly to see her friend's face, which resulted in the leaning Rosemary falling on her back.

"Oof."

She stayed silent, making Meara fear she'd hurt her friend. Her nails bit into her clenched fists. "Are you hurt?"

Rosemary managed a slight chuckle and pushed into a sitting position. "No. If you're going to move like that, I'd appreciate a warning. What was that about anyhow?"

"I must have over-reacted. The idea that people were badmouthing me when I was trying to save them startled me." She took a deep breath.

"Truth?"

"I'd like that."

"It made me mad." The realization surprised her since she spent most of her life suppressing any emotion. Anymore she was a bubbling pot of emotions. Anger, considered to be the devil's tool, she'd worked the hardest to control, but had failed obviously.

Rosemary's tinkling laugh sounded again. "Who wouldn't be mad? Sometimes, you must accept that people don't always appreciate the good you do for them, but you must keep believing. Keep going."

It didn't seem worthwhile. Why labor all your life for those who gave no recognition of work done or even belittled it. A masculine voice, she knew to be her father's sounded in her head.

It's the right thing to do.

Right thing to do. Was that enough to get her going? Blundering across the Irish countryside with all sorts of creatures trailing? A few weren't human, she suspected. Another voice sounded, a low feminine voice full of warmth and love.

The right thing is never easy. Still, it is for the good of mankind, even if humanity is deep in strife and hatred and fails to prevent the sacrifices you make.

Meara sat stunned for a moment, not reflecting on the words, but the voice. Could it be? "Mother?"

"No, it's me, Rosemary. I thought you didn't have a mother. Thought she died."

Her first impulse was to hush her friend so she'd be able to hear her mother's voice. The sweet, gentle tone with love shimmering through it. In her mind, she called for her mother, searched for the sound of her voice. Nothing.

What had she even said? The thrill of hearing her mother's actual voice caused the short hairs on her neck to come to attention. All she could remember was something about doing the right thing was never easy. That she could accept, but she was still battling with knowing what the right thing was.

Just as the wailing dissipated not so long ago, the rocking motion did, too. They must have stopped. She could feel the dip as someone stepped down from the driver's bench. She hoped that someone happened to be Jane, but so far nothing was ever what she suspected it to be.

Chapter Fourteen

THE WAGON DOOR swung open and someone stood there. That Meara knew. She placed her hand on Rosemary, stilling any action she might make to rush to the door. It would be natural to assume that Jane and Olio still drove the wagon, but it had been quite a while since she'd heard their voices. It would be easy enough to have taken their place, leaving them trapped like birds in a cage. They'd already be in a handy package ready to deliver to whoever thought she knew where these magical horn pieces were.

"Meara? Rosemary?"

Jane's familiar voice relieved some of her fears. Light spilled over her rescuer as Olio strolled up with a lantern. He inserted the lantern into the wagon, illuminating the interior. There were clothes on the floor, along with cooking pots and a thick quilt.

Meara stared at the quilt that looked heavy. Could that had fallen on her? Was that the heaviness she felt? It made sense, but her intuition didn't accept her logical conclusion. It knew what it knew.

Olio gave a head nod in her direction and held up his index finger to his eye, which she interpreted as he could see her.

Why shouldn't he be able to see her? He'd thrust the bright lantern inside, which caused her eyes to burn after being in the dark so long.

Jane gestured to them to come out. "The look away spell has worn off. As it should, since we've been on the road for a while. Come out. We can have a cold supper and set up camp for the night."

Anything involving food sounded good. Anxious to get out of the cage as she now considered the wagon, she stood, bumpind her head on a framing beam. Not hard enough to knock her out, but enough to remind her of the usefulness of moving slowly in the cramped quarters. Her hand went to her head and rubbed the sore spot. No bump yet, but one might come. She waved away inquiries about her health, too embarrassed to answer them.

The cool air brushed away the last tendrils of fear that had wrapped around her. The smell of desperation and hopelessness might leave with the gentle breeze. The stars sparkled overhead in a cloudless sky while a half moon presided over them all. An owl hooted from a nearby copse of trees.

Everything appeared so normal, so peaceful. Olio retrieved another lantern from inside, lit it, and handed it to Jane. Rosemary and she followed Jane to the front of the wagon. Seymour was out of his traces and grazed nearby. The three of them stretched and chattered about inane matters until Olio returned with a water skin and a basket.

They all sat in a tight circle and the water skin made the rounds. Rosemary and Meara drank greedily, until Jane warned, "Not too much. I'm not sure how far we are from fresh water. Since there is only us, we could probably water at a village."

This was quite a change from travelers avoiding villages. "How so? I thought I understood that many people were uneasy when travelers were nearby. Afraid they might steal the children and the chickens."

"Many still feel that way." Jane took a sip from the skin and wiped her mouth with her wrist. "Still, we won't be showing up as travelers. None of you are, except for myself. I've thought about this. Got it planned. You have a big part to play, Meara."

"Should I ask?"

Olio pulled a loaf of bread out of the basket, broke off a small bit, then handed it to Rosemary. When it came to Meara, she took only a tiny piece, unaware of how long the bread should last. The next item to come around were potatoes. She took one still a little dirty from being dug out of the ground. What was she supposed to do with it?

Jane took a bite out of her potato and chewed before speaking. "You and Olio will be newlyweds traveling through the countryside to visit your family. At least half of it is true. My da always told me always add a bit of truth to a lie to make it work."

Rosemary rubbed the potato against her tunic, cleaning off the dirt. Meara followed her example, before biting into her spud. The inside was crisp and wet, but tasted mildly like dirt. She forced herself to finish it. They couldn't afford to waste food. This may be all they have. After a few minutes of wishing for salt, she pondered their lack of fire.

"Do you think the travelers are following us?"

Olio answered before Jane could. "They won't cross the cursed land."

The one thing she had learned from her short association with Olio is whatever he said would be true. Apparently, his lack of parents meant he'd never learn the art of embellishing any story.

"What do you mean cursed land?" She had an inkling it was pretty much as the name indicated.

Jane used her thumb to indicate the dark area behind them. "The land we crossed is claimed to be haunted."

Olio coughed on the word *claimed*.

"Once," Jane continued, "there was a battle, a feud of sorts. No one knows exactly what it was about, but some figure a woman was involved. Others suspect it was about gold or power. In the end, one group waited for the other family burdened down with their goods and their family members, both women and children. The evil ones swept out and attacked. There was a valiant fight with the men of the family trying to save their own. It is said they took many of the evildoers' lives. They died unsanctified with sin on their souls. They are the sluagh, the sinners, who wander, hoping to steal other souls."

The idea made her shiver. "Weren't you afraid to travel across such a place?"

A metallic jingle sounded as Jane pulled up a clump of talismans and pendants from underneath her shirt. "I put on every protective amulet I had, and Olio did the same. I had hoped that the wagon with all its magical elements would protect the both of you. We made it over the cursed land. When I decided to take a short cut across the area, I believed it was nothing more than the travelers were a superstitious lot, fearing the place when there was nothing to be afeared of. I've changed my mind now."

"Did the screaming come from the soul stealers?" There was a question of why they'd want to steal her soul. Hadn't they one of their own?

"No." Jane shook her head and took the last bite of potato and chewed in silence. "That was beansidhe. Sometimes, in England and other countries, they pronounce it banshee."

She must have noticed the blank look on Meara's face, because Jane went on to explain. "A beansidhe or a banshee is the sound of a woman wailing. You usually hear it on the outside of your own home when someone you know is going to die. I heard it before when my grandmother died."

A chill pebbled her arms as she considered the wailing woman spirit. "You think one of us was meant to die?"

"That's what I thought. It could have been someone in the camp. I could have misunderstood. It had to be someone I knew or the beansidhe wouldn't have followed."

Olio steepled his fingers together and looked thoughtful in the lantern light. "Ghosts, maybe, of the women crying for their men killed in battle, for their children."

"It's possible," Jane agreed.

Rosemary, who had only listened until now, joined the conversation. "Is that why we didn't build a fire? We didn't want to attract the spirits?"

Jane smiled. "That might be a wise action, too. We're trying to be hard to track by anyone. A dead fire is the same as waving a flag or shouting, 'We're over here.'"

The uneasiness that had followed Meara slowly broke up and drifted away on the night breeze. A battle that had happened years ago had nothing to do with her. "Why do people worry about crossing the land? There probably have been battles all over the place."

Jane held up her index finger for attention. "The attackers were said to be possessed by a dark evil that turned good men into ruthless killers. Not quite mortal men and more substantial than ghosts, people fear the evil, afraid it is still out there, waiting to attach to someone."

No reason to tell them that it was still out there waiting. The thought made her want to leave the area. Even though they may be out of the haunted area, it wasn't far enough.

"Are we going any farther tonight?"

"Not unless we pull the wagon ourselves and Olio carries Seymour on his back."

The man snorted his opinion of doing so.

"I see. So, what are we going to do?"

"Sleep. We can post a guard or do it in pairs. When you do duty as pairs, one can wake the other up if she falls asleep. The down side is longer hours since doing everything together means less people to go around."

Meara held her hand up. "I volunteer because I know I won't be falling asleep."

"I'll do the first duty with you."

"How will you know what time it is?" The convent had a sundial they used to tell time. The ringing of the bells was based on this. When it was cloudy, they depended on the bell ringer's stomach to determine the right hour. This was effective, at least three times a day.

"You have a sense of it. Living outside among the trees and nature, I've learned the patterns. Even the night birds stopped calling by four in the morning. Could be they've given up hope of being answered. All I know is it is very still at that time of night. When it seems like you're the only person in the world or that everyone else is sleeping, it's a magical time."

Rosemary grinned around a mouthful of potato and tried to speak. "Tout da midnight."

"Midnight is a liminal period, which makes it important to the fae-ries, who are often about then. Midnight is also important to those who practice lunar magic."

"I'm guessing that has something to do with the moon."

Jane arched her eyebrows, visible even in the dim moonlight. "You guessed right. It is based on the cycles of the moon. When the moon grows large, that's when you work on things you need or want. When it grows lean, your spells should be on those things you want to eliminate in your life."

"Evil?" Wouldn't that be grand if she could speak a few words under a full moon, clap her hands, and all of this would be over. People would go back to being kind to one another and beaches would no longer have barbed wire on them to slow down would be spies and invading soldiers.

"Something smaller, more personal. Maybe you want to eliminate self-doubt or even not having enough money to pay for the ordinary things you need."

"I can see that being useful," Rosemary concluded and yawned.

Jane gestured to the wagon. "You're welcome to sleep inside. It looks like Olio has already bedded down underneath the wagon."

The man had slipped away without her even noticing. A long dark form could be spotted through the wheel spokes, the rest fading into shadow. Rosemary brushed off her hands on her skirt as she sprang to her feet.

"I'm not sure about you two, but I'm knackered. Could fall asleep standing up. It's the wagon for me tonight." She reached for a lantern, leaving one behind as she circled around to the wagon steps.

The night closed around her a little more tightly as Rosemary re-treated into the dark, becoming a tiny orb of light rather like a spirit or a star. It made it easy to understand why people preferred a fire at night to keep away four-legged predators, but also anything else that might be lurking in the dark.

The insects continued their nightly chorus. Back in the convent, she had longed for a night such as this. Not that she wanted to flee travelers or play hide and seek with the sluagh. No, she wanted the freedom to be under a star-filled sky, listening to nature, possibly be in tune with it.

Now, that she was, it was a bit overwhelming. The trees sprouted up in different spots as silent sentinels, and whatever creatures lived out here knew they were there.

"Do you think there are any wolves or the like watching us?"

"There might be a hare or a deer. No wolves. It's no wild west like America with all sorts of beasties roaming all over the place. Most of the beasties here end up in the stew pot. They know this and make a point of avoiding people. Occasionally, we might attract a feral cat or dog. They're only hanging around for the scraps."

"Not too much to worry about then?"

"Not from the animal kingdom. People are the real problem, those who think travelers are dirty bandits."

"How are we going to fool these people?"

"Well, now." She crinkled her nose as her lips tipped up. "You have to sound less British. If there is someone an Irish villager likes less than a traveler, it has to be a Brit."

Meara splayed her hand against her chest. "I say that's not sporting of them. They don't even know me."

"Talk like that will do you in. It doesn't matter if they know you. They do know your people. The Brits took over their country and made up rules about what the Irish could do. About hundred years ago, the Brits took away the right to govern ourselves. The Irish have very long memories. A hundred years might as well be yesterday. It might be best if you don't talk. Just look up at Olio adoringly."

"We have to depend on the man who hardly speaks more than a dozen words to do the talking."

Jane shrugged. "He hardly talks to us. I'm not sure how he is in the towns. We always send him on ahead since no one would connect him with us. He even has a set of clothes that are less..." She paused, allowing Meara to finish the sentence.

"Less colorful."

"That works. I was thinking flamboyant. Joyful. Clothes that enjoy being. I'm not saying your typical Irish person is afraid of color, but they like it to be all the same. Not so much mixing of colors. That's why we have to paint the wagon tomorrow."

There was travel, evading people who wanted to impede their traveling, along with unearthing some hidden faery whistle pieces, but she'd never considered painting in the mix. "Why?"

"I just told you. Too much color. Too much design. The plainer the better. It's not the first time my grandmother's wagon has been disguised. She wasn't one to inscribe various symbols and designs on her wagon, believing being a good person should be enough to keep a person safe not all these various symbols. My mother also thought it had a bit to do with she wasn't a good artist, either. The few designs that are on the wagon, I did."

"Here I thought they were just to be fancy."

"They are that. Never pass up an opportunity to pad your luck. With that in mind, we'll cover up the remaining symbols with the paint I saved from last time. It should be enough."

Her lips pursed as she considered a wagon with splotches of new paint on it. "Won't it seem obvious that we covered stuff up?"

"The paint is the same color. Besides, as newlyweds you wouldn't have a brand-new wagon. The caravan is only for right now until you build your cottage."

"That makes sense."

"We only need it for Rosemary and me to hide in."

"What if they spot you?"

Jane shrugged. "Then, we'll be your cousins coming along for the ride. There's plenty of dark-haired Irish. Even call them Black Irish. That's what we'll be."

It sounded workable. The feeling that it could all go horribly wrong stuck to her like a bur. When she'd stepped in the car with the stranger, she hadn't immediately sensed it was wrong, but her feeling grew. Deep inside she knew this wouldn't work, but what other choice did she have?

Chapter Fifteen

THE MORNING SUN and a joyful bird chorus woke Meara from her sleeping place beneath the wagon. She came awake slowly, shaking off the tendrils of dreams of confused images. She'd opted for sleeping outside, feeling safer underneath the wagon than inside. If she were inside, it would be easy for someone to block the door and ride off with her trapped inside. Worse yet, it would be easy for someone to knock Jane off the driver's seat if taken unaware and take the wagon. Olio, she imagined, might be a little harder to push off the seat.

Her eyes narrowed against the light as she attempted to remember her dreams. She could have sworn Braeden was in one of them, but she wasn't sure. As she struggled to remember, she heard her father's voice, or did she just remember it from a dream?

"Anyone can be a threat. Even those close to you. Too often people convince themselves they are doing the wrong thing for the right reasons."

Did her father talk to her or did she simply imagine he did? If she was making up stuff, why not make up something more cheerful. Talk about disconcerting. Was running away the wrong thing to do? Grandmother Biddy was in favor of it. At the current time, she was the most knowledgeable person Meara knew, especially when it came to other worldly matters. Then again, if she was supposed to trust no one, could she put her faith in even the wise crone?

The best thing to do would be to ask her father. She'd whisper the words in an effort not to wake Jane, who slept beside her.

"Did you speak to me last night?"

Nothing. No response. None verbal and none in her mind. That didn't necessarily signal no. It could be her parent was busy doing other things in the spirit world. He'd mentioned something about it being hard to penetrate the veil and how it was easier when she was asleep. Maybe when she fell asleep tonight, she'd receive her answer.

For now, she'd have to wonder who might betray her and how they would do it. As far as she knew, she had no value here in Ireland. Back in England, there were those who suspected she started the convent fire, but since they were a cloistered order, none of the sisters were left to identify her.

An uneasiness rolled about in her stomach. It was hard to decide if it was hunger or anxiety. Her Uncle Simon came to look for her, which meant he'd wanted to find her. Still, she tried to remember the name of his wife, but couldn't. Maybe she wouldn't be too thrilled about the prospect of another mouth in the household.

At her age, they would probably expect her to marry or at least have someone in mind. She did, in a way. The distance between her and Braeden made her doubt her attraction to the handsome farmer more and more, but still Meara wanted Braeden to stay safe. If fate would have it, they could meet in the future, perhaps by happenstance. By that time, he could be married with a baby on the way. It would be a tough time to test if the attraction behind them still held. She sighed heavily as she decided to devote her prayers to Braeden's safety as opposed to returning to her.

"You're thinking so hard. I'd swear I saw smoke coming out of your ears. What's on your mind?"

Jane's voice startled her, since she hadn't assumed her companion was awake. "Oh, nothing."

"Nothing doesn't make you sigh like that."

She blew out a long breath, before propping herself up on her elbows. "Braeden. I think I dreamed of him, but I can't remember, which is frustrating. What if I forget his face? His voice? When the war ends, he could walk up to me on the street, and I wouldn't know him."

Jane rolled to her side to face Meara. "Yours is a normal fear. I'm sure many a wife and girlfriend has had similar ones as the war stretches on. You won't forget, but people change, too. The Braeden who comes back won't be the same man who left. You may not feel the same about him."

It sounded a bit like her previous advice to get to know more lads, about flirting with them, and kissing a few to test her feelings. Her lips pursed as she considered a changed Braeden. "Eleanor said the same, although I think she meant that Braeden might regret his hasty proposal. Apparently, men faced with death will do impulsive things such as proposing to women they barely know."

"There's some truth there. It's been my experience that men do rash things all the time. This explains the broken noses and battered knuckles. The next day, they can be singing with the same man they were using as a punching bag the previous day. There's no logic in the gender. We lasses tend to be the long thinkers. We have to. Else how would humanity survive?"

Long thinkers? Was she one? Her reactionary responses to everything didn't reflect this. Maybe she needed to do some long thinking.

"What's our plan for the day?" It would be her first step toward planning.

"Paint the wagon. I think you could benefit from a knife throwing lesson. Maybe Rosemary, too. We can forage and see if we can find anything edible. Mainly, we need to find water. With any luck, a stream might give us a fish meal. We might also stumble across a village. This will allow you and Olio to use your newlywed act. It could be beneficial in gaining food and water."

"How so?"

"Most won't begrudge you water, and a few mothers will feel a tenderness for the newly married and invite you to a meal."

Personally, she didn't see that happening, but the Irish could be more trusting and generous than those of her previous experience. "Those men who approached the caravan with pitchforks and guns didn't appear to be thick with tenderness."

"Bad sorts those." Jane continued to talk. "The women fix the food, which means they have the food to give. Some of the men are little more than bandy roosters strutting right proud in their territory, but possessing little more than pride."

"Avoid the men."

"Most of them. Olio can pick up a job as a day laborer. Most won't pay him in money, but they pay in whatever they might have, which can be anything from hay to potatoes. A happy farmer could bless us with eggs or even a fat hen." Her lips tilted up as she described the possible forms of payment.

"We work our way through the countryside doing odd jobs?"

"Pretty much. What skills do you have?"

She blinked at the notion she had any useful skills.

"You had to do something at the convent."

She grimaced, considering what she could do. "I'm good at polishing altar candelabras. I can sing in Latin."

Jane shook her head as Meara scrounged for whatever talent she might have.

What had she done at the convent? "I can feed livestock, gather eggs, and pick berries."

"All good, but the children would do those things."

It made her skills sound like something only youngsters did. "I'm good at gardening and mixing up jellies and jams."

"Most mothers can handle this on their own. There might be a few widows who do this for them to get by. We don't want to cause trouble by taking away their income."

That left nothing. All her life, she'd been training to do nothing. "I'm not good with children like Rosemary. I can't sew a fine seam or drive a team of horses. All I can do is read and write."

"That might be useful. Plenty of folks can't or can read very little. Maybe you can help at a school or a store or even volunteer to read to those who can't."

The idea didn't appeal overly much, but everyone had to do their part. It made her wonder what Jane would be doing while they played out their charade. "What about you? What are you going to do?"

"Forage, fish, stay out of sight. I might be able to patch together some items you could sell or trade in the village. People generally welcome the opportunity to get items they don't easily find."

Rosemary bent down to peer under the wagon. "Do the two of you want to break your fast?"

"I do." Meara crawled out from under the wagon, trailing her blanket behind her. Once on her feet, she accepted the water skin and took a swig. She never knew how much she missed tea until she didn't have it, and her brief interval with Eleanor had introduced her to many flavorful brews.

Jane followed her, saying, "We are fortunate that when Olio chose to leave he brought his jerky with him. He does make a good jerky."

"Jerky?" The word was unfamiliar to Meara.

Rosemary handed Jane what looked much like a twisted stick. Jane waved it about. "It's a way to dry meat to preserve it. Olio met up with an American who explained it to him. Well, enough for Olio to try. The first few batches weren't that good, but he kept trying and finally hit upon the right way to do it."

Rosemary raised an eyebrow and added, "It's hard leathery, smoked meat. You'll need water to get it down. I can see the benefit of having some while traveling though. We didn't have to make a fire to cook it."

Taking the offered brown stick, Meara bit. Her front teeth had no effect, which forced to her resort to her back teeth to get a grip as she used her hand to twist off a piece. It had the consistency of bark, only saltier. "Now what?" she inquired with the chunk still in her mouth.

Jane winked at her and added, "Chew. Pretend you're a cow chewing its cud."

Of all the things she wanted to pretend, being a cow chewing its previously digested grass supper was not one of them. Her mission had certainly introduced her to many new experiences. They came so fast she never had proper time to reflect on them. A whistle caught her attention as a man emerged from the woods.

He was dressed in plain clothes with his sturdy brown pants tucked into his boots. His plain homespun shirt had no embroidery of any kind on it. A battered hat crammed on his head shadowed his face. In one hand, he carried two dead rabbits. As he drew closer, he flourished the rabbits.

Meara glanced at Jane, who did not appear to be worried. In fact, she smiled at the stranger.

Then he spoke. "The traps I set up, provided."

It was Olio. What a difference a change of clothes made. She should have realized there was no one else around, but still. A nervous laugh erupted as her sudden fear bled away. "You fooled me. Gussied up in your town clothes. Makes me appear the dunce."

Rosemary patted her on the back. "No need to be embarrassed. I had no clue who he was, either."

The rabbits were passed off to Jane, who vanished behind the wagon with them. Olio smiled at the two of them and laughed. When he stopped, he held up one finger as he caught his breath. "I've never encountered anyone else like me."

Blond giants were probably a rarity most places. "It must be the clothes."

"You have some, too."

"Really?" She had wondered how they'd explain her own colorful wardrobe.

Before Olio answered, Jane came around the wagon holding a stiff, and unattractive brown dress. "A perfect ensemble for a young bride."

Rosemary hooted and elbowed her friend. "Perfect if you mean it won't show the dirt."

While Meara had similar thoughts, she couldn't help noticing it was the same brown of the tunic she used to wear. "The brown color is practical since it won't show stains or even wear too much."

"Bang on. You're thinking like an Irish woman now. Finish your breakfast. After, we'll paint the wagon and then begin your transformation. I'll need to find some pins to fix your hair."

The simple words reminded her what it would be like to be back in the regular world. Uncomfortable clothes and restrained hair along with repressed sensibilities was not something she looked forward to, but it would only be for a few hours, then they'd be back at camp.

The wagon painting and the transformation process, which involved a great deal of teasing by both Jane and Rosemary, didn't take too long. The sun was still east as they made their way across the land looking for signs of civilization. The hedgerows that marked property lines served as their first marker. A cottage with a long curl of smoke coming from its chimney was the second. Jane's vote for continuing to an actual village won since it was her horse and wagon.

When they finally spotted a village, Olio climbed onto the bench as Jane vacated it. Meara scampered up to the seat in the restrictive dress with a push on her bum from Rosemary. Her convent tunic was comfortable compared to this monstrosity. She never asked Jane where she got it, but she was sure someone either gave or threw it away. The dress had nothing to commend it, with the exception that it wasn't worn looking.

Olio guided the horse to the village and headed for the main square to a trough and hand pump there. He pulled the brake and filled the trough for Seymour. Meara moved her leg sideways testing out the width of the skirt to see if she could descend without any trouble. It could work. She was ready to scoot to the end of the seat, when the shutters opened behind her, and Jane passed out the water skin. Staying on the seat, Meara twisted to take it and directed her attention to Olio. She did her best to look adoring, pretending the striking man was Braeden.

The sight had Olio reaching for the water skin with a smirk, possibly a reflection of her acting abilities.

Sounds of cooking and conversation emanated from the cottages surrounding the town square, along with scents. The smell of baking bread and sausage made her stomach protest its earlier meager breakfast.

Perhaps one of the generous mothers would appear at the door and invite them in for tea. A door opened. Here it comes, the invitation to come inside and experience some Irish hospitality. A man stepped outside carrying a shotgun and wearing a disgruntled expression. The uneasy feeling she had before she went to sleep last night returned.

Another door opened and another gun-toting man exited. She did not expect a huge welcome, but she hadn't expected this either. At this point, she'd have to say the British were friendlier, and that wasn't saying much. All her hopes of a nice biscuit, even a meaty sandwich she didn't have to chew for ten minutes dissipated faster than the smoke coming from the snug cottage chimney.

"Hallo there." One of the men approached with the breach of his shotgun open, showing it was unloaded. The hand in his pocket probably fingered a shell just itching to insert it.

Olio smiled and waved. Her pretend husband replied in a broad accent she'd never heard before, matching the man greeting them. "Greetings friend. I appreciate the use of the water. My bride and I are off to visit her family."

"That's nice." The man's shoulders relaxed a little. "Forgive us for being on edge, but things haven't been grand lately."

From the opposite side, the other man moved in closer. Meara couldn't help noticing his gun wasn't open, which meant it was probably loaded.

"Women folk are jumpy since you could hear the spirits from the cursed land howling all night. Not a good omen."

"Farmer Bruce lost all his eggs and two good layers. Got up in the morning and they were gone," explained the first.

Meara forced her face to stay emotionless, but she had her suspicions that the chickens ended up in an empty stew pot, possibly the one emptied by Olio.

"Hooligans," said Olio. "Do you have any more advice?"

The first villager, the one Meara had labelled the friendlier of the two, shook his head and turned away. He made a sudden pivot and narrowed his eyes in Olio's direction. "You're not one of those rabble rousers? Come around to stir people up to revolt against England?"

"As a newly married man, would I be wanting to leave my bride?"

Both men chuckled, gave Meara an assessing look, and laughed again. Olio handed the filled water skin to her and climbed up on the wagon. Obviously, they would not be getting work here.

A red-faced woman with her hair hidden by a scarf came out carrying a basket with a napkin tucked over it. "Here's something for your travels."

Meara reached for the basket and had her hand on it when she thanked the woman.

The woman whisked the basket out of reach. "I'll not be giving my food to any English."

"My mother is from Ireland." The comment came out almost as a wail as she saw whatever savory treats the woman had packed were out of reach.

Olio urged Seymour into a slow turn around the water trough, while the formerly generous woman yelled after her. "Your mother should have stayed in Ireland."

A few curtains twitched as they rode by to see who was causing such a ruckus. The sweet couple act hadn't worked out that well. Meara did her best to contain her composure and keep her mouth closed, although it was a little too late for the latter when she'd been so close to a late breakfast, it'd almost made her salivate.

Olio urged the horse faster by flicking the reins and clicking his tongue. They crossed the road into the green fields where Olio finally decided to speak. "As a bashful wife, a smile would have been thanks enough."

"It would have been helpful if you had said something earlier."

He grunted, which as a response could have meant anything.

The shutters swung open behind them, and Jane held out her hand for the water skin. "Too bad that didn't work out."

Rosemary joined the conversation. "I could hear you in the wagon, and you sounded more British than normal."

"Yes, I know. I guess it was all that concentrating on not sounding British just made it worse. Did you catch the part about the chickens?"

Jane gave a brief snort. "I did. I do suspect it would have been travelers, which means they aren't that far away, or the men took the horses for their foraging trip."

Jane confirming her previous thought that sometimes the travelers helped themselves to a few things now and then didn't bring any joy. Instead, she was trying to use her long thinking skills. The one thing she did know was she didn't want to run into the travelers again. It didn't take any vision to know it would not end well.

"Do you think it is wise to travel over the fields as opposed to the main roads?"

Jane pushed her torso through the shutters. She twisted in both directions to survey the landscape. "I don't see any troubles."

"Yet. You're driving the path a traveler would take. It makes sense we could encounter them eventually. Why not take the main road? A path a traveler would avoid?"

Jane gazed off in the distance, while Olio answered. "It might be a straighter way to Galway County."

Rosemary added with an amused tone, "I'm sure it is smoother."

They headed back over the hills to a dusty road they had crossed earlier. Olio turned Seymour in a northwest direction.

Even though she'd never been to Ireland before, she still asked, "Are you going in the right direction?"

Olio remained silent, but gave her a knowing glance. Jane nudged her shoulder. "I'll translate for you. That means I know what I'm doing. You should know better than to ask a man if he knows where he is going."

"Why is that?" Asking just made sense. Why wouldn't she?

Rosemary joined Jane in the open window, causing Jane to move to the side to give her room to look out. "Remember, Meara doesn't have much experience with the vagaries of men. She doesn't know they operate on an entirely separate set of rules."

"They have rules? How am I supposed to know this if no one tells me? What are the rules?"

Jane held up her index finger. "Men are always in charge, until they're not."

Both women chuckled as Meara tried to untangle the meaning behind the rule.

"Number two," Rosemary continued, "a man is always right, even when he is wrong."

Meara glanced at Olio to see how he felt about the rules. He looked straight ahead and didn't show any distress about rules that appeared to be unfavorable to his gender.

"Rule number three is the man is never ever lost, even when he is." Jane said the words with a certain amount of glee that had Olio pulling on the reins and stopping Seymour.

"Anyone who wants to drive, feel free." He applied the brake and wrapped the reins around the metal bar in front of the wagon for such purpose.

If he expected to get a general refusal and begging for him to continue to drive, then he'd be disappointed since Rosemary squeezed through the window to take his place as driver. Olio descended to walk with a parting sally, "Don't get lost."

"As if I would. I'm very good at directions."

Meara hoped that was true, because she hadn't a clue where she was going. To her family, to Galway, to find the missing piece of what she now called the faery horn, but those were ideas, ones she was told. The physical body of Meara Cleary did have certain deeds to perform while the spiritual one was lost somewhere in the ether. With any luck, she could unite the two.

Chapter Sixteen

THEY TRAVELED A few miles down the road, acknowledging fellow drivers with a wave or a smile. After traveling more than half a day, they pulled off on a grassy area that bordered a stream and had a few sheltering oak trees. A spirited discussion ensued between the advisability of should they have a fire or not to make rabbit stew.

From their spot near the water, they could see the patches of the road. The traffic was sparse with not more than two vehicles passing since they'd stopped. Jane wanted the fire, knowing that the meat would not keep forever. Olio felt it was a mistake that would give away their location. Both points of view had merit. While Meara chose to remain silent and see how they worked it out, Rosemary placed both hands on her hips and waded into the argument.

"Anyone who cares can see us from the road. They won't give much thought to a family having a bit of meat or tea. This type of thing is expected when folks travel. You keep forgetting people see what they want to see. As a party of mainly women we are no threat."

She gestured to Olio. "There will be some that will even feel sorry for you."

He chuckled and threw up his hands. "Build your fire."

The night ended well with full stomachs and easier minds. Olio took the first guard shift, allowing the women to sleep inside the wagon. Still, the fact they were so close to the road and other people made them vulnerable. Jane barred the door, which made Meara feel even less secure. The brief time she'd been with Jane, she had never done that.

Perhaps noticing her curious stare, Jane remarked, "Desperate folk travel at night."

"We did."

"Just my point." Still standing, she tapped her finger against her forehead. "What most people call lucky is simple planning. I lock the door against any who might think to enter and help themselves to all we have."

"What about Olio?"

"He could be knocked out, went to check on the horse, or stepped away to relieve himself. I also suggest we should all sleep with our knives on us."

On that note, sheathes were passed out. Jane lifted her skirt about her knees to expose the sheath strapped to her thigh. "Don't make the mistake of strapping the sheath to your calf no matter how long your dress is. The muscle flexes too much, and you'll end up with it dropping to your ankle and tripping you. Besides, most of your trouble will come from men. If they see you lifting your skirts, that will be enough to distract them to get a good shot. Women and animals, not so much. That's why you should make the shot count. There will be no second chances."

Meara had to rock to her knees to attach the sheath. The dark leather case stood out like a bruise against her pale thigh. She wiggled it around until it faced out. Jane handed Meara a throwing a throwing knife, hilt first.

"Try this to see how it fits. Make sure your hand just brushes it when you're standing. No need for all this bending and twisting to reach it, which might end up getting you killed."

Sometimes the more she knew of the world, the more she wondered if she wouldn't have remained safe behind the convent walls. That would only work if the place hadn't gotten bombed. Still without the bombing, there would be no adventures, stolen kisses, sweet treats, or friendships. Wearing a knife strapped to her thigh might be a price she had to pay.

"Jane, did you ever kill anyone?"

"No." She shook her head and handed Rosemary a knife. "Hope I never do. When you can control the knife, you can make it go where you want. Depending on the danger, sometimes I just want to scare the person. A knife close to a man's head does that or anywhere else he might value. Men don't expect women to know how to handle a knife, which means a knife in the hand of a female is doubly dangerous. There are a few men who might think differently, but something unlucky usually happens to those braggarts."

Rosemary patted her newly sheathed knife. "I feel safer already."

"Keep in mind," Jane gave them both a stern look, but lingered a little longer on Rosemary, "having a weapon is for defense. It is a last resort. If you think you're in a tricky situation, try talking yourself out it. My da taught me that enclosed spaces are the worst for escaping. When you enter someplace, make sure you have spotted more than one exit. Be aware of who is by you. Often you can watch the eyes of whoever you're talking to and see when someone significant enters the room behind you."

The thought of always being on alert presented some challenges. Does everyone she meets want to harm her?

As if reading her thoughts, Jane smiled at her. "Often, if you're aware, you'll find opportunities as opposed to threats. Now and then, you learn something. Instead of Dame Fortune shining more brightly on some people, it's awareness, grabbing opportunities, and planning."

Rosemary wrinkled her nose at this comment. "I've always heard that fortune favors the bold."

"That's because the bold are willing to try something over and over again until it does work. The average Joe will give up after one try or possibly two."

Meara had been guilty of that. Not that she had tried all that many things. Still, there was an entire world of possibility for her to try once the war ended. She smoothed out her pallet made of folded blankets and fluffed her pillow.

"Not sure about you two, but I'm going to sleep before I have to get up for guard duty." She closed her eyes, suiting her actions to her words.

The lantern winked out, making the interior dark. A lavender scent wafted over Meara, relaxing her, which meant she was probably right next to the herb storage area. The chorus of frogs near the stream began their evening warm-up with throaty warbles that hung in the air. How many things had she missed because she was too involved in something else? What if she missed something important? Wondering if she'd passed some significant sign nagged at her until she stumbled into a deep sleep.

A RHYTHMIC KNOCK woke her along with Jane's aggrieved voice beside her. "Meara, it's your time."

She rolled out from under her blanket and crept to the door. She pulled the heavy bar back and swung the door out. Olio held out a hand to help her down the stairs.

Once her feet touched the ground, Olio released her hand and stepped back. He gestured to under the wagon. "I'll be there. Put out the fire since it will attract folks hoping for a bite to eat or tea."

What was wrong with that? Before she even voiced her sentiment, the answer made itself known. They were on a mission, and they didn't know who they could trust. No one who had a lick of sense would show up and announce their nefarious intentions. Instead, they'd either sneak in or be an unassuming person, perhaps a sweet old lady or even a woman of the cloth. Still, she should know better than most that appearances can be deceiving.

"I UNDERSTAND. NO light?"

He shook his head and pointed to the moon. "See where it is now?"

"I do."

He sketched his finger about six inches in the night sky. "When it reaches the point right over the stream, then it is time to wake Jane."

"Will do." She gave a slight wave before Olio turned and crawled under the wagon. "Hey, can I ask you something?"

He had already pulled up his blanket and it was difficult to determine his mood from the night shadows, but he still answered, "What?"

"Why do you talk so much now?"

"Do I sound like a woman, now?"

"No, of course not."

"Good. I talk when there is a need to."

Being alone in the dark caused her to pace. She circled the wagon with what she assumed was stiff military precision. It had to be the way guards performed their evening patrols of the grounds.

A grunt sounded first, before Olio called out, "Would you go sit down on the boulder? I can't sleep with all the marching."

Meara slipped away to a dark shadow that marked what she knew was a boulder where he'd sat earlier. The rock had a smooth place on it that worked well as a seat. Dozens, possibly hundreds of bums had sat in the very same place. A few might have even stood watch as she was. Maybe standing watch was common enough.

Near the top of the tree she thought she saw a flicker of light, then another. She blinked. The lights flitted at the top of the tree. They vanished, making Meara think she never really saw them. Widening her eyes didn't help her to distinguish anything in the dark, gray night except for silhouettes of the wagon and the trees. The moon illuminated the water, making it appear like a silvery ribbon.

Meara used her feet to pivot around the rock while remaining seated. How Olio entertained himself on watch with no one to talk to perplexed her. Back when she was in the convent, they spent a great deal of time like this, being silent, doing nothing. At the time, she was supposed to be praying, and she did try, using the prayers she'd been taught, but it hadn't felt real. Instead, her imagination had roamed. Sometimes she'd wondered about ancient lands of the Bible. Other times about the dangerous people in the village. Once she found the bolt hole and slipped outside the walls, she thought about nature.

How the sunlight filtered through the tree canopy touching the delicate wild flowers made everything special and sacred. It felt holy and authentic to her, so much different from the damp chapel with its modest altar crowded with ornate candelabras and a chalice. All the sisters in their dark clothes hadn't helped much, either. If she ever prayed from the heart, it was to be out in nature, free from the gloomy confines of the convent. She was, though she certainly hadn't planned on such a dramatic exit.

Something buzzed by her ruffling her hair. Her hand went up to her head in reaction, but whatever it was had moved. Too big to be an insect, too low for a bird unless it was attempting to land. No stunned bird flapped nearby.

"I didn't mean to alarm you."

The voice again? Was it her mother? She'd only heard it once. "Mother? Sorcha?"

"It is me. As much as I tried, it hasn't been easy to reach you."

"Have you been trying?"

"Yes. I was there in the wagon with Grandmother Biddy. She saw me or felt me."

She remembered Grandmother Biddy's Tarot reading and her certainty that they were not alone. "That was you?"

"Yes. Grandmother Biddy felt me. It made me sad I couldn't reach you. I did enjoy hearing how the fairies arranged our meeting."

That meant she heard the story about the faery horn and could probably explain more about it. "You heard the story, too."

A gentle laugh sounded on the wind. *"Faith, I did. One summer day we were exploring the ruins, and we found the faery horn. I guess more appropriately, we were led to it. A sunbeam pointed to it, lighting up the area and drawing our attention."*

"Did you know it was special?"

"In a way since it was beautiful and ornate. Fulmen even put it to his mouth to blow, but we both heard a voice that said now is not the time and he wasn't the person. We were told that honor belonged to our child. This surprised us both."

Meara's heart beat faster with the thrill of talking to her mother. If her mother was seated beside her, and she could physically touch her, it would be everything she prayed for. As much as she wanted to ask her if she'd seen her growing up or if she was proud of her, she needed more information about the horn.

"What did you do with it?"

"The faeries told Fulmen to separate the horn into three pieces. It came apart easily enough. We were to hide it in three different countries, starting with Ireland. Were told when they would be found when needed. Didn't write anything down to keep the wrong sort from finding it."

"Where did you hide them?"

"The first I hid in my favorite wishing place. My brother Simon and I used to go there to hide when the house was full of company. Sometimes, I'd climb the ash tree and pretend I was a pirate on a tall ship."

It was lovely to imagine her mother as a young girl in a tree pretending to be a swashbuckler. Maybe they were somewhat alike, not that she ever wanted to be a pirate, but she'd climbed a tree or two.

"The first piece is on your family's property?"

"Not exactly our property, but close enough."

"Meara, who are you talking to?"

The unexpected voice of her friend, interrupting her conversation, startled her. It meant she must have been speaking aloud. Did her mother also? "Did you hear anyone else?"

"Just you. I came out to make use of the bushes and didn't expect to find you chattering to yourself. If it keeps you awake. Fine. Maybe I should take Jane's place. That way you can scamper back into the wagon, and I'll stay out here once I get my business done."

A quick glance at the moon indicated it had moved enough for her duty to be done. "Go on."

Rosemary shot her an odd expression before she strolled a short distance away, possibly still in hearing distance.

"Mother? Mother?"

No answer. Inside she could feel the absence of the nurturing presence that had been beside her only seconds ago. Might as well let Rosemary take duty, and she could consider the almost clue about the horn being hidden close to Cleary land at the base of an ash tree.

Chapter Seventeen

MEARA PEGGED UP the wet nappy beside the other on the line. Next came a long sleeved shirt and some socks. Childish screams of delight drew her attention. The young mother she'd agreed to help was spinning in circles with her children until they all fell in a heap on the grass. A breeze sent a leaf dancing through the air until it hit the ground near her feet.

"Fall's not too far away."

Rosemary stopped cranking the clothes through the wringer to reply. "Too close, if you ask me. We should have been at your uncle's house already."

"I thought we'd be there long before now. With us stopping every two or three days to work for feed and pay, it slows a person down."

"You can say that again. Your idea of being a mother's helper by doing the household work to allow the mothers time with their children is a winner. We have so many mothers wanting to take advantage of our services there will be gnashing of teeth when we leave."

Meara grinned at what she knew was an exaggeration. Sure, word had gotten around that the two of them could be had for a meal or two. They really needed to start insisting on groceries as opposed to meals, though. At least Olio earned some money, helping erect a new steeple on the church. Jane received a length of fabric, a box of nails, and a live chicken for her efforts as harness repairer and knife sharpener.

Even though Jane had no real use for the nails, she kept them to use for barter somewhere else, since nails could be dear. The length of cloth would be turned into dresses or skirts for Rosemary and Meara. The chicken was stretched out into three dinners. Most of the villagers they met didn't have money lying around, but they were willing to share what they did have.

"Oh, a few might weep at our exit, but we can't expect the village to support us forever. I talked to the town priest, and he knows the Cleary family. He told me we're only three days' ride away."

Rosemary threw a wringed garment in the basket to hang. "That should only be two weeks, the rate we're going."

No need to answer since she had a similar thought. She pegged up another tiny shirt. Her fingers moved over the almost invisible stiches. Would she ever be a mother and a wife? Plenty of women were both. It was the rare woman who was neither. Meara made a mental note to ask tonight when they'd be moving on. It could be that Olio and Jane had a fondness for the village. They might want to stay. Then, she and Rosemary could strike out on their own, which would seem odd to the villagers since she was supposed to be the wife.

If the journey had accomplished one thing, it forced Olio to speak even more than before. Sometimes, she wondered if it was because the setting was different. There was no normal among the four of them. They were all misfits in one way or another.

A wet slap of a towel alerted her that Rosemary was up to her old games. "Stop! No one wants you snapping their towels."

The young mother who had been playing with her children walked up to the clothesline in time to hear her words. Rosemary sucked in her lips while Meara flushed, wondering if they'd get anything for their efforts. Lorna, the mother, took the towel from Rosemary, spun it until it was a nice tight rope, and whipped it out to crack in the air.

"You northerners don't know much about making a good towel snap." She laughed and whipped out the towel again, almost hitting Meara. Meara imagined the woman could hit her if she chose to.

Northerners is what the villagers had taken to calling them, with their British accents mellowed some after being surrounded by the lilting

Irish. A few of the men teased Olio about marrying a northern girl, but joked about love being blind and deaf. They were accepted since the two things that separated the north and south regions, besides geography, was the north's allegiance to England and religion. When it came to saying *Our Fathers* and *Hail Marys,* she proved herself. Apparently, repeating prayers six times a day did have some benefit.

"That, we don't," Rosemary teased back. "You could school us?"

Lorna shook her head. "Tempting as it is, I have a meal to make. Made an extra loaf of bread this morning. You're welcome to it."

Meara wanted it, but didn't want to appear too anxious. "That's very kind of you."

"Yes, we'll take it and be glad of it, too." Rosemary grinned at Lorna. "Let me finish wringing out these clothes, and I can help you with dinner."

Lorna surrendered the wet towel for Meara to hang. "You'd be more useful to me if you just watch my darlings, instead."

"Will do."

Meara watched her friend finish her job in record time to frolic with the youngsters. Here in the country, life was serene. There were shortages of some things, but she couldn't determine if they were war related as in England. The only time the mention of war came up is when someone was in their cups and cursing about the possibility of England taking good Irishmen for soldiers. So far, that hadn't happened.

They'd come across some actual rabble rousers in their travels, rough men talking about revolution and revolt. Olio's unusual size usually attracted attention. They tried to recruit him, but the clever man pretended to neither speak nor hear. Jane chased them away by yelling at them to leave her simple brother alone.

She would have sworn a gleam appeared in one of the men's eyes at the mention of simple. It wasn't hard to figure out they'd hoped to manipulate Olio. They did the only thing they could when they encountered the firebrands, they moved on.

That night after they filled their bellies, courtesy of the villagers,

Olio sat with the townsmen and smoked a pipe that someone had provided. Normally, the man didn't smoke, but he explained he'd soon discovered all the town news was dispensed at these get togethers. He probably did a great deal more of gesturing with his pipe than smoking, while the men assumed—wrongly—that the women had no clue what was said.

The three of them worked on cutting out patterns from old newspapers the local priest gave them. That he was a newshound and had the news mailed to him surprised her. Though it often arrived a few weeks late, making nothing current, it still allowed him to be the center of the all-male gatherings as he read the paper aloud.

Rosemary held up a pattern piece to her body. "I think the skirt is a little narrow for comfort. Maybe we can just make a pinafore out of it to cover my dress. People seldom look past an apron. Plenty of women back home wore an apron all the time."

Jane pursed her lips and held up the cloth. "It's a busy pattern. It could clash with whatever you have on."

"That might make us seem ordinary, then. The local women often wear skirts, blouses, and aprons that didn't coordinate. Only those with money appear to have an ensemble that goes together."

A short snort came from Jane, who feigned shock. Even though most of the traveler women wore white blouses and solid skirts, they usually had some type of embroidery that united the pieces.

"Except for the travelers, they always appear coordinated."

Jane laughed. "We may not have much, but we do have an eye for color and a way with the needle."

"I'm hoping you'll use that way to make me a new pinafore," Rosemary quipped as she put down the pattern to pick up a hand mirror and peered into it. "I'm getting too dark. No wonder I've not attracted the attention of any of the men."

"Be glad you haven't. It would not go well for you," Jane commented, placing the pattern against the cloth.

Rosemary whirled around so fast that her skirt fluttered. "What do you mean? I'd make as good a wife as most. A man would be lucky to have me."

"It's not the man you need worry about. It's the women. The town isn't thick with single, unmarried men. I suspect there are more women than men in that respect. Plenty have already eyed the men and decided which one will do for them. Now they're in the stage of convincing the man. If you snag an available man, not only do you earn the ire of an expectant girl, you get her family's disfavor, along with her friends and anyone else in the village who might decide to dislike you because you're not a local."

Rosemary put down the mirror and sat. Feeling sorry for her friend, Meara drifted over and put a hand on her shoulder. "My mother married a stranger, a non-local."

Before Rosemary could reply, Jane did. "It's different. She moved away, and your father was not the target of a local girl's affection. Did they move back to his town?"

"I have no way of knowing. If they did, I guess my mother could have felt a similar dislike that you described from a designing woman. If so, it was no wonder they were anxious to move to the farm my father inherited."

Talk of her parents' brutal end never was something she discussed with others. Destiny divined it, which wasn't the same as telling. The most she'd tell anyone was her mother gave birth at the convent, then died.

"Do you know where the farm is?" Rosemary asked as she stretched and tried to find a more comfortable position on her rock seat. Not finding any, she slipped off to sit in the grass.

"No. Uncle Simon got a letter from someone in Beacon, Wales that explained my father's death. Whoever wrote the letter confessed that their own relation took over the farm."

"It's yours. You should take it. March up there and thank them for keeping the farm for you, and you'd like it back."

Jane coughed, although Meara suspected it was forced, and shook her head. "Even I know the Welsh can be a dangerous, unpredictable people, and I've never stepped foot in the country."

"You're right." Even though Meara agreed, she also knew the farm was her birthright. She had to visit. Maybe she'd feel closer to her father there. It's also possible that part of the horn was there.

The sound of masculine singing drew their eyes as Olio sang about a lass dying of heartbreak because her man deserted her. They watched the man weave as he walked toward camp. A few times it appeared he stumbled, but he never hit the ground. The closer he came, the steadier his gait became, until finally he walked upright without a stagger, and the song died before he entered camp.

"Someone enjoyed himself." Jane smirked and continued to cut carefully around the pattern pinned on the cloth.

"I did, but not as much as some. Old Tom brought out his special homemade whiskey. I was beholden to sample it."

"I'm sure you did more than sample."

Urgency made Meara interrupt the good-natured bantering. "What news?"

"Nothing different. There are still revolts against the English. Small skirmishes popping up here and there. With the war going on, Britain doesn't have the manpower to put them down. The leaders of the rebellion are calling the lack of action a victory."

It wasn't anything new. She'd heard more of the same. It didn't have any impact on her plans. "Anything else?"

"Travelers in the area. We need to leave before we're accused of stealing anyone's chickens. While we were sitting and drinking, I saw Leon peering at me through the bushes."

"You saw him? That was sloppy work." Jane folded the fabric she'd been working on and stood. "We'll leave tonight."

Olio gestured to Seymour, who was grazing nearby. "I'll get the horse ready." He looked in Rosemary and Meara's direction. "Help break down the camp. Light the lantern before you put out the fire."

They were finally heading out with the traveler on their heels. She suspected Grandmother Biddy had passed since a blue bird had alighted on her shoulder a few days earlier. The birds normally avoided people. Not only had it stayed on her shoulder a few seconds, but she suddenly thought of leaving too. It wasn't the first time she thought of departing, but there was a new urgency as if the bird told her to *go now*.

Faeries could take the shape of birds, and sometimes they could use them for transport. It could have been Grandmother Biddy's soul directing the feathered messenger, or it could have been faeries. Whatever it was, she didn't share her experience. Instead, she waited for someone else to mention something similar. No one had.

In less than ten minutes, they had the wagon hitched and everything packed up. After dousing the fire, Rosemary started kicking dirt over the ashes and scattered the stones from the fire ring. Jane grabbed her arm.

"Leave it. There'll be no hiding our presence since Olio was spotted in the village. They lost a good tracker and spy in Olio. The fact they'd resorted to Leon, who has no skills, makes me wonder if they haven't splintered into smaller groups. There were those who were plenty greedy. They'd feel no guilt about taking our wagon and all that we have."

She gave Rosemary a slight push to the vehicle and turned to climb onto the driving bench.

Meara, already in the wagon, helped Rosemary in and barred the door. The forward jolt sent them both wind-milling in the dark wagon. With any luck, they were headed the right direction to reach the Cleary homestead. While the priest offered up the information that they were near, he hadn't specified what direction.

In the dark, Olio led Seymour, urging him into a light trot. The man could only jog so long. She suspected the horse even less. What would they do if the travelers caught up with them? The thought kept her uncomfortable company.

Chapter Eighteen

THE TWITTERING OF morning birds woke her. Meara wiggled her toes and stretched her arms as she contemplated all that had happened. The lack of motion meant they'd stopped somewhere in the night. She should get up and unbar the door. A closed door kept Olio and Jane away from the food they'd stored inside to keep it safe from wildlife.

Sunlight filtered in through the shutters illuminating the interior. A few steps brought her to the door where she wrestled with the heavy bar. Meara opened the door slowly, just in case she might need to close it in a hurry. Seymour was grazing not too far from the camp while Jane rested against a tree trunk holding a flower.

"Morning, sleepy head," she called out when she spotted Meara. "Bring out those muffins I made yesterday and wrapped in a blue scarf."

A quick search yielded the bundle, which she carried out and handed over.

Jane brandished the bundle. "Breakfast. Good thing I had the foresight to make them. I had a feeling we might be moving on sooner than we thought."

"Why didn't you share that feeling?"

Her shoulders went up in a shrug. "That's a funny thing about instinct. Sometimes it is hard to know when nature is guiding you or if it's your own desires. One will get you where you need to go. The other will just cause trouble."

It made her wonder which one she'd been listening to.

Jane held out the opened bundle to her, and she picked out a round-ed corn muffin. The dry cornmeal was a little hard to swallow.

"Any tea?"

"Can't make a fire. It would be the easiest way to trace us. All Olio's work of breaking branches on paths we didn't take would be wasted if we lit a fire. We already know they're using the overeager Leon for spying and tracking. If they're tracking us, they'll turn the wrong way." Jane passed the heavy water skin to her.

The memory of the angry women screaming about poisoning chil-dren presented itself along with the anxiety that came with it. "I was only trying to help."

"I know you were. Logic never can find its footing when it comes to raw emotion."

"What do you mean?"

"People don't listen to sense when they're riled up. Now that every-thing is over, there might be a few who understand. Some may have even let it go."

The possibility that the travelers had buried the incident under more pressing concerns cheered her. She uncapped the water skin and took a drink. At least something was looking up. Meara glanced up into the interlocking branches of the tree. A black and red bird regarded her with a fixed gaze. She returned it, trying to determine if it was simply a bird or a messenger. It acted like it was aware of her and not in the easily frightened way most birds had.

If it came with a message, what was it?

Jane continued to talk as Meara closed her eyes, searching her mind for a message. An image of a stone house with green shutters and smoke curling out of the chimney presented itself. The word, home, resonated in her mind. Whose home was it?

A silence of the human variety meant her companion had stopped speaking, which meant she should say something, but what? Difficult to come up with a response when she had missed most of the conversation. The last thing she mentioned was something about the travelers forgetting about her prediction that their children would die, if they ate the tainted stew.

"Do you think they let it go?"

"No. Some have need to hold on to it." She sighed heavily. "My da told me once that some people have a need to hate something or someone. There's this part of them that wants to hate. It needs a target. I imagine that's how they get soldiers to fight. There wouldn't be any desire to fight the Germans if they thought of them as someone like themselves, a person with a family, possibly a wife and child. Still, some folks are good at hating. It's like they practice. All the dreadful things that happen in their lives, they take no responsibility for, but blame others instead."

"Would the sheep have been eaten if everyone approved of it?"

"Possibly, but that wouldn't have happened. Anyone with sense knows you don't eat an animal conveniently found dead in the field. It would have been different if we knew how it died. Whoever made the decision to pick it up decided to wait after everyone ate their fill and announce their great find to an appreciative group."

"It would have been too late then."

"I know, which would be only another reason to hate you. By preventing the group from eating the tainted food, it throws the blame right back on those who picked up the convenient mutton without a word to the leaders. Could be those allied with Leon were thrown out of the group."

The bird gave her a long look before it flew off. Tension returned to her body as she pushed up into a sitting position. "I imagine those people would be very angry if they were kicked out of the group."

"They'd refuse to accept any blame. It would be all your fault, Rosemary's, or both."

"I noticed you didn't include yourself."

"They fear me."

"Why?"

"They suspect that Grandmother Biddy taught me the old ways."

"Did she?"

"Some and it's time I teach you what little I know. As for the other, I suspect you'll find teachers as you go. When a student is earnest, a teacher presents herself."

Even though Grandmother Biddy had sent along her books and cards, there had been very little time to look at either. "What should we start with?"

"Knowing which way to take." Jane grasped a chain around her neck, undid it, and pulled a green and red pendulum from underneath her shirt. She held it up and allowed it to swing free. "Back in the day, many knew the art of knowing, but people forgot. Some priests even discouraged the craft, saying it was of the devil. Too often people are afraid of what they do not know."

Grandmother Biddy had spoken about the Tarot cards and the pendulum both being tools. "How do you use it?"

The pendulum consisted of two rounded spheres. The smaller one stacked on top of the larger one which had a metal cone attached to it. "The pendulum is carefully weighted. Most people use anything for a pendulum, including a needle on a thread to tell the sex of an unborn child, but they're players. They don't care half the time if they are right or not since it is merely entertainment. It can't be entertainment for you. You can use the pendulum to warn you of danger. Before we left last night, I used my pendulum to determine if we were acting rashly. It told me to go."

Meara's gaze fixed on the pendulum, swinging slightly from the chain. "You wear it all the time?"

"It's best to have it close. It's like your knife in that respect. You can't go looking for it when you need it. If you do, it might be too late. I usually keep the pendulum part tucked between my breasts since there are those who'd condemn me for wearing it. Even that priest back in the village you impressed with your catechism could be one who might accuse us both of consorting with the devil for having a divination tool. My pendulum and I have been together for years." Her voice turned affectionate as she looked at the swinging object.

"What should I do first?"

"You'll need one of your own. I'll let you pick one out of the box Grandmother Biddy sent with us. You'll know the right one. It's a feeling. Then you'll need to cleanse it. You can do this with a flame, leaving it in the sun, burying it in the earth, incense, or fresh water. The water would be the simplest and the quickest. Then you consecrate it with a prayer."

"A prayer?" Her eyebrows shot up.

"People have been praying for thousands of years to various gods and goddesses, sometimes to the Earth itself. Better, they've received answers to their prayers. The important thing about the pendulum is safety and love."

"How so?" The more Jane talked Meara felt like she understood less and less. It went against everything she knew before.

"Love comes from the gifting of a pendulum. It should be given to you by someone who loves you. In this case, it comes from Grandmother Biddy, who loved you so much before she'd even met you that she managed to delay her own death. I'm certainly glad of that because I learned much while waiting."

"The safety part?"

"You consecrate it in a safe place." Jane turned slightly to look to her right, then left. She even twisted to look behind her. "Everything looks good. This should serve. Slip inside and get the box Grandmother Biddy sent. It's on the left side of the wagon tucked under the herbs. Bring it out to me. Try not to wake Rosemary since this ceremony is only for you."

"Why just me?"

"I have nothing against Rosemary. Like her. Still, she would only use the pendulum to ask if a certain man fancied her or how many children she might have. She'd probably use it every second of the day."

True enough. Meara found herself nodding in silent agreement. Jane continued her explanation as Meara pushed to her feet.

"I know some people regard the pendulum as a tool. It is in a way, but in another way, it is a living energy. Some say it has a spirit, which is what I believe. I prefer not to annoy it with silly questions."

Excited to learn more, Meara crept into the wagon and located the box with some odd symbols painted on it. Her friend murmured in her sleep, but did not wake as she removed the box and exited on cat's feet. Maybe her pendulum would look like Jane's.

Once outside, she carried the box to Jane, who placed it on the ground beside her and opened it. A whiff of a potent perfume thick with spices and a shimmer filled the air. "Grandmother Biddy never left anything to chance. She enchanted the box to prevent it from being opened."

"You opened it."

"I did, but I was meant to. What she enchanted it against was those who would have opened it with mercenary purposes. Many came to Grandmother Biddy for cures and potions. Some of the other women of our group could do a fair reading, but our small tribe depended on Grandmother for her insights as opposed to their actual leader, Red Monesha. As you remember, there were some things Grandmother Biddy kept hidden."

Jane stopped and made a face before continuing. "I'd call it hidden in plain sight because plenty came to her for help. Despite all their two-faced talk about not believing in magic or the old ways because the church condemns it, they'd raid her wagon, looking for magical items once she passes."

Jane pushed aside some books and papers written in spidery handwriting to reveal some brilliant crystals and some pendulums. The colorful crystals sparkled in the morning sun, and there was one just like Jane's made up of two perfectly rounded crystals of differeing sizes. Her hand hovered over it, until her companion spoke.

"Close your eyes. Use your heart to find it. The first pendulum I chose shattered on me. It wasn't for me, and I assume it had sacrificed itself rather than be used. Startling for a young girl."

Look with her heart. Eyes closed, mentally, she chanted the words, as her fingers glided over the smooth pendulums. With each smooth form under her finger tips, she had the impression *not this one*. Her fingers encountered something colder and smaller than the rest. Was it a pendulum or something else? A tingle shot up through her fingers, across her palm, and up her arm. She stilled her search, knowing she'd found the right one.

It was time to look at what she'd chosen. She hoped she had chosen one that had one of the flashy stones embedded in the chain or the crystal shaped as a pendulum. Underneath her fingertips rested a slender metal cylinder. Time had tarnished it a bit, and it was smaller than the rest. She lifted it to examine. There were some slight curves to the object, a rounded top and nine separate rings. It didn't look anything like the other pendulums. Why had her heart picked this one?

"Ooh. The Egyptian Goddess Isis Pendulum. I always wanted that one."

"Why?" She attempted to suppress the disappointment in her voice.

"It's the most powerful of the lot. Even though I wanted it, I knew enough from my first experience not to go picking what appealed to my vanity. Haven't you heard of Isis?"

"Any knowledge of anything outside of scripture is a bit lacking."

"She's an ancient Egyptian goddess."

"That explains why I've never heard of her," she said, holding up the pendulum to watch it twirl. Every now and then it would reflect the sun's light on a tiny untarnished area. What it needed was to be polished.

Let's rinse it." The water splashed on Meara as Jane poured. After wetting the pendulum moderately, she stopped. "You can wipe it off on your clothes, since we don't have much else."

The tiny pendulum already looked brighter. Meara held it out, feeling better about it as it twirled in the sunlight.

"Are you ready?" Jane asked.

"Ready for what?"

"To consecrate your pendulum."

"Yes."

"Place it in your open right hand. Use your left hand to cradle it." She demonstrated the action with her own pendulum. "Normally, we ask the universe for assistance. In this case, we'll ask Isis because as goddesses went, she had a way of getting what she wanted and needed. Often, she is called the Mother of All or the Goddess of All, because there is nothing she can't do. How does that sound to you?"

"Wonderful." It really did sound wonderful. Who wouldn't want to be aligned with a goddess who could do anything.

"Repeat after me. I ask Isis to charge my pendulum."

"Isis, charge my pendulum." She wasn't sure if she should be demanding that a great goddess to do anything.

"Allow me unclouded vision."

She repeated the words.

"Clarity of thought."

She murmured those words. It would be nice to know what she knew as opposed to second guessing everything.

"Allow me to act with boldness, but for the highest good of all."

What was the highest good? She undertook the mission certain it was the highest good. Honestly, the mission chose her as opposed to her picking it. "Allow me to act with boldness, but for the highest good of all."

Jane lifted her cupped hands into the air. "So, mote it be."

"So, mote it be."

She watched her companion until she turned and smiled at her. "Ready to use the pendulum?"

"I am. What does mote it be mean?"

"I asked Grandmother Biddy that once, she told me it was like amen and meant so it is." Jane allowed her pendulum to slip through her fingers, and she caught it with the ball at the end of the chain. "First, you ask it to show you yes. Not all pendulums work the same."

Her pendulum hung straight down from her fingertips not moving.

Even though she felt a little ridiculous, she asked, "Show me yes."

The pendulum made almost infinitesimal movements that arched into an ever-growing circle. "I'm not doing anything, and it's swinging."

"I know. You have an opinionated pendulum. Now, let's move on and ask it to show you no. You have to stop it first."

She stilled it with her opposite hand. The object she had shunned in her mind, suddenly took on new importance. Did it realize her feelings, although, she didn't feel that way anymore? Should she apologize? She held out her arm straight after stopping the pendant. "Show me no."

It swung back and forth in a hard line. At the top of its arc, it would give a tiny jump, then swing back. "Straight line is no. Circle is yes. What do I do now?"

"Think of yes and no questions. Sometimes, it is good to start with a simple question. Something you know the answer to such as your name."

"What if it didn't agree with my name?"

"Then it's not the one for you."

She cut her eyes both ways to determine if anyone else was near, nothing, except for two sparrows nearby that were probably more interested in crumbs as opposed to whatever she might say. She took a deep breath, already anticipating a fail. "Is my name George?"

The tiny metal amulet swept back and forth in a direct line, denying George as a name. So far, so good, but maybe she should try another one. "Is my name Eleanor?"

Another no answer.

Jane gave a long-suffering sigh. "Ask it something real. Something you care about."

There were plenty of things she cared about, including her continual survival, but she didn't ask because some things you were better off not knowing. She considered several questions about the faery horn and Rosemary's marital prospects until she finally came up with one.

"Is Braeden still alive?"

Her pendulum swung in a beautiful perfect circle. She closed her eyes in relief. "Thank God." Maybe she should ask if the two of them would ever meet again, but before she could Jane spoke.

"Be careful what you ask. Be sure your heart can take it. The pendulum can be like the Tarot, changing from day to day, depending on your actions or another person's."

That tidbit of information did nothing to reassure her. "What is the purpose of asking anything if it changes?"

"Everything changes to a certain degree. Once I asked if Hayden would pledge his troth to me. The answer was yes."

"Yet, here you are unmarried."

"Hayden did ask to marry me, but my da refused him. At the time, I refused to speak to my father for weeks. Eventually, I saw all the other fathers were refusing him, too, which made me think something was up. I should have asked if my father would accept Hayden. You can only ask yes and no questions and only one at a time. Some questions are everyday questions."

"What do you mean by that?" It was hard to imagine anything she'd be asking every day. If she was pulling out the pendulum and consulting it on what to eat or wear, she'd not get much done, or it would take much longer. It didn't seem a practical thing to do.

Olio sauntered by, stilling any other protests she might make. Jane held up her muffin bundle, and he selected two. He nodded toward the wagon. Even though he was more than capable of speaking, Meara had learned most of his non-verbal signals.

"She's not up."

He told her, "We need to hit the road soon if we want to get to your family."

"Today?" The possibility had her mentally dancing a jig, but she wound down fast enough when she realized Olio hadn't answered her. Instead, he popped a muffin in his mouth and chewed. Jane shrugged her shoulders. After seventeen long years of having no one, it had been some rough months knowing she had a living and breathing family, but she couldn't quite get to them.

Jane handed Olio the water skin to wash down the muffins. He gave it back and then wandered off into the woods without answering her. Her shock must have shown because Jane chuckled and leaned forward enough to tug her skirt.

"There's no way he could know the time to get to some place he has never been. We'll have to ask questions. The closer we get, the more likely your relatives will hear of it and come looking for us."

That solved that issue. In a few days, she'd see her uncle and her cousins, Ronan and Brigit. Sometimes, she chanted the names right before she went to sleep along with her mother's name, Sorcha, and her father's name, Fulmen. It reminded her that she did belong somewhere.

Olio's appearance made her forget momentarily she was about to ask the pendulum about the possibility of Braeden and she reuniting. The pendulum must have sensed her question. When she held her hand out, it shook, but didn't swing.

Jane's eyebrows lifted. "I see you didn't bother to say your question aloud. When the chain shakes like that it means the question can't be answered now." She wrapped the chain from her own pendulum around her neck and secured it. "As you probably already guessed, you can't use a pendulum to determine all your actions, but by using it daily it improves your intuition. In the morning, when I wake, I ask if I should be on my guard? If it is a good or difficult day? If it is a dreadful day, I can ask questions knowing what to avoid. Sometimes knowing what to look for helps turn a difficult day to good."

That would be useful. Maybe if she'd had a pendulum she would have known Taylor, who said he was from her uncle, was a liar. Who knows, she'd might even be at her relative's home by nightfall.

Chapter Nineteen

B Y DAY THREE of their hasty flight, Meara concluded the priest hadn't been very good about his directions. Either the Cleary family had moved along with their village or they were lost. Since all they truly knew was they were in Ireland, it could have been the latter.

At least the sun was shining, and they were beside a small stream that had bunches of blue wildflowers beside it. The jingle of harnesses reached them from the nearby road. Olio stood beside Seymour as the horse drank his fill, and Rosemary collected wildflowers. The nearby copse of trees provided enough privacy for Jane to do her business.

Meara missed the comfort of an outhouse as opposed to squatting near a bramble bush and baring her backside. The charm, if there had ever been any, of life on the road had grown thin. There was something to be said for a bed that wasn't on wheels. At least, they were no longer being followed by the travelers. Jane assumed because they'd lost Olio as a tracker, they didn't have anyone with the skills to follow them. Meara secretly hoped they'd lost interest in doing so.

The horse hooves sounded closer, drawing her attention to the road to view possibly another farmer heading to market or a family out for a visit. Instead, two draft horses came into view along with a man driving an empty wagon. He pulled the horses to a stop, stood up, and waved his hat as he yelled. "Hoy there. Are you the folks looking for the Clearys? I was told to look for a traveler wagon and a yellow-haired giant."

So much for disguising the wagon. Meara stood and waved back, certain this man had come to lead them there. Olio abandoned his post by the horse to come stand by her. Instead of answering the grinning man, he uttered a sober, "Who wants to know?"

Somehow, he managed to endow the question with an underlying threat. Meara hadn't traveled this far to have her chance to connect with her relations ended before it happened. A hefty shove budged him not. Different tactics would be needed. She approached the man with a smile.

"Hello. I'm Meara Cleary from England. I've traveled far to see my family."

The man placed the hat back on his head, tied off the horses, set the brake, and jumped down from the wagon. He strolled toward her, and they met halfway. Once close enough, his eyes combed over her, starting from her head to her feet then once again. His hand went up to stroke his graying beard.

"You have the look of a Cleary. The female side, of course." He laughed as if amused by his own wit.

Meara laughed with him, but failed to see the humor in his remark. "Do you know where we might find the Clearys?"

"That I do." His eyebrows took a dive toward his nose, and he took a step back as Olio's shadow fell over them. "You might want to tell your man we're relatives."

She'd witnessed Olio's effect on strangers more than once. Women instinctively knew they had nothing to fear from him. Many women attempted to flirt, but it never worked out well since it involved him keeping up his side of the banter, which he seldom did. The men reacted strongly when they spotted him.

She rushed to the side of the bearded stranger who implied they were related. She hooked her arm in his. He tried to shake her off without success. She'd been traveling forever to meet an actual relative and wasn't going to let go.

The man stammered as he tried to free himself. "It's not what it seems. My wife, Nessa, asked me to go see what was what when we heard about someone asking about the Clearys."

"Nessa," she repeated the name. It had a gentle sound to it. Surely, someone with such a pleasant-sounding name would be kind. "How is Nessa related to me?"

The man stared at her arm hooked over his. Reluctantly, she released her arm and stepped back. Even if she hadn't been out of the convent long, she still knew grabbing a man's arm, especially a stranger's, was not the thing to do.

"Don't know. I'm Malcom Weber. My wife Nessa was originally a Cleary, so it's possible you two are cousins. Who are your folks? I thought I knew all the Clearys and their kin."

Excitement bubbled through her when she realized this time she could name her parents. "My mother was Sorcha Cleary and my father was—"

"Sorcha. Yes, I remember." He gave her another long look. "That's who you look like. I was trying to put a name to a face. She left more than a decade ago. Fell in with one of those Druidish fellows. Normally, I don't begrudge them being all about the sanctuary in the woods. Don't figure walking inside a church makes you any better than those who stay without, but my Nessa doesn't feel the same way. She'll be happy to see you, but first you should meet your closest blood, Erin and her brood. If you want to join me on the wagon, I'll drive you there."

Meara started toward Malcom's wagon, but a heavy hand on her shoulder stopped her. Olio announced, "We will follow in our own wagon."

Normally, he didn't use his deep, commanding voice, but when he chose to, it was effective. Meara smiled at her cousin. "Looks like we're following."

"All right. I'll wait for you." Malcom gave them a wave as he headed for his wagon.

Olio kept an eye on him as if expecting the man to twirl around and charge him. Without being asked, she rounded up Rosemary and Jane. There was no way she wasn't going to see her family.

Once everyone was rounded up, Meara climbed up front on the bench seat next to Olio. She wanted to make sure they kept close to her cousin. Seymour broke into a rough trot, probably as a form of protest at having his break interrupted.

"Olio, why were you so mean to my cousin?"

"I was cautious. You seem to forget your safety is my responsibility. Anyone can say he is your cousin. People know you're trying to find your cousin. If someone wanted to harm you, it would cause you to drop your guard."

"Maybe." She didn't want to admit he was right, but he was. "I don't think things are as bad as when I was in England. I may be safe here."

Olio snorted in response.

"What's that supposed to mean?"

"I grew up with the group of travelers who were ready to tear you and Rosemary apart. There could be occasional disagreements, but nothing like what I witnessed. I would have sworn some of them lost their minds. Like when the lost souls invade a drunk person, making them act the fool."

It explained some of the weirdness, but made her feel worse. It made her into the catalyst that caused all the trouble. Jane had rationalized that some of the women were jealous of Rosemary riding with Hayden. She'd accepted that, even though their departure had more of the air of people fleeing for their lives. Had she gotten so used to it that she failed to notice what was going on?

"What do these people want from me? The ones who would trick me?"

"They want the faery horn."

This mysterious instrument had to be kept hidden from those who would use it for nefarious purposes. She'd assumed the Germans wanted it. Didn't see why, since it was rumored they were winning the war.

"Why?"

"To have the faeries do their bidding. A farmer could have a wonderful crop with the use of faery helpers."

"Are you telling me that someone would connive to have a bumper crop of potatoes?"

"Some have done so before. I'm sure you've heard of the stories of why the humans and faeries parted."

"I have. A few wanted faery gold. The others wanted the ability to read minds to control others."

"Aye. How do you know this man is not one of them?"

She twisted on the bench seat to give Olio a long look before answering. Everything he said had merit. They could be riding into trouble, deceived by a helpful manner and fed by a desire for this part of their journey to end.

"I noticed you're still driving the wagon, despite not trusting Malcom's words."

He gave a small cough. "I did not say I didn't trust him. You have to consider all possibilities."

Even though her companion had his doubts, she didn't. No evil had wafted off the man as he'd spoken to her. There was more than a healthy curiosity, but she had yet to determine exactly what it was. "He could be exactly what he appears to be."

"There is that." Olio concluded without bothering to look at her. The way he said it told her the conversation had ended, at least for him, not surprising since it had been the longest conversation she'd ever had with the man.

Green fields marched along with the road. Most had hedgerows while a few had stone walls. Every now and then there'd be a spot of color to relieve the vivid brightness of the grass. Usually, it was a sheep or two. On occasion, there'd be a handful of goats or a milk cow.

A beautiful chestnut mare and her foal stood behind a blind rail fence and welcomed them with a whinny as they passed by. Meara found herself smiling. She could have sworn the horse said something such as what took you so long. Everyone knew horses didn't talk, but if any creature could, it would be a horse or a dog.

The thought of a dog preceded the barking of a black and white sheltie. He raced past Malcom's wagon to keep pace with theirs. Seymour gave him the eye and sidestepped once before resuming his steady gait. The sheltie was content to trot beside them as if shepherding them.

The appetizing scent of baking bread floated out to greet them as they neared a two-story wooden home. Large oak trees shaded the house while clothes flapped on the line on the side. A woman in a red apron exited the house and used the flat of her hand as a sunshield to look in their direction.

"What have ye brought me, Malcom?" She asked the question with a hint of amusement in her voice. Her lips were up in a smile as if Malcom was in the habit of bringing oddities to her house.

"Good day to you, Cousin Erin. Remember your husband searching for a lost relative?"

Her smile vanished. "I'd ask you not to speak of it. The poor man's heart practically broke when he found the girl, the very image of his dead sister, only to lose her in some freak fire while he went up to London to see about his expedition funding. You do me no favors speaking of that."

"Sorry I am to be poking at a sore spot. Is Simon home? I have something guaranteed to cheer him up."

Erin dropped her hand and tilted her hand. "Didn't you hear? Angus forced Simon to go on the trip over there in Egypt. I wanted him to, since work might get his mind off the niece he so briefly met and lost. The man has been looking for that girl as long as we've been married or close to it."

"No. When did he leave?"

"A week."

Meara winced, remembering their leisurely pace across Ireland. If only they had been faster. Since they were working their way across the country about the only way they could have been faster was stealing a team of young horses or possibly a car. Would anyone welcome her here?

Malcom shook his head and cast his eyes downward. "That is a shame, because I've found her."

"That can't be."

"Aye, it is. The image of a young Sorcha or at least all I remember of her before she left for the blasted island. The girl even has a tinge of the unfortunate accent although she tries to hide it."

It wasn't that she was trying to hide her accent, but making it less noticeable giving the general populace's negative attitude to anyone or anything British. Now, that she'd come so far, why this? She knew her uncle had planned an expedition. He even mentioned it in his visit. Everything would be so much easier if Simon and Angus were here.

It was easy to read Erin's body language as she drew closer. The narrowed eyes and hands on her hips shouted suspicion as she approached their wagon. She gave Meara a thorough once over and asked, "What's your name?"

"Meara." Then she figured she should add a last one, too. "Cleary"

"I have to agree with Malcom. You do have the look of her. You even have the same name as Simon's mother. How do I know you aren't clever travelers here to trick me? Maybe you heard about Simon's search? It wasn't exactly a secret."

All this effort, only to be turned away caused her hand to tremble as she reached under her shirt for the locket. Even though Grandmother Biddy warned her not to remove the locket, she felt this time could be an exception. Using her thumbnail, she opened the locket to reveal the photos of her mother and father and handed it to Erin.

"Would a stranger have my mother's locket with her photo and her husband's in it?"

Erin accepted the locket and peered at it. "That's Sorcha, for sure. We didn't have too many folks taking photos around here. I suspect that is from her wedding. Still, that proves nothing, you could have stolen it."

"Dear Lord." She thought she muttered under her breath, but the censorious look she received meant she'd been heard. "I thought you were a kind woman since you nursed my mother and uncle's da, but I'm not sure. You're a hard-headed woman who won't listen to common sense. I have no clue why the faeries thought I could accomplish anything here."

"Did you say faeries?" The irate expression smoothed from her face as she tapped her index finger to her temple.

"I did," she answered hesitantly, not sure what difference it would make. "My father, Fulmen, was a great friend of the faeries."

Erin acknowledged her statement with a head nod. "The Clearys are known for their affinity with the faeries, too. Some say there is even a strain of fey blood in the clan. No good Irishman or woman would turn away someone on a faery mission. Besides, that spark of fire you displayed reminds me of your mother. Sorcha was a fiery one and had no problem putting people in their place."

Had she done such a thing? She hadn't meant to. The house door banged open before she could apologize and a tall lad exited with the look of his father. He already had the broad shoulders of a man, but his face retained the soft, unlined look of a person untouched by hardship.

"Ma, I thought I heard wagon wheels—" His speech faltered and stopped when he spotted them. He held up one hand in greeting and moved forward. "Yes, hi."

Meara smiled, while Olio twisted to gaze at the lad, straightening to his full height. Even though the boy's eyebrows went up a bit, he held his ground. Much more than most men did when meeting Olio.

The proud father had mentioned his children's names. Brigit, she remembered easy enough because of Saint Brigit and the son was Ronan. She should remember them well enough since she whispered them to herself before falling asleep to remind herself that she did belong somewhere.

"I'm Meara. If you're Ronan, then we're cousins."

"It's my bad luck to be Ronan."

"Why bad luck?"

He gave a dramatic sigh. Before he could answer a young woman came around the side of the house toting a laundry basket. She waved in their direction. "Ignore Ronan. My brother is full of theatrics. He should go act in The Abbey Theatre. Everything is so fraught with feeling." She placed the basket on one hip and placed the back of her free hand against her forehead and uttered in a melodramatic manner. "Woe is me. All the pretty girls are related to me."

Erin tried hard to suppress a smile. "Leave off. Your brother isn't the callous brick that you are."

"Yes, I noticed. Who might our company be?"

Erin nodded in Meara's direction. "This is your cousin, Meara. Perhaps the handsome man beside her is her husband. So far, he's said nothing for himself. Malcom, you know."

"How are you?" She directed the question to Meara, but surprisingly, Olio answered.

"I'm better seeing your fine face. Meara isn't my wife if you were wondering."

Brigit colored under the blatant flattery, but Meara's jaw dropped in surprise. What had come over her traveling companion?

Erin, the mother, took control of the situation. "Well, now, instead of conducting our business out in public for everyone to see, why not duck in for a cuppa."

Malcom responded with an enthusiastic yes, tied off his horse, and jumped to the ground. Meara knew she couldn't leave her friends in the wagon. "I'd welcome some tea, but only if my friends, Rosemary and Jane are invited, too."

"Where might they be?" Erin swiveled her head in several directions.

The shutters behind her back opened, and Rosemary poked out her head. "We're in here."

Her friend thrust out half her torso, forcing both Olio and Meara to move. Her attention went to Ronan, standing there with his brows lifted and mouth slightly opened. She commented possibly to Meara, but loud enough to carry. "Now, he's a fine one,"

Rosemary disappeared back inside the wagon with a grumble as Jane took her place. The woman grinned, which was unusual, and waved at the Cleary family. "Too young," she announced and popped her head back inside.

Erin sucked her lips in and placed her hands back on her hips. "The faeries never do anything in halves. Everyone come in. I'll put on two kettles." She moved toward the house to do so.

Brigit had dropped her dramatic pose and turned to follow her mother. "I could use some tea, too."

Her mother must have heard her declaration since she turned so fast her skirt belled out. "Laundry first, then tea."

Ronan smirked at his sister, but was caught by his mother, who reminded him, "Chickens don't feed themselves."

He gave a sigh and headed off.

That was her first official meeting with her young cousins and aunt. Meara was anxious to know more about them. The only contact she had with people her age, besides Braeden and Rosemary, was at the few barn dances she attended. Technically, she should count Adelaide and her friends, but she chose not to. It would be like calling a hungry a bear a friend when all it really wanted to do was eat you. Here she was in Ireland at her uncle's home. The future was definitely looking up.

Chapter Twenty

THE LEAVES TURNED and fell as summer turned to autumn. Erin welcomed Olio's help on the farm since Simon had left. Ronan and Olio put in fence posts and created a new hen house. There were shingles on the roof that needed fixing. While the weather remained mild, the four girls slept in Brigit's room, often giggling and talking way into the night.

It was easy to ignore her father's urgings that came while she slept. The guilt would sometimes stab at her at unexpected times, making her determined to do something the next day, but her intentions lessened each morning at the thought of leaving her new-found family. A disturbing dream featuring a faceless soldier with Braeden's voice who demanded she resume her mission or hate would triumph forced her doubts to the surface, not that they had been buried that deep. It would be lovely to stay here with her newfound family doing whatever families did.

The next morning had a hint of frost in it. As the group huddled around the table, nursing their morning tea, Erin came into the room brandishing several mismatched worn gloves. A huge moan came from her cousins who recognized the significance of such items.

"What is it?"

"It's time to harvest the potatoes." Ronan explained.

His sister joined the conversation. "It's backbreaking work, but the spuds see us through the winter. At least with the four of you, the work will be less. We'll be asked to help at other places such as the Widow

Mclaren's. Then it will be the second haying season."

Her brother groaned, as Brigit continued. "It's a good thing you got the other things done around the farm first. There will be no time now."

Meara listened to the verbal recitation of everything that needed to be done before the snow flew, aware that if things went right, they'd be long gone before the first snow. At least, she could be. It didn't feel right to ask so much of others.

Erin circled the table, placing a pair of gloves on the table for the first two. When she came to her, Meara, anxious to prove her determination to her father, the faeries, and the faceless soldiers, almost shouted her question.

"Do you know where there is an ash tree big enough for my mother to climb when she was young?"

Erin hesitated, with the gloves in hand. Her eyes rolled back in her head as she talked to herself. "Ash tree, big enough to climb." She shook her head. "Can't think of any."

Well, that hadn't worked out well. Why had she expected it to be so simple?

Erin continued around the table until she handed out the gloves. "I was friends with Sorcha as a child. I'd imagine any tree that was big enough to climb when she was young would be bigger now. That was so long ago. Ronan might know were there any some similar trees."

Ronan looked up and managed a grin. "Those days are gone. Now, I'm a working man. Why do you want to know?"

She shrugged her shoulders not wanting to reveal the story. Erin clicked her tongue and gave her a bit of the fish eye. "I raised a pair of wily devils, these two. So I know when the truth isn't being told to me."

Olio put his cup down hard enough to draw her attention. His stern look served as a reminder that the more they were told the harder it would be. You could never tell when someone might break under pressure, but she had to say something. To say nothing would be rude and suspicious.

Meara gave a dramatic sigh, learning much from Ronan over their short association. "It's silly really. I had a dream. Maybe a vision. Whatever it was, I knew my mother had buried something near the ash tree where she used to play. Maybe it's nothing, but I'd like to try to find it."

Erin appeared thoughtful as she returned to her seat and poured herself some tea. "I can understand how something like that can be precious, even more so having never known your mother. How does this fit into your mission?"

Why had she even mentioned the mission to begin? Not knowing what to say, Meara remained silent using Grandmother Biddy's technique of stillness that supposedly unnerved people. Unfortunately, Rosemary hadn't been introduced to the technique.

"There's some artifact that has been buried and has to be found to end the war."

Both she and Olio regarded the chatty brunette with a mixture of astonishment and shock. Meara hadn't been too forthcoming with the facts, certain her friend would leave her at any time, trading their adventures for a missus in front of her name. Yet, somehow, she'd unearthed enough facts to have an inkling of what was going on.

"It's too bad that Simon isn't here. This is his strong point hunting out hidden artifacts. Both he and Angus attended archeology schools and have gone on digs for ancient relics. That's where they are now. You'd think England would have its fill of everything Egyptian, but they haven't."

"What would he tell me to do?"

This time Brigit answered, her hands fluttering through the air as she spoke. "You got to make a grid as much to scale as possible. Mark each square out where you've searched, to make sure you don't go back to the same spot."

That made sense. She could do that. All she needed now was the location of the ash trees. "So, are there many ash trees on the farm?"

Ronan chuckled, noticing her puzzlement, he explained, "Ash is one of the trees sacred to both the Druids and faeries. Plenty grow on their own, but a few have been planted here and there."

Every step she took forward resulted in her taking two back. There had to be a better way. Erin slapped the table with her gloves. "Those potatoes aren't going to get themselves dug. We got work to do. Ronan can get out the dowsing rods later, and see if he can't find this thing you seek."

Not knowing how to answer, she managed a smile for Ronan, who looked agreeable to the idea. Surely, they'd use the dowsing rods, whatever they were, and find the horn piece. With her mind a little more at ease, she settled into a long day of combing the earth with rakes, shovels, and pitchforks looking for the elusive potatoes. Rosemary got the easy job of throwing them in the baskets while Jane drove the wagon.

It was a dirty job, but not one she minded. It made her feel in touch with the earth. Some of her happiest times were when she'd had her hands immersed in the convent garden. While a contented feeling wrapped around her and soaked into her bones, something else needled her. It felt like something was watching her.

It wasn't anything as simple as a bird or a dog, but something evil. It had the heaviness of sickness and the smell of decay. Whoever the owner was of such a thing, she was certain she'd prefer not to meet. Still, she made subtle sweeps of the area as she knelt to pick up a potato. In the brush, there weren't any evil eyes staring out at her. No strangers standing in the shadows. Nothing.

Her gut told her something was wrong, and Grandmother Biddy reminded her to trust her gut. If she had pulled a card or used a pendulum, she'd know what was up. Whatever it was, it was waiting for her to find the artifact. It would wait until she found all three, because without her it could do nothing. This meant if she found nothing, she was fine. The thought eased her apprehensions a little, but she knew finding nothing was not an answer.

The potato harvest took days. When the Cleary farm was done, Olio, Ronan, and Jane went to help the neighbors with their crops. The rest of them stayed to clean and sort potatoes and help carry them to the root cellar. Erin told tales about each of the relatives. She even remembered a little about her parents' courtship. Erin and Simon hadn't been courting yet, but in a small area everyone knew everyone else.

Just when Meara thought the harvesting was over. Brigit informed her, with a smile, that there was still carrots and turnips to dig. Since they hadn't put in massive amounts, the women could get the work done on their own. The days tended to run into each other with the digging, cleaning, cooking, and canning. Most of the root vegetables weren't canned, since they kept moderately well in the cellar. Others were mixed together and canned perfect for a rich stew or soup.

The work was satisfying, but exhausting. Each night she tumbled into bed. Jane would often tease Rosemary about a handsome lad she'd met that day, doling out information that the man was single and in need of a wife. When Rosemary was squirming with interest and begging to know more, Jane inevitably added something about the man being toothless and almost eighty-five.

It was hard to know if there was even such a man or it if was all a game. She fell hard asleep never hearing the result of Jane's latest tale. Often, in her dreams, she worked. Sometimes, she even dreamed of harvesting, other times traveling, but this time she found herself in a low fog unsure of her way.

A gentle voice called her name. "Meara, where are you?"

"I'm here."

Even though she was lost in the mist, she felt no fear. The voice sounded familiar and loving.

"Where?"

"Over here," she shouted again, certain that the owner was drawing closer. The hair rose on her arms as she tried to peer through the mist. Her heartbeat doubled as she tried to identify the form moving toward her. The slender silhouette was female. As she drew closer, the light in the distance lit up the fiery mass of hair. Her breath caught. It was her mother. She knew it,

instinctively.

The woman gave her a wishful smile and held open her arms. Meara catapulted herself into them. "Mother."

"Yes, I'm here." She brushed a kiss on Meara's hair.

Tears filled her eyes. She tried blinking them away, but her eyes filled again. What was wrong with her? She could feel her mother's hand smoothing her waves and the warmth of her body. "You're here."

"Hush, child. Don't take on so. The faeries helped me reach you. Your mind is so busy that sleep is the only time your mind is free."

She pulled back enough to look at her mother's unlined face. "You look so young."

"Not too surprising. I died only a few years older than you. Often, spirits retain the same form as when they lived, but some choose to go to happier times when they can walk without a cane or a younger version that their loved ones who have gone before will recognize."

"Oh. Are you floating around in a white robe playing a harp?" That was part of what she was taught in the convent. The departed were also supposed to be part of a celestial choir that sang day and night. While most of the time she hadn't minded singing, doing it non-stop would be boring and a bit overwhelming.

"Goodness. No. Spirits have lives, rather busy ones, which surprised me. We have spirit schools, spirit hospitals where we heal the mental trauma people still hang onto when they passed. Most of all, we help our loved ones that still remain on the other side of the veil."

Until recently, she couldn't remember any contact with her mother. None. Her lips pulled down in a frown at the realization.

"No sad faces, daughter. I did try to contact you, but it was difficult. At the convent, you were so busy with your various tasks and your mind was seldom open to other things. The fact you never knew me meant when I did come, you'd not recognize my face or voice. It was only in the forest that I felt I made some progress in reaching you."

"That was you? I always felt when I was there under my favorite tree that I wasn't alone."

"Sometimes, it was me, other times, your father, and always the faeries who loved that particular glen."

A pleasant feeling had always drawn her back to the place. She'd initially assumed it was a feeling of belonging. If her family was with her, that explained it. "I always loved it there."

"I know."

She drew back again, enough to see her mother who so much looked like her, but different. An air of peace and tranquility wrapped around her mother, something Meara did not have. "Why have you come now? I'm glad you did, but why not before?"

Her mother reached for her hand, entwined their fingers and gave a small tug. "Walk with me."

They turned and walked through the mist, which shimmered and changed colors as they moved, going from a ruby red to bright orange, then settling into yellow, before turning green. She found herself watching it with one eye as they strolled, waiting for the next color and wondering about its meaning.

"You never answered me."

"I did. I was there, but you couldn't see or hear me. We spoke briefly before. Even now, there is your father and several other spirits assisting me so I can have this face to face conversation with you. Normally, the best we spirits can do is give a word or two, a thought or a feeling. Long conversations are difficult."

"Father did."

"Yes, he did, when you escaped the bombing, but you noticed he hasn't lately. Such work takes a great amount of energy. Personally, I think he had been saving up energy for that moment."

That would mean he had to know there would be a bombing. "Do you know the future?"

"In some ways. Every day, everything you do changes the future. When you wake up tomorrow the future will be different than it was today."

Her impulse to ask if she could accomplish the mission she was given faded. To say anything would sound like whining. If she knew her mission never succeeded and she stopped right now, would it make the current situation worse than it was? Not knowing what to say, she squeezed her mother's hand.

"I understand. More than you expect. When I met your father, I was ready to be madly in love. I had grown tired of the local lads trying to catch my interest and fell headlong for your da. He did likewise for me. All was good, fiery and intense. I hadn't expected to find a horn while we were exploring."

"Why did you two find it?"

"Good question, one I asked myself more than once. Apparently, it had been hidden from human eyes by faery magic. It had been created by both human and faery hands, fashioned for human use. Despite the falling out between the two races, the faeries had never hardened their hearts. It's incomprehensible for them to do so."

"They can't blow this horn themselves and come to the rescue?"

Her mother gave a small sigh before continuing. "I wish they could. It would make things so much easier. I hate for my darling daughter to face all these trials. When your father and I fell in love, we thought that was it and our lives were perfect. No more needed to be done, but evil exists in the world. Even though it might not have been my wish to fight against evil, it was our fate."

"Couldn't you have just ignored it? Lived a quiet life?"

Her mother bestowed a sad look upon her. "In some ways, you are so like me. That's what Fulmen and I hoped to do when we moved to the farm he'd inherited. We foolishly believed that by moving, we'd fool fate. I'm not sure if we would have died if we stayed at our other home or if our actions caused it to happen. Hiding from evil doesn't make it go away. Doing nothing is not a solution, either."

The comment pierced her like an arrow. It wasn't so much that she was not doing anything, it was that others were too busy to help her. "Ronan is going to use his dowsing rods to help me find it."

"That's all well and good. Don't wait on others to do what should be done."

Her mother reminded her of Erin. She had the same tone her aunt used to scold her children. Instead of being upset, the notion rather pleased her. She'd had enough of do this, don't do that in her life, but a maternal scold came from love, wanting what was best for the children.

"Are you saying I should try the dowsing rods on my own?"

"You could."

The possibility thrilled her. Each day, something new unfolded, teaching and revealing the magic of her heritage. "I will!"

A light tinkling laughter filled the air between them. "I have absolute confidence in you. I know you will."

Ronan's complaint about the dozens of ash trees on the farm came to mind. "How will I know which ash tree it is?"

Her mother placed her free hand over her heart, and her lips moved.

A violent shaking occurred, moving her whole body while her name was repeated.

"Meara. Meara. Did you hear what Jane said? There is a pair of brothers nearby, only in their twenties. Can you believe that?"

She blinked. Rosemary's face came into focus as her mother's faded, then disappeared. What had happened? Meara lay there in a daze as she tried to recall what her mother said. Her friend poked her.

"Didn't you hear me?"

Upset that her visit with her mother had ended abruptly, and she'd missed a major clue, she snapped at her friend. "Are men all you think about? There's more in life. Maybe if you weren't so gung-ho to get married, you'd meet someone, become friends, fall in love. With your wide eyes and gaping mouth, signaling your attentions, the men all run and hide."

Her friend's complexion whitened with each word until she finally burst into tears.

Jane gave her a reproving look. "Don't you think that was a bit harsh?"

Rosemary ran from the room crying. Meara started after her, but

Jane grabbed her arm. "Let her go. Even if you spoke in haste, your words were true enough. It may have been something she needed to hear. Give her time. I didn't expect such a snap of temper out of you, but Grandmother Biddy warned me it was there."

Her shoulders slumped when she realized she may have severed the friendship between Rosemary and her.

Jane patted her on the back. "No worries. Sometimes being a friend means speaking the truth."

Is that what she did or had she just barked at her friend out of frustration? Either way the results were the same. Had her parents' move hastened their fate or would they have lived out a long, happy life together? Nothing came to mind. If intuition was supposed to be helping her, then it was failing dismally.

"Meara, it does you no good to blame yourself." Jane pushed up on her elbows, nudging Brigit in the process. The other girl grumbled drowsily. "Here I thought it would be fun having sisters. I had no clue how much sleep I'd sacrifice."

Sacrifice, the word resonated inside of Meara. Relationships had rewards, but they also demanded sacrifices.

Chapter Twenty-One

A STRONG CHILLY WIND rustled the leaves on the trees. Ronan, in the process of buttoning up his jacket, gave Meara dowsing lessons before he left to help a nearby neighbor with his feed corn harvest.

"Hold out the rods straight. Don't let them touch."

She held the willow wands in her hands. Each one had a natural grip formed by branches that grew in a Y shape. The bark had been peeled off and the limb whittled down to a tip on each one.

"You're holding on too hard."

His rushed instructions made no sense. "I have to hold on or the rods will fall to the ground."

Ronan reached for the rods to demonstrate. "Like this. Keep your fingers loose to allow for movement. When you've found what you're searching for, the tips come together."

"I think I understand." She reached for the willow sticks and practiced her hold. "Like this."

"Much better."

An horn sounded outside, causing Olio to bolt from the table. "That's our ride."

A truck rumbled in the driveway. Inside the fenced sides around the truck bed, see the hats and heads of the various male neighbors bobbed about. A few of the men smoked while most of them conversed. Ronan and Olio burst out of the house. Some comments were called out, but she couldn't hear them well.

Brigit joined them at the window. "It's a blessing old man Henry doesn't believe in women working the field."

"That means we have an entire day free, then."

Erin entered the room carrying an armload of baskets. "Not so fast, girls. We have nuts to harvest before the squirrels steal them all. Go get your coats on."

Since both Rosemary and Meara had arrived in warm weather, they brought no coats. Rosemary had one of Erin's old coats while Meara had Ronan's outgrown jacket. The dark, rough wool was none too attractive, but it was warm. When the winds blew, that was all that mattered.

There were a couple of walnut trees on the property and hickory and chestnut trees in the woods. Since Jane had complained about being cheated out of the chance to work the fields, Erin encouraged her to climb the trees and knock down the nuts. After a busy day of nut collecting, the women walked back to the house with heavy baskets.

Jane was the nearest to her. "I know things have been hectic, but we need to dig into Grandmother Biddy's boxes. There has to be some useful spells in there."

Erin glanced back at them. "You girls talking about spells and charms?"

Aware such talk could get you imprisoned and possibly hanged in some areas, Meara said nothing, but Jane felt the need to answer. "Yes, we were. Meara will have to be off on her mission soon enough. It would help if she had some useful charms and spells."

There were a few seconds of silence, which felt longer since Meara was holding her breath.

"I agree. I may be able to help. My granny gave me her books of spells. Can't say I've even opened it for years. With a family and the threat of the church hanging over me, I put it away, but I know where it is. Maybe we can get it down and look through it."

Even though their hostess's response shocked her, it was nothing compared to Brigit's gaping mouth astonishment.

"Mother, I never knew anything about this."

"No need for you to. Every now and then, a mother can come up with a few surprises. Let's put the nuts in the wood boxes and latch them well. Later, we'll shell them, probably on a winter day."

Their steps picked up as they hurried to the house, determined to see what other surprises awaited. Once the nuts had been stored, and jackets hung on the hooks, the girls gathered around the table to wait. Erin had forbidden anyone helping her locate the book since she wanted to keep her hiding place secret.

Brigit pushed up from the table. "I'm going to fill a kettle. Anyone else want tea?"

After several ayes, she puttered around the kitchen putting the tea together. The wind whipped around the house rattling the windows.

Jane glanced toward the outside and grimaced. "I'm glad I didn't go with the men. I imagine it will be a chilly job."

"Aye." Erin agreed as she entered the room with a massive, dark book. "Afraid winter might be coming early. Means everyone will be frantic to get their crops in. Imagine we won't see the men until after dark."

"Makes me even more glad to be here at the table then," Jane commented. "Some of the fellows can be a bit short when tired."

"I bet I can name some names," Brigit called from her place at the stove.

Before she could, her mother hushed her. "It's always better to focus on a person's good traits, than his bad moments."

"Yes, Mother." Brigit answered dutifully, but made a face as soon as her mother's back was turned.

"I saw that." Erin spoke without turning around. She winked at Meara and smoothed her hand over the book.

"That's one big book."

"It is. My granny not only wrote down recipes for medicine, but she had concoctions for getting stains out of clothes, a rinse for making your hair shiny, how to keep your garden bug free."

Brigit interrupted as she poured hot water into the teapot. "Why is this the first time I've heard of this?"

"It might not have been the first time I talked about it, but it is the first you've listened. Much of the stuff I do comes from this book. A good part is in my head. Now I decided it was time to have a look and see if there might be anything useful for our guests."

Rosemary put her elbows on the table and leaned forward to peer into the book. "Might there be a love spell in there?"

It was hard not to sigh since, obviously, Rosemary hadn't taken anything to heart that Meara had said the previous evening.

"No need to look. There is none. Granny was not one to believe in making someone love you. Most young girls would pick a fine-looking fellow without an ounce of ambition. In the end, that would be something you'd be regretting. Before long, you'd look for a spell to get rid of him. Does anyone really want someone who doesn't love you? Someone who has to be tricked into forming a bond? Someone who, if they could be forced under a spell to join with you, could easily be taken from you with another's love spell."

Rosemary grimaced and sat back in her chair. "When you put it that way, I'm not interested."

Inside the book was heavy parchment paper and spidery handwriting. Erin slowly turned the pages her eyes moving across them as she read each heading before moving on to the next page. She murmured the names.

"To keep your focus."

Meara thought she might need that one. Was it more of not keeping her focus or things not coming together to keep her going?

"Protection spell to fight against envy."

If only envy was all she had to worry about. "How does that spell work?"

Erin stopped turning pages, and looked around for who asked. Meara waved her hand and angled her head to look at her as she spoke.

"Not sure if this is the one you want. You have to know the name of whoever wishes you harm."

"That might be a problem."

Erin arched her brows and turned the page. "Here is a Balefire spell guaranteed to banish your worries."

"That sounds wonderful. Why doesn't everyone do that one?"

Jane wrinkled her nose. "There is the issue with persecution. In case, you forgot."

She, of all people, should remember. "How does it work?"

"Let me see." Her finger moved down the page as she read. "It involves a large fire. Slips of paper on which you write down your worries, a bundle of weeds, some yarrow and an orange."

Brigit carried the tea tray to the table and bent to move it to the center. "I have an orange Kenny Foster gave me. Probably thought I'd turn my affection his way. Does it matter if it is a little withered?"

"Shouldn't since it is going into the fire, anyhow."

A discussion erupted about which troubles or worries they should burn. Jane was in favor of everything they could think of including war, famine, and disease. The idea conflicted Meara. If it did work, why hadn't someone done it already? Still, on the other hand, it couldn't hurt. Might try the focus spell, too.

When the men arrived home, they were gathered around a bonfire throwing in slips of paper they'd written down individual worries on. Olio walked by without a comment, but that wasn't Ronan's way.

"You're too early for Guy Fawkes Day."

Brigit gave her brother a disdainful glance. "Move along idgit. We're ridding ourselves of worries."

"Well, then, continue. I'll have to see what I can find to eat."

Not done with tormenting her brother, she called out. "There are nuts in the barn."

The rest of the women continued the spell, ignoring the banter the best they could.

Rosemary threw the weeds on the fire. "By this bane, I cancel."

Jane added the yarrow. "By this boon, I cancel."

They each named their worries, before tossing the slip into the fire. Then they took turns peeling the orange and throwing the peel into the fire, saying, "Troubles begone. Sweetness begins."

Meara slept well that night and for several nights afterwards. She'd forgotten her troubles and was content to help her Aunt Erin with household matters. Jane on the other hand was restless since a traveler was not a settler. She mentioned this several times within her hearing.

There seemed to be something she should be doing, but Meara couldn't quite remember. The heat from the fire, the smell of baking sweets lulled her into a half-sleep.

The voice poked at her and irritated her. "Do you have my dowsing rods? A neighbor's well has gone dry."

Another joined it.

"Can't you see she's asleep?"

Yes, sleep, that's what she needed. She tumbled back into the land of slumber where whirling mists and whispering claimed her. At one point, she thought she was flying as her body drifted through the air, but then she settled into a comfy bed.

A cool hand settled on her head. "She's burning up. I hope it's not the influenza."

For days, she floated in and out of wakefulness with proddings and probings disturbing her. Liquids both warm and cool poured down her throat. The overwhelming smell of onion poultice almost brought her out, but the lure of the safety of sleep pulled at her.

For one moment, a clarity ensued, and she tried to push upward into wakefulness. The moment vanished as abruptly as it came, sending her spiraling back into slumber.

In her sleep, she enjoyed a picnic with Braeden, picking flowers, walking in the sun dappled woods. Everything good happened when she slept.

Jane's voice penetrated her slumber. "I think she's been bewitched."

"Doesn't she wear all those charms to keep her safe? Shouldn't that have protected her?" Rosemary's question resonated.

"Those are to protect the body. We assume danger would come in a physical form, but it hasn't. Someone or something has attacked her mind. This is dark magic perpetuated by someone who knows only fear and hatred. I have no clue what has been done, but we have to find some way to make Meara want to come back to us."

Burnt feathers and ammonia capsules were waved under her nose. Meara to rolled away in protest, but never waking. Stomping and pans banging annoyed more than anything else. Why would she want to go somewhere where they made so much noise?

"I'll go get Grandmother Biddy's box. There is bound to be something in it." Jane called out as she walked to the door.

"No. Wait. We're forgetting all those who care about Meara." Erin explained in a somber tone. "We need to call on her parents. All who love her. The faeries. Anyone you can think of."

Yes, call my parents. I'd like to visit with them. Haven't seen them in quite a while.

Amid stomping, and hand clapping, and the smell of candles lit, she could feel the vibrations surging through her body when her mother and father shimmered into existence. They held out their hands to her.

"Come, sweetheart, you've lingered too long in this place. It's time to go."

Each parent took a hand, pulling her upward out of her nice, soft bed.

"It's nice here," she whined. *"Out there it's loud, bright, and smells bad."*

Her mother spoke in a comforting voice. "Maybe so, but you belong out there. A spell has been put on you. One I don't understand. Once you wake up, you'll need some Tiger's Eye, Black Tourmaline, or Peridot to protect you from another psychic attack."

"I suggest you wear all three, and hematite, too," her father added.

They kept pulling her upward out of her cozy place, out of the warmth, and her drowsy state until an icy splash of water awoke her.

A circle of concerned faces surrounded her, but she noticed the empty bucket was in Rosemary's hand.

"I see you waited your time to get me back for my remark."

"What remark?"

Her friend picked up her hand and knelt beside her bed. "You've been like a dead person these weeks. We've tried all sorts of remedies. Even broke down and called the doctor, who acted the fool, hurrying out of the house as if afraid. I came up with the idea of ice water. Thank Mother Mary, it brought you about."

It hadn't been the water or Mary, but her parents, but she decided not to mention it. If Rosemary wanted to think it was water, then why not? Meara attempted to push herself into a sitting position, but found herself too weak to do so. What had happened to her?

Chapter Twenty-Two

CHRISTMAS ARRIVED WITH MEARA still in recovery mode. Olio carried her to the living room where they lit candles and sang traditional songs and a fast-paced one Meara had never heard about bells and horses. With the smell of warm gingerbread tantalized her nose, Erin allowed her to deviate from her invalid diet of broth for a bite or two.

Recovery took longer than her illness. Each day she'd push herself even if it was as simple as walking across the room. Winter hit with a vengeance, but Erin, a firm supporter of the healing benefits of fresh air, bundled Meara up for a short walk outside.

Without the distraction of green grass, flowers, or bees, the outdoors resembled a ghost land dusted with white snow. The trees with barren branches would make it hard to identify an ash. As soon as the thought entered her head, she knew immediately where the horn was hidden.

"I know." She stumbled off in the direction with Erin and Rosemary yelling at her to stop, but she couldn't. If she did, the direction might stop, too. A stitch formed in her side, but she kept on going.

"You're leaving Cleary land."

Erin's comment reached her, but she knew what she was doing and where she was going. At one point, she'd have sworn there were eyes in the bushes watching her. Ireland has no real predators. If she discounted people, she had nothing to worry about.

Her hand pressed against her heart, which was guiding her. It felt like there was a magnetic pull between herself and the object she was bound to find. The item called her, and she was helpless to refuse. Her feet came to a stop in a clearing where no trees existed, but there was a stump of what may have been a sizable tree.

Without a thought, she dropped to her knees and pawed at the frozen ground until her hands were bloody. The tips of her fingers were raw and her nails ragged as she attempted to locate the missing piece.

"Stop it!" Rosemary grabbed Meara's shoulders in a tight lock.

"I have to find it. It's here at the foot of the ash tree."

Erin joined them and knelt beside Meara examining her hands. "You'll not be undoing all the work I did to get you well."

"I have to find it."

Erin shook her head. "We'll send Olio out to dig. If anyone can penetrate the frozen ground, he can."

How could she make them understand that the faeries wouldn't allow anyone else to find it? She knew. Didn't know how, but she knew. "I have to find it. Me. It's my mission."

Rosemary loosened her hold on Meara and plopped down beside her. "If you and the faeries are such friends, why not ask for their help in digging up the thing?"

"Oh, yeah, that'd be rich. What should I say? Dear friend faeries, I need your help, I've come this far, but can do no more." She started the words in a sarcastic vein, but found her intention and voice changing as she went. "Help me, please."

A buzz of power shot through her. She rested back on her abused hands.

"It's beautiful." Erin stretched out her hand toward Meara's lap and pulled it back. "I shouldn't touch it. It isn't meant for me."

In her lap, was a beautiful silver column about eight inches long. A tiny ivy vine swirled about it. She tentatively touched it with her index fingers just to see if it was solid. It was—and surprisingly alive. It pulsed under her fingers.

"We found it."

An awe-struck Rosemary clarified the situation. "You found it."

"I did in a way. It's time to leave. I have to find the second one."

The wind blew, cracking the ice coating on the branches, reminding them with a touch that it was very much winter. Meara wrapped her fingers around the horn section, obtaining strength from it. Contact allowed her to see what the entire horn would look like when assemble. As she fingered the column, an impression of a Scottish glade came to mind.

"I know where the second piece is."

Erin helped her up, muttering about Meara undoing all the work she had done in making her well, and then asked, "How do you know this?"

"I don't, but this part of the horn does. It can feel the other part calling it. They want to be together. I need to go now."

Even though the urgency to leave was so real, no one else felt it, resulting in a delay. Erin insisted she needed to get better, and unfortunately, Meara's body gave all sorts of signs the woman was correct. If that wasn't enough, Seymour, the wagon horse was in no condition to make the trip to Scotland across Ireland, the water by ferry, and then more land. On top of that, Olio announced he couldn't accompany them. He'd fallen for a local girl while harvesting and had received permission to court her.

How could she be given a mission and no way to complete it? Personally, she wouldn't have picked herself, but someone more suitable such as Olio who was strong and formidable. Why was he leaving her now? Wasn't his job to protect her?"

"People come into your life for a purpose, but when that purpose has been served, they leave."

She knew that wasn't her own thought since she had no desire for Olio to leave. *"Can't you see I need him to complete my task?"*

"He would be a liability. A man as big and strong as him would be memorable. His leaving makes space available for someone new."

It wasn't like she was advertising for people to help her rid the world of evil. Even if she was, she had no way to pay them, which usually killed anyone's desire to assist. In a world that tended to value men over women, three women alone would not fare well, despite their knife-throwing skills.

Brigit provided the first light at the end of the tunnel. "Maybe you could take one of the draft horses. We won't need both, and you should be back before too long, right?"

Draft horses were valuable creatures, especially to farmers. Aunt Erin would turn down the generous offer. With her husband gone, she might not even have the authority to make such a decision.

Erin said, "Those draft horses can be a handful. It would take someone familiar with them to handle them."

Jane tensed up, probably assuming her driving skills had been called into question, while Meara thought it might be Erin's roundabout way of saying no. Erin pinned her son with a significant gaze.

"I'll go too," Ronan volunteered. "I always hoped for a bit of adventure."

"See, another one was provided."

Meara ground her teeth, wishing she knew who was speaking. She was sure she'd recognized her father or mother's voice, but this was a new one altogether. Her head had become a meeting place for disembodied voices, or she was going crazy. Both options held equal weight.

Over the ensuing week, they prepared to leave. Brigit made a small box for the horn piece, even including two more compartments for the missing pieces, despite having no clue what size they might be. She assumed they'd be similar.

Erin gathered up food stuffs including smoked meat. One evening she surprised them by showing up with a pile of cast off clothes, battered work boots, and a pair of scissors. "Ladies, it's time to get transformed."

Jane stopped sharpening her knives long enough to listen. "What do you mean? I've traveled enough to know I don't need to be transformed."

"You're wrong." Erin still clutching the scissors in one hand, placed her balled fist on one hip. "Since you've been hanging out with country Irish, you probably figure everyone is alike. They aren't. You'll be going through Dublin to catch the ferry. My son, no matter how clever he thinks he is, will not provide enough protection for three women. It would be best if you go disguised as boys."

A low growl from Jane greeted this pronouncement. Meara, however, could see how it made sense and plopped down in the kitchen chair. "Do me first. I can't wait until I have the freedom of wearing pants and not caring how I look."

"Hey!" Ronan complained, because he did take a lot of care in his appearance.

A few scissor passes rid her of her wayward hair, exposing some quarrelsome cowlicks that caused her hair to stick straight up. Rosemary chuckled at the sight.

"No girl would ever go out like that. I'm next." She made a show of kissing her curls goodbye before she sat.

Meara joined Jane in picking out some clothes that might suit and carried them off to the bedroom to try them on. Ronan sat back and watched the show, joking about the procedure.

"There was many a time I dreamt about girls taking off my clothes, but never putting them on."

Brigit gave her brother a hearty shove. "Stop it. I'll hear none of it."

After their transformation, they sat around the table wearing battered hats that hid their newly shorn hair as they studied a map. Ronan put his finger on one road that led to Dublin. "Easter Sunday comes on the twenty-third this year. It's my hope to be in and out of Dublin before that happens. Every good Catholic will be in church. Us wandering through is bound to strike someone as peculiar. Our goal is to be in Scotland by Easter. The Scots won't notice us not being good Catholics and all, since they are few and far between. I also heard they may claim religion, but seldom bow to it."

Uncertain what her cousin hinted at, Meara chose to ask. "What do you mean?"

"Most aren't known for attending mass on a regular basis. If they saw us, it wouldn't cause any suspicion like it would here."

Jane frowned as Ronan announced their plans as opposed to asking for suggestions. Later, she'd grumble about how the boy felt he could take the lead since he'd been born with different plumbing. When it came to travel about the isle, Jane had the experience.

Instead of listening, Rosemary was admiring herself in a mirror. "I do make a rather handsome boy. It might be hard for the girls not to fall in love with me."

Knowing her cousin expected feedback, Meara was happy to give it. "Sounds great, Ronan. The sooner we're in Scotland the better."

He gave a nod and folded up the map. Erin bustled in and shooed them all off to bed. The incongruity of being treated like a child, then expected to accomplish a mission no adult had so far hadn't escaped her. The weight of such an undertaking settled on her making each step up the stairs arduous. If a person was doing the right thing, shouldn't everything be sweetness and light? Maybe it was her attitude. Another balefire ritual would have served them well.

Once they arrived in the room, Meara lay down, but she couldn't get to sleep with Jane grumbling about Ronan's cocksure attitude. Brigit provided several examples of the cousin's cockiness only whipping Jane into more of a mood.

She tried to close the two out by rolling the other way only to meet Rosemary's gaze. She pulled out the hand mirror from under the covers and stared at herself.

"I do make a handsome boy. Don't you think so?"

"Yes, you're a very pretty boy." She agreed, thinking the world needed much more than this rag tailed group to save them. With any luck, the faeries could pull it off.

"Handsome," Rosemary corrected.

Meara closed her eyes. If there is anyone out there on the other side who can help, we sure can use it.

Chapter Twenty-Three

T HE MOMENTOUS DAY dawned gloomy and dreary. With the temperatures dropping to frigid levels, she knew rain was the last thing she had to fear. As they prepared to leave, Olio managed an apologetic hug for the three of them while giving Ronan an impromptu lecture about life on the road. There was a chance it had more to do about living with three women than the various hardships that came with it.

A crow huddled on a bare branch and stared at them as they loaded up. Eleanor, the woman who'd sheltered her after the convent burned down, was fond of pointing out animals as messengers. She wondered what this one meant. Mentally, she imagined him saying, "You'll be sorry."

Her attitude was the problem. That was it, although it was a trifle hard to get excited about traveling in the tail end of winter. Add to that a cryptic mission. Then there was the issue that someone was attacking her psychically. She probably had about twenty pounds of protective amulets on including the hematite ring Brigit stuck on her finger just before leaving.

Meara climbed up to sit by her cousin as the wagon lurched into action. With Hercules in the traces, he pulled the wagon along as if it were little more than paper. The downside was the horse seldom broke into a trot. He could do it, but didn't like to. Jane kept the shutters opened behind the bench seat to call out instructions whenever she thought they were needed, which appeared to be whenever she could.

While Meara had absolutely no desire to be a leader, she had even less in being a peacemaker, but found herself in the role despite her preferences.

"I think Hercules is doing a wonderful job at keeping a consistent speed. With his stamina, we could probably get in a few extra hours today."

Jane snorted, then closed the shutters. If asked, she'd make some comment about it being cold as the reason, not that the conversation didn't suit her. It would be a long trip. Before Ronan was manipulated into coming, Jane and he used to get on very well.

The road to Dublin appeared to be much more traveled than she expected in the winter and so close to a major holiday. It could be that people were trying to get home for the holidays. Several carts passed them, the drivers usually men who asked Ronan his destination. Seeing no reason to hide it, he volunteered, "Dublin," whenever asked.

Some praised him for his attitude, while a few reminded him that he was too young to go so far from home.

Announcing where they were going didn't strike her as smart, but she needed to approach the topic gently. "Why are you telling everyone our destination?"

He shrugged. "They're strangers. Why should it matter? Besides, we're on the road to Dublin. People might think it strange if we tried to go somewhere else using the Dublin road."

There was some merit in his reasoning, but still they had no way of knowing who they could trust and who they couldn't. "Why not say we're going to visit relatives? That's believable."

"Why should I?"

Before she could explain, the shutters opened, and Jane stuck out her head. "What's she's trying to say is if you keep to your country boy ways, we'll all end up dead. Great Scot, Meara was raised in the convent and knows more about the world than you do. Consider all those you exchanged words with that one or two of them was eyeing Hercules. You might consider that the next time you feel the need to announce our destination."

Instead of being angry as Meara expected, Ronan appeared startled. "Jesus, Mary, and Joseph, I had no clue. I'll be more careful."

Jane, not appeased, continued talking. "It's too late. You told would be horse thieves where you will be. They'll be waiting."

Ronan threw Hercules an anguished glance. "What should I do?"

Meara shrugged. She wasn't the specialist at avoiding people. "Jane has spent a good part of her life outsmarting people that wanted to do her or her family harm."

"What should I do?"

Jane allowed just enough silence to make the male squirm before answering. "Take another road. One that doesn't go to Dublin. We can cross over in a day or so as long as we're sure the would-be horse thieves are gone. As a traveler, we usually told people we were going somewhere other than where we were going."

"You lied?" Ronan asked as if such a thing was unheard of.

"We survived." On that note, Jane closed the shutters.

The next man who greeted them asked where they were headed. Ronan froze up, then spit out the name, Newport.

The stranger cocked his head a little. "Not sure if they'd need much help there. It's a tiny fishing village."

Meara could tell that the situation unnerved her cousin. "We're headed down there to meet relatives for Easter."

The man cracked the whip over his team as his voice drifted behind him. "Enjoy your holiday."

"You're so much better at this than I am." Ronan gave her a sideways glance before successfully urging Hercules into a trot.

"You mean lying?"

"Yeah, I guess."

"It gets easier, especially once you realize everyone does it to a certain extent to keep peace. People never tell their bosses the truth, because they don't want to get fired. Many an intelligent husband tells his wife she's beautiful even when she isn't. If there's a bully in the local pub itching for a fight, you probably play along so as not to be his first fight."

"When you put it that way, it's not lying, but good sense."

"Yes," she agreed readily as the wagon turned into the side road. "Do you know where you are going?"

Her cousin gave her a dark look. Apparently, it was true. No man liked being questioned about his sense of directions.

"I'm going on a road that isn't the Dublin road." He pushed out his chin as if he expected her to call him on it.

She said nothing that day or the next when it looked like they were truly lost. Two days later, they discovered the Dublin road once more, making sure to say nothing. By day three, Jane couldn't take it any longer and climbed up to the bench seat before Meara could. They headed in the right direction, but even Jane was surprised by the amount of people on the road.

"Most of the time we go overland, but we still have a good view of everyone going over the road. This is a fair amount of people."

"Yeah, you can be sure of that. All this asking me where we're going is a bit odd. Back home, they never ask my destination."

"Maybe they don't need to, because they already know."

Meara kept the shutters open for the light and to listen to their banter. Not too surprising, they were getting along since Ronan tended to follow Jane's direction after his last fiasco of driving in circles.

Rosemary was curled up asleep, which would make her a good choice for first night guard duty. Their directional misstep had them in Dublin on a Monday, which was good since they needed the ferry, and they didn't run on Sundays.

The sun had been playing peek-a-boo with the clouds all day, but suddenly a stream of sunlight appeared, highlighting their cart. The sun should have lifted her mood, but all day she felt an ominous pall hanging over the day. The streets of the city were unusually quiet. There was a hiss. Someone popped out of a pub.

"Get off the street. What are you, an idgit?"

Jane attempted to direct Ronan to where the ferry would be. He turned the big draft horse who made the turn none too fast, until a shot rang out startling the horse into a run. A British soldier showed up in the street and attempted to flag them down.

More shots sounded. Some even peppered the wagon. Meara boosted herself just enough to see Hercules running. Ronan stood with his legs spread, sawing back on the reins with no luck. Jane had her fingers clamped around the bench seat and her shoulders hunched, trying to make herself as small of a target as possible. Gunfire rang out behind them as Hercules ran full speed to the dock. The ships bobbed on the water in the distance. It looked like Hercules would run right off the pier.

Why hadn't she taken the opportunity to learn how to swim when she could? It was going to be the water or gun shot. Rosemary might want to be awake. She lurched across the wagon to wake her friend just when the wagon became airborne. Supplies flew in a slow arc as they tumbled. Meara grabbed the horn box as it flew by and tumbled with it using her body as a shield, but then everything went black.

To Be Continued

Glimmer

by
Rayna Noire

Chapter One

England 1915

A SNAP OF a tree branch signaled Meara wasn't alone. Her breath caught and swelled her belly as she waited. A tiny thrill danced across her skin, leaving the hairs on her arms upright. Mother Superior strictly forbade the sisters from entering the woods. She called it *going into the world,* and they'd renounced the world when they entered the convent walls. The rule was for the sisters, not her, an orphaned child who by chance had been born within these same walls.

A speckled fawn stepped into the sun-dappled clearing, allowing Meara's breath to escape in a whoosh. A deer, a baby, which meant the mother wouldn't be far behind. The doe stepped out from the brush, giving the girl leaning against the tree a speculative glance before foraging the mosses and delicate wildflowers. If she stayed still, the skittish forest inhabitants would ignore or possibly accept her. It meant a great deal that they accepted her in an offhanded way.

Birdsong accompanied the play and the chuckle of the nearby creek. The area around the convent walls drew her. Here, she felt at home. It certainly felt more right than walking in straight lines with the sisters, chanting somber words to an unseen male deity who demanded constant homage in the form of prayers six times a day. Her hand covered her mouth, hoping she hadn't said such a thing aloud. Even thinking it was a sin, but speaking it would result in excommunication and horrible punishment.

Sister Phillip reminded her—anytime she'd made the mistake of complaining about the endless monotony of convent life—that her mother had died a painful death in childbirth due to her sins. A few sisters whispered *bastard, changeling, dark whelp* within her hearing. Perhaps they needed to point out she was different, as if she couldn't have figured that out herself.

Outside the walls, she'd slip off her shoes, feeling the cool spongy moss under her feet. It tickled, but more importantly, it lived and touched her. The lack of physical touch within the cloistered walls intensified her yearning for something to touch her, even if the touch was passive as she trod upon it.

The tiniest shift of light motes moved through the air, forming and reforming, tumbling through the air. The grass beside her pushed down similar to something landing beside her. Although her eyes did not convey such information, she knew. The same as she knew her mother did not die from any great sin. Dozens of Hogstead village women died in childbirth, Sister Gabriella explained, when she found Meara crying in the garden shed after another verbal attack on her parentage.

A warmness crept over her body, a comforting peace that somehow came from the unseen presence beside her. To speak of it would destroy it. Even Sister Gabriella, who was bolder than the other sisters—since she took an angel's name as opposed to a saint's—wouldn't understand.

The lengthening shadows indicated the vanishing afternoon. Soon the bells would toll for the three o'clock service, and her absence would be obvious. She stood, brushing the leaves off her plain brown tunic before giving a head bob to the area where she'd been sitting.

"Good day to you."

Even though no words rode the air, she felt a response, one of respect and care. Her measured footsteps allowed her to move past the wildlife without sending it fleeing. Once she cleared the woods, she grabbed the hem of her tunic with one hand and clutched her shoes in the other. Meara's loping sprint carried her across the open, green space. Her most ardent prayers happened outside the walls as she mentally bargained with God to allow her to slip back in unnoticed once again.

The high convent walls kept out intruders, according to Sister Bartholomew. Of course, it made her wonder why intruders would want in. A large locked gate was the only entrance and even then, the visitors came no deeper than the antechamberwhere the Mother Superior greeted them. The temptations of the world did not overcome her, as it might a lesser sister.

A horseless carriage chugged, snorted, and belched noxious smoke as it trembled on the narrow convent road. The black vehicle had shiny sides, roof, and a glass shield at the front that would provide protection from the rain.

Meara forgot about her tardiness as she stood in the shadow of the trees and watched the vehicle lumber closer. The convent only possessed a dog cart and a mule for transport, which they seldom used. Amos, the mule, grew more cantankerous, forgetting his real purpose.

Even more curious were the two individuals riding in it. They both possessed beards, which would make them men. Not counting the various saint statues scattered across the grounds and inside the sanctuary, it was her first glimpse of an actual male. The beards were the only thing the saints and those men had in common. As much as she wanted to see what happened next, she knew time was a priority.

Staying in the forest's shadow, she dashed for the bolt hole. The tiny opening came about from overzealous vines pulling the bricks apart in the gardens. A particular large blackberry bush hid the opening. Since her job included picking the berries, no one else had any reason to be near the hole. Would any of the sisters be tempted to squeeze through for a look at the world they left behind? They might not be as interested since they voluntarily left it.

A quick glance assured her no one observed her outside the walls as she wiggled through the tight break. The tunic caught on a brick and tore. *Oh no*, she only had one. The tear would be noticeable and would invite questions. A moment of indecision had her half in the hole and half out.

Sister Gabriella's voice called, "Do hurry. Mother Superior is asking for you."

What was more surprising? That Gabriella knew she snuck out on a regular basis or that Mother Superior requested her attendance? Her left hand smoothed down her tunic and pulled it off the evil brick that had snagged it. The fact Mother Superior asked for her could be connected with her outside visits. An image of her gate into the natural world slammed shut.

Inside the cloistered walls, running was forbidden, along with talking in a loud voice. It didn't matter now since she had no desire to do either. A sense of foreboding pressed down on her shoulders. Her already sedate pace slowed more. A desire to escape back to the forest glen tugged at her. Back underneath the trees, she had felt safe and welcomed, but years of obedience kept her feet moving forward, despite her desire to do otherwise.

The sisters kept her out of Christian charity. They fed, clothed, and even educated her, a luxury for many of her gender. All she ever read were the scriptures, but even those were limited t for fear she might tear or soil the delicate pages. Sister Gabriella once spoke of a wonderful place called a *library*, full of books, but it existed outside of the walls. What would it be like to read into the late evening hours? The possibility distracted her a little from the upcoming meeting. No books would be allowed or the extravagant use of lamp fuel.

Once she'd picked up a shiny scrap of metal on her unsupervised walks outside. The piece was smaller than her fist. When she held it up to her face, she could see one eye staring back at her and the bridge of her nose. It fascinated her since the sisters were not permitted to look at their own reflections. To do so would cause the sin of vanity. No mirrors existed anywhere. Meara had never seen her face, except for that one wide, unblinking eye.

The scrap metal would have caused trouble if found in her tiny cell of a room, but it had vanished mysteriously. She suspected Sister Gabriella. The woman gently guided her more with actions than words.

Often, she felt the youngest sister there was her only true friend. As there were no very young nuns in the convent, Sister Gabriella was closer to her age than any other sisters, although her face was unlined and her eyes lively, Meara had no clue of the kind nun's age.

A large door with an arch at the top separated her from Mother Superior and whatever edict she would issue. Someone as low as she never received too much of the good Mother's time. When she did, it was never good. The last time she'd entered the hallowed room was in reference to her habit of whistling, her poor efforts were to mimic the birds, perhaps even call them to her side. Someone heard her whistling while gardening and reported it. After doing a three-day indulgence that included crawling to the chapel, which made her knees bloody, she never whistled again inside the convent walls.

Mother Superior believed whistling was associated with the sins of vanity and pride. After all, it drew attention to oneself. Her eyes narrowed as she searched her memory for any recent whistling. None that she could recall.

Her raised fist hesitated before knocking the prescribed three knocks of medium force. The door swung open before she had mentally prepared herself for the ordeal. No matter what the infraction levied against her, she couldn't show any emotion. Any tears, pleadings, or remonstrations fell under the sins of pride and falsehood.

The tall robed figure of Mother Superior filled most of the doorway, but the sliver of a pants leg of a seated man drew her eyes more than the frowning matron.

"Mary, you are late."

The name always grated, giving her a mental jar strong enough to bring her back to the current situation. Her gaze dropped to the floor. "Sorry, Mother. I came as soon as Sister Gabriella told me." She sucked in her bottom lip, wondering if Gabriella had been searching long. It was not her intention to transfer blame to the kind sister.

Mother Superior snorted her disbelief, but rather than say anything else, she stepped aside and gestured for her to enter.

Meara's shoe stuck to the stone floor, akin to stepping in spilt honey. Both men stood and turned curious gazes her way. Her eyes traveled over them both, memorizing their features and their strange clothes. Later, when she was alone in her cell, she'd reexamine it.

A flash of white teeth showed in one man's beard. A smile, she recognized it without being told, although smiles were rare inside the walls. It was a sign of frivolity, a lightheartedness that did not become a bride of Christ.

Even though the sisters accepted that their God took male form, they seldom spoke of the male gender at all. This other sex could roam free outside the walls without worrying about falling prey to the temptations of the world.

"Make haste, Mary." Mother Superior slapped her hands together, which bespoke her irritation.

Meara shook off her initial fear and strode into the room, stopping short past the door. The smiling man's expression changed as he sent a sharp look at the Mother Superior.

"You told me her name was Meara."

Her heart leapt. Outside of Sister Gabriella whispering that name when she asked for details about her birth, she'd never, ever heard another person say it. Mentally, she called herself *Meara* in an effort not to lose that slender thread that connected her to her mother.

The woman swung around so fast her black veil fluttered from the motion. Even though she couldn't see her expression, Meara knew it would be stern enough to cause trembling in the most stalwart of the sisters. The man did not seem intimidated. *Strange.*

"Meara is a heathen name. Even though her mother chose to name her Meara, I chose the name of Mary to inspire the child who came from a sinful union."

A low growl emanated from the man's throat. The other man placed a hand on his shoulder while speaking loud enough for her to hear. "Careful, Simon, don't be doing something you might regret."

He shook off the man's hand before addressing Mother Superior.

"Meara is my mother's name, a good Celtic name my sister chose to keep in the family. It means the sea. As for my sister, you slander her good name. She was married to one of your kinsmen, an Englishman." He spat the last word as if it were poison and needed to be out of his mouth. "Meara, come closer." He gestured to a nearby chair.

She regarded it the same way she did the large cat she'd encountered in the woods. It was an unknown and possibly dangerous creature. Once she reached the hard wooden chair, she slid into it since her legs had turned weak.

"Could you give us a few moments alone?" He directed the request to Mother Superior.

"Certainly not. I have the girl's welfare to consider. Whatever you have to say can be said in front of me."

The man called Simon mumbled some unfamiliar words. They were enough to make the abbess gasp in consternation, which made them very powerful words indeed. She wished she knew them.

The other man touched his companion. "Remember where we are. This isn't a public house."

"Sorry, Meara." Simon nodded at her and smiled again. The simple lifting of the lips caused his face to light up. Even his eyes sparkled. He studied her as if she were an unusual bug. "You have the look of my sister, Sorcha, when she was younger. Doesn't she, Angus?"

The other man gave her a measured look before replying, "She does indeed."

"My mother's name is Sorcha. I've never heard it before," Meara told him.

This somehow angered Simon. He threw another accusing glance at Mother Superior, who huffed, making no verbal reply.

"You are," she tried to shape the word she wanted, but it eluded her since all talk of families were forbidden. That was the past. "Family?"

He reached for Meara's hand, clasping it in his large, masculine one. Warmth flowed between their hands along with a sense of connection she'd never felt before.

Mother Superior moved faster than Meara had ever witnessed and pulled their hands apart. "No touching is permitted."

Her hand felt suddenly alone after the brief touch. Worse, she'd lost the connection, the only time she felt a sense of belonging, outside of the forest. Mother Superior spoke truly. Touching was never permitted except in dire circumstances, such as healing or catching a sister who might be falling. Even then, if the sister was only falling a little distance, helping could disrupt a divine lesson. Many a sister had tripped on the uneven stones and tumbled headfirst to the hard floor.

Simon's lips pulled down in a forbidding frown as he glanced back at the older woman. Meara watched with interest because she'd never witnessed such a display of emotions. She had never seen anyone go up against whatever pronouncement Mother Superior made. Inside the convent walls, she served as a direct extension of the patriarchal deity they bound themselves to, which meant this god had to be a stern, unforgiving figure who hated laughter and frivolity. The men, what did they have faith in?

Simon turned to face her, his former smile returning. "I can't believe I finally found you. Sorcha wrote me that I'd be an uncle years ago." He looked past Meara's shoulder as he took a long, unsteady breath.

Angus stood and dropped his hand on his friend's shoulder and squeezed. He nodded his head at Meara. "It's hard on your uncle. Travel is never that easy between countries, but now the war and the various navies crowding the sea made it a diabolical trip, fer sure. Simon never gave up on Sorcha. We came on the university's coin to join a team heading for Egypt."

"Egypt." She repeated the word, remembering it from the scriptures. A noise caused her to look back in the direction of Mother Superior, who'd managed to shuffle closer while Angus spoke.

Simon transferred his gaze from the wall to her. He threw a dark look at the hovering nun, daring her to say anything. "Forgive my behavior. It's just that..." He paused, gulping loudly. "I always assumed Sorcha lived. My sister, your mother could be a stubborn one. She gave her love freely and strong. On the other hand, no one could hold a grudge like her."

Angus leaned in to add, "Sorcha was known to be right grudge holder of Galaway County. People did not cross her."

"That she was," Simon agreed. "My sister did everything with passion. I remember when she met your father, who was visiting his people nearby. She marched home all smiles and told me she intended to marry Fulmen."

"Fulmen." She said the name slowly, sounding it out. Never having heard her mother's name, and now having an actual father's name made her beginning more tangible. She wasn't a changeling, a gypsy's git, or any of the other unflattering terms whispered about her.

"Aye, I asked her what type of name was Fulmen."

Meara wondered too, although the only male names she knew belonged to the saints.

"Ah, Sorcha put both hands on her hips and proudly announced the name was Druidic."

A feminine gasp emphasized Mother Superior's location.

Simon continued with a sad smile. "She told me it meant lightning. He stole her heart just that fast. Sorcha, proud as the day is long, threw her flaming hair over her shoulder and declared she'd have no man but him. I should have realized she meant what she said."

"What happened?" The love story of her parents fascinated her, the first love she'd ever heard of due to the sisters never mentioning their past. As green as she was, she knew if a woman had a great love, she wouldn't become a sister, or if she did, her love must have perished.

"Da forbade the union."

Before he could continue, Mother Superior harrumphed her way into the conversation. "Well, he should. No good would come from hooking up with a heathen."

Simon threw her another ominous look that had her sliding back a few steps. "My da, your Grandda, was a great one for the church, although he attended the services only on the high holidays. In his grief over my mother's death, he turned bitter and hard. The only thing that mattered to him was family. All he saw in your father was an English-man who would steal his daughter away, one of the last living remnants of his beloved Colleen."

Meara knew the couple must have continued to see each other or she wouldn't be here. "Did they run away together?"

"I figured they must have. Since one day she was at home, the next day not. Over a year later, a letter came from Beacon, Wales. Sorcha told me how happy she was and that she was expecting a babe any day. My first impulse was to find a freighter heading that way, but I couldn't leave."

"Why?" The question popped out of her mouth before she fully thought it through. She'd worked hard to correct the habit. Her saying what she thought was a sign of an uncontrolled spirit. Her shoulders hunched for the expected lash she'd receive, but it didn't come. Neither did the verbal reprimand.

"When Sorcha left, me da took to his bed. Some say it was his heart, which I know to be true. It was broken. Da lingered on death's doorstep for many years. In the intervening time, I met my wife, Erin. She helped care for Da and even urged me to seek out Sorcha, which is what I did."

Meara squirmed in the hard chair wanting to ask what had taken him so long, but she'd already had one outburst. Instead, she asked with her eyes full of pleading, hoping for more details.

Angus answered instead. He leaned forward, resting his large hands on his knees. "This isn't Simon's first trip. The first one took place about six years after your Grandda died. He went down to the Brecon area, but mouths were tight, and none mentioned Sorcha by name."

Simon shook his head. "If only I had taken more interest in Fulmen. I didn't even know his last name. As extraordinary as the name sounds, there were more than a handful of Fulmens in the place, but none was Sorcha's Fulmen. I did offer to pay people for information. Even though they were Celts as much as I, they told me nothing. Erin was expecting our own babe so I returned to Galway. The next trip was two years later with the same result. It was as if Sorcha and Fulmen vanished from the earth. I made up cards with my name, contact information, and passed them out. This year I received a letter for my efforts."

"What did it say?" Meara pressed her hands together in a prayer-like position against her heart, forgetting her vow to forgo any future outbursts.

"The sender refused to give his name on the grounds his own relatives took part in a dastardly act. Fulmen's cousin died had without any children and left prime farmland to Fulmen. It was a big holding sought after by many. Along with it came the house and outbuildings, some of the best in the area. A few offered to buy the land from Fulmen, but offered an insultingly low bid. Fulmen intended to stay on the farm until Sorcha delivered, maybe indefinitely. The writer didn't know. All he knew was his da and uncle were worked up about it. The squatter wasn't welcome there. The writer claimed he was only a child at the time and overheard talk when they thought he was asleep."

As much as she wanted to hear about her parents, this tale was not going the way she wished. It didn't seem like her parents had a fair life the short time they were together. Her mother had abandoned her family for love and apparently stepped into a desperate mess in England.

Simon stopped talking and glanced back at Angus, who cut his eyes in Meara's direction.

"Go on. I want to know," she urged, knowing they had reached a difficult point in the retelling.

Her uncle cleared his throat. "To put it plain, they meant only to scare Fulmen off the land, but he was determined to protect you and your mother. Your father's death may have been accidental, but the results were the same. Your mother must have fled the scene. Somehow she came across this convent where she had you."

The brutal ending didn't surprise her, but waves of sadness buffeted her. She'd hoped her mother had lived a happy life until the time she died. Unfortunately, that hadn't been the case. Instead, she'd had a slim escape after witnessing her husband struck down. A sigh escaped her.

"Poor Sorcha. Poor Fulmen. What happened to the farm?"

Angus raised his eyebrows. "Now, that sounds like something a Cleary might ask." At Meara's surprised look, he explained. "You're a Cleary. It's the family name of both Sorcha and Simon. It means *clerk*, which suits since the Clearys always know the bottom line."

Simon's hand covered his face. He brought it down slowly and gazed at Meara with eyes that reminded her of the eye she had seen in the tiny reflective fragment she'd found.

"Aye, that's a good question. I expect those who cut down Fulmen now sit on the land."

A rush of outrage filled her, causing her to shake. What justice was there in her father's inheritance taken by the same greedy villagers who killed him and caused her mother's horrible run across the countryside? "That's wrong."

"I agree. My concern wasn't about land, but about my own blood, which you are. I came for you to take you back to your family. My son, Ronan, is a few years younger than you are. I have a daughter, Brigit who may be your age or a few months over. You have a family waiting for you in Galway. I have work to do for the university, but I'll come for you when I'm done. It will be less than a month."

A home, a family, someone near her age. Her heart swelled with joy, making Meara wonder if it could burst out of her chest. "I'll be ready." Truer words she'd never uttered.

Simon held up his hand, signaling the interview was over. She stood and looked at Mother Superior who made a slashing movement with her arm, which meant she should leave. Meara hurried to do so, knowing she'd already broken several rules with her unruly tongue.

She stood for a moment outside the closed door, listening for the sound of her uncle's voice.

"I'd like to see Sorcha's grave."

Her mother had a grave on the grounds? This was news to her. Looking both ways to be sure she wouldn't be seen, she rested her ear on the door to hear better.

Mother Superior's strident voice conjured up a mental picture of the angel barring Adam and Eve from paradise. She would have made an excellent avenging angel with righteous certainty filling each word. "Your sister was not buried on sacred ground."

"Why the hell not? She was as good a Christian as you are. I suspect better."

"Now, Simon, calm down. Don't go forgetting where you are."

She recognized Angus's voice and the fact he was trying to placate her uncle. Obviously, she wasn't the only one in the family who had difficulty holding their words.

"Sir, remember we had no way of knowing the identity of a dirty, battered woman. She collapsed on the doorstep, similar to a stray mongrel ready to whelp."

"I thank you not to refer to my sister as a dog."

Meara wished she could see the tableau taking place on the other side of the door. It was as much emotion as she'd ever heard from Mother Superior.

"I will speak plainly. We tended to your sister. Brought your niece into the world and cared for her these last sixteen years, for which you owe us. A hearty contribution to the convent would be in order. If we had known she was a Druidic get, we would not have raised her."

The indrawn breath had to be her uncle or possibly Angus, maybe both. The sisters would have let her die due to her father being a Druid. She didn't even know what a Druid was. Maybe Sister Gabriella did.

"I'll be back in two weeks or more. I expect my niece to be ready to leave. No doubt, you'll be anxious to get her off your hands."

The words signaled the end of the conversation, which sent her rushing down the hallway. There had to be something she could busy herself with to appear as if she hadn't been eavesdropping.

If you enjoyed this book, why not sample the entire Pagan Eyes series.

Leah Carpenter thought being the only witch in her local high school was hard. That was until she inexplicably found herself in the past, running from an angry mob, which turned out to be much harder. Lionel, the man in charge of the mob, holds a grudge against a girl he calls Arabella. He thinks she's Arabella.

Luckily, just about the time it looks as if she's done for she pops back into her century. This causes trouble at school, but at least she has an understanding family. What happens in the past can hurt her. The whiplashes covering her body are proof enough.

Her Nana believes she must right a wrong in the past to stay in the present and go out with her crush, Dylan. What she discovers in the past is an evil so pure that it makes her blood run cold. She might not ever make it back to geometry class or more importantly a possible date with Dylan.

Nora Carpenter is a trainee assistant physician, a part-time diner chef…
and a witch. Hiding from the memory of a traumatic rape – fueled by
prejudice over her eccentric reputation – she keeps to herself. Demanding work, study, and a cold shoulder to any guy that crosses her path,
seem like her best defense until she starts having vivid dreams about a
compelling, mysterious stranger with dark curls, sexy eyes, and a
charming Irish lilt, her defenses seem to be breaking.

He says he is her soul mate – that he has conquered many centuries
to contact her. Can this be real? Or is she going mad? Nora tries to fight
the gentle seduction that threatens to thaw her icy façade. But when
she's forced to come face to face with real evil she must call on all her
magical resources, including her lover from another life, to save her.

Ethan finds himself trapped between the world he knows and the world that could be. A sadistic bully, an unsympathetic principal, and an unreachable love interest make high school difficult for Ethan. He feels like he's living a lie, trying to blend in at school to keep his head attached to his body.

Fear that he's not the son his father wants negates the support his Wiccan family offers. An impromptu trip into the future saves him from an enraged bully while instilling doubts about where he really belongs. Somehow, he must find a way to survive in his own world tossing aside his mask and doubts.

Stella's college life transforms from sweet to rancid when her boyfriend asks her to do the unthinkable. How did she end up holding her best friend's future in her hands? Anything she does will trigger the disastrous conclusion.

If that isn't bad enough add in a lunatic minister, a demi-goddess, and a walk through another dimension full of vindictive shrubbery and wildlife. It's a freshman year she may not survive.

Author Notes

Stop over at www.raynanoire.com to see what books are out, what contests are happening, and if I'll be making a personal appearance near you.

Make sure to sign up for the newsletter on the website too. It is a wonderful way to get free stuff included stories, swags, books, and Amazon gift cards.

Check out my blog www.raynanoire.weebly.com, which features a weekly Totem Animal Blog and Friday Book Reviews.

You can hang out with me at:

Facebook
facebook.com/AuthorRaynaNoire

Twitter
twitter.com/raynanoire